Veiled Visions of Love

Secrets of Roseville • Book 4

Betty Bolté

This is a work of fiction. Names, characters, places, and incidents are a product of the author's imagination. Locales and public names are sometimes used for atmospheric purposes. Any resemblance to actual people, living or dead, or to businesses, companies, events, institutions, or locales is completely coincidental.

Betty Bolté
www.bettybolte.com

Copyright © 2018 by Betty Bolté.
ISBN-13: 978-0-9981625-9-1
ISBN-10: 0-9981625-9-0

Author's Note

Dear Reader,

Writing Beth and Mitch's love story involved more research than expected. I'd like to thank Suzanne Ramsden, owner and Black Belt instructor at the Maverick Training Center in Huntsville, AL, for her insights about training in Brazilian Jiu-Jitsu. She also took some of her precious time to read the relevant scenes for accuracy. Any errors remaining are purely mine.

I'd also like to thank my beta readers—Danielle Bolté, Anne Parent, Sue Moynihan, and Suzi York—for their keen-eyed read to help me make sure the resulting story is both authentic and entertaining. They each used their professional and personal experience to correct my inexpert portrayal of airplanes, guns, motorcycles, and more. Thank you all!

I also visited a state-of-the-art indoor shooting range, a Harley Davidson store, an airshow, and watched a class at the Maverick Training Center, all of which took me out of my personal comfort zone. But if Beth could venture out to new experiences, then I had to as well in order to share her experiences with all of you.

I hope you enjoy reading Beth and Mitch's story as much as I enjoyed writing it.

Betty

Chapter One

A wave of frustrated longing crashed and churned inside her chest. One day she'd make her fondest wish come true. But that wouldn't be today. Or this week. She huffed in disgust. Or this year. But one day.

Beth Golden flipped the page of the travel guide to peer at the pictures of pyramids and colorfully bedecked camels standing against a deep blue sky. Closing her eyes, she imagined the grit of the burning sand and gusts of a searing zephyr. The lurch of the animal as it carried her over dunes. A half smile formed as glimpses of an Indiana Jones type of pursuit using trucks racing across the desert played across her mind's eye. Or perhaps risking everything to rescue someone in trouble. Like in the latest romantic suspense novel she'd devoured. Living life to the fullest, surrounded by strong, daring men and smart, sexy women. The perfect lifestyle.

"Beth! We need you down here."

She sighed and forced her eyes open. Back to reality. Instead of a desert, she stood in the travel section of the Golden Owl Books and Brews bookstore she and her two sisters, Tara and Roxie, had run for the last several years without their mother. Beautiful and savvy, Peggy Golden had started the shop as a focal point in the small town of Roseville. She'd loved to keep up with their neighbors, treating them as family more than customers. Providing a uniquely welcoming experience in the store by including baked goods and coffee to enjoy while they browsed for their next great story. She'd taught her daughters how to suggest new books to people to help them find something of interest. If only Beth could find something interesting, she'd be far happier.

"On my way." Her raised voice seemed small and insignificant in the open space. Much like she felt.

The upper floor of the Civil War era building housed the nonfiction selections. Everything from cookbooks to animal husbandry to psychology to witchcraft. The last a particular interest of the three sisters, especially since her mother had literally written a book on the subject. She laid the brochure on top of the stack on the table, nudging it into alignment with the others, and then turned away to trudge down the steps. She had work to do despite the fact her heart and mind journeyed about the world without her.

Her entire life had been lived within the boundaries of the county. A day trip to Nashville didn't count as adventure. Far from it. While the atmosphere in the Music City was different from the small town vibe of her hometown, it still didn't satisfy the need for something else. Despite the increased hum of activity, she wanted more. More surprises. But of course her gift of vision meant she could tell what was about to happen to those around her, even if not her own future. She could still sense what was in store for others, whether she wanted to know or not. She'd learned to mute the ceaseless images so her emotions weren't overwhelmed, but the visions clamored for her attention.

Rounding the corner of the checkout counter, she cringed at the long line of customers waiting at the coffee bar. If she didn't know better, she'd think her neighbors came to the bookstore for their morning rush, either caffeine or sugar. In fact, much like Edna's Supermarket across town, the store served up local gossip as well. Usually purely curious exchanges about what was happening in the town which helped the three sisters keep their fingers on the town's pulse.

"Glad you found your way back to help." Roxie, dressed in the same khakis and black polo all three sisters wore, pulled the tap on the soda dispenser to fill a cup. Her chestnut hair pulled into a short ponytail, Roxie watched her with concern in her hazel eyes.

"Sorry. I got distracted." Beth didn't want her sisters worried about her. She could take care of that all by herself.

"Let me guess." Roxie splashed soda down the outside of the cup with a short exclamation of disgust. She grabbed a paper towel and dried off the cup before addressing Beth. "Daydreaming of faraway places?"

"I can't help it." She glanced at Tara, standing by the bakery counter. Her younger sister had blossomed since marrying Grant Markel earlier in the year. She'd done her hair in a chignon, a different look but attractive on the slender woman.

"You're not trapped here." Roxie tossed the crumpled paper towel into the trash. "You could take a trip."

Beth shrugged as she scooted behind her sisters. "What fun would it be to go by myself? Besides, how could I go and not feel guilty leaving you both shorthanded here?"

"We'd manage." Tara folded a pastry box and then selected an assortment of muffins to nestle inside. "Or is that an excuse?"

"I'll know when the time is right. Which isn't now." Beth donned a lightweight apron with the Golden Owl logo—a Great Horned owl holding two crossed branches inside an inverted triangle—emblazoned in the center and quickly washed her hands.

She stepped up to the bakery display to take the next order from Sue Grimwood. Mother of three and grandmother of one, her trim frame proved a woman could live a full and happy life without looking old and worn out. In fact, she continued to be Max Chandler's legal secretary at the law firm down the street. He ended up marrying Meredith Reed, the sisters' new-found cousin. Family ties had grown rather knotty in Roseville upon the discovery that Meredith and her sister Paulette were indeed related to the three Golden sisters. Sue made it a habit to stop in for her daily breakfast purchase on her way to work. Giving everyone the perfect opportunity to stay in the know about doings in the town.

"Good morning, Sue. How may I help you this morning?" Beth rested her fists on top of the glass case, a smile aimed at the spry older woman.

Sue brushed a stray wisp of chin-length brown hair off her cheek and then pointed to the bagel shelf. "I'd like one of the poppy seed bagels, please. Oh, and a decaf coffee."

"Do you want cream cheese?" Tara pulled a piece of waxed paper and grabbed the bagel, slipping it into a white paper bag. At Sue's nod, she added a tube of cream cheese and then lifted a brow at Sue. "Have you tried the eclairs?" She motioned to where the custard-filled, chocolate-iced pastries were lined up beside bear claws and glazed donuts. "The best I've ever tasted."

"You're such a temptress, my dear." Sue grimaced, deep curved dimples on either side of her mouth, and slowly shook her head. "I'm sure they're delicious but not for me. Too rich for my taste."

"I know you love chocolate." Tara folded the bag closed and then spun away to snap up a cup and fill it with hot coffee. She handed both the bag and cup to Sue. "Do you have plans for the Memorial Day weekend?"

The town excelled at celebrating every holiday, big or small. Some stemming from the town's history, like Founder's Day and Strawberry Festival. Memorial Day brought picnics and outdoor concerts, car and tractor shows, and yard sales on every street. The town square stood festooned in red, white, and blue decorations on every light pole and strung across the streets. Everybody anticipated the fun and frolic of the weekend events planned months in advance.

"Yes, I do. I'm taking my grandson, Jeremy, out to the new airfield for his first flying lesson." Sue scrounged in her voluminous purse for her wallet. "He's wanted to try flying for months and I finally figured it would be better to let him try, get it out of his system."

"That sounds like fun." Tara took the plastic card from Sue and rang up her order.

What an idea. To be able to fly off wherever and whenever. A tantalizing prospect she'd never considered. But how much did it cost? When would she ever have the time to do such a thing? She mentally shrugged off the slight hope that had lifted her spirits for a fraction of a second. No, she was pretty much stuck in sleepy Roseville.

"I bought him a lesson for his eighteenth birthday last week and it's scheduled for this afternoon." Sue tucked her card away and hung her purse on her shoulder. "It may be his one and only, or he may fall in love with the thrill of flying."

"If it makes him happy to do something like that, I say go for it." Beth wiped her hands on her apron. "A bit of excitement never hurt anybody."

Sue grinned at Beth. "Sounds like you're envious. Would you like to go with us? See what it's like to fly?"

"Thanks, but I have to work." She glanced at her oldest sister, Roxie, who had just popped out of the back room with a box of recent arrivals to shelve.

Roxie cocked her head, studied her for several seconds, and then plopped the box of books on a table and sauntered toward the bakery. What had she noticed that made her come over? Beth hadn't done anything, hadn't sent any secret messages her way to ask her to stop what she was doing and intervene. Nothing needed her attention.

Beth shrugged off the questions rattling in her brain and addressed Sue. "I'd like to, just to do something different. But we have a bookstore to run."

"Surely you could slip away for a little while." Sue waved a hand at Tara and Roxie and then gripped her purchases. "There are three of you, after all."

"I appreciate the offer, but we each have our tasks to complete to keep everything running smoothly." Just another cog in the wheel. She usually enjoyed her work, but lately she couldn't stop thinking about having an adventure of her own.

Roxie stopped beside Sue with a nod of greeting. "Hello, Sue. How are you this fine Saturday morning?"

"I was hoping Beth would go to the new airport with me this afternoon. Keep me company while my grandson takes a flying lesson. She might even find she'd like to try it herself. Could you spare her for a few hours?"

Roxie tilted her head, crossing her arms as she considered the question. She aimed her hazel eyes at Beth and then smiled. "I don't see why not. Go have fun."

"Are you sure?" A surge of excited energy sizzled through Beth at the idea.

The new Roseville Regional Airport had been advertised as a modern facility that would enable the further growth of the economic and government sectors of the region. Having a place for the big wigs to fly in and out of town made it possible for increased access as well as easier development and management of businesses. To introduce the services available to the general public, the owner had arranged for a small airshow. The flyer hanging in the front window advertised the vendors and planes waiting for people to come out and see. Maybe going outside of town for a little while would scratch the travel itch consuming her head to toe.

"I think it's just the thing for you." Roxie folded her arms over her chest. "You deserve to have an afternoon off to do something fun."

Sue nodded, her short hair floating around her chin with the movement. "We'll have fun. I'll make sure of it."

The sparkle of Sue's eyes reminded her of the time when Beth was a mere slip of a girl and her mother took the three sisters to the circus. Mom had promised them they'd have a good time and she carried out that promise. Only not the way she'd foreseen. During the acrobatic demonstration involving a pony, one of the acrobats fell off when the horse shied sideways at the entrance to the ring. The lithe girl landed in a moaning heap near where they sat in the front row. Tara leapt up and ran to lay hands on her, using her secret healing powers to restore the girl before even the first responders could reach her. Roxie calmly chanted a protective spell for the woman, a shield to see her through the rest of the performance. Beth sensed the woman would be fine and envisioned her continuing in her acrobatics. Their mother, eyes glittering with tears of pride, couldn't have been more pleased at the sisters working together on the stranger's behalf. Beth remembered the entire episode as the most fun she'd had.

"I may as well go see if there's anything interesting out there." Beth untied her apron strings and hung it up. "What have I got to lose?"

The signature throaty rumble of the Harley died away, consumed by the louder whine of plane engines and the whir of propellers. Mitch Sawyer removed his helmet and smoothed his hair back from his face. Tired and grumpy from the long ride on the bike, he took a moment to absorb the layout of the airport. He'd bought the comfortably outfitted bike for long-distance travel, particularly its cushioned seat and compartments for his gear. Spending days on the road made such a luxury a necessity.

His contact had sent him to the insignificant airshow to do a job. Otherwise, he'd never have known about—let alone attended—the paltry affair. He perused the nearly empty tarmac with a variety of planes parked along either side. A smattering of people of all ages visited the handful of exhibits, children breaking free from parents' restraints to run across the fields edging the airstrip. Several hangars huddled at the end of the open space with a handful of small buildings on either side, presumably offices of one kind or another. He inhaled, sampling the combination of sharp scents. Home again.

Not that he actually thought of any town as home. Instead, airports had been his surrogate home ever since he'd first joined the Air Force fifteen years ago. He'd thrilled to the speed and daring associated with fighter jets and excelled at every aspect of flying and maintaining his aircraft. He even fought his way through a master's degree in aeronautical engineering and earned the designation of Distinguished Graduate at the Squadron Officer School, which enabled him to qualify for the top job in his field: Executive for the Operations Group. He'd beaten out all of his peers for the coveted position. Which didn't make him any friends. Even cost him a few. But he'd enjoyed his time in the OG.

After fifteen years of active duty service, he'd started contemplating his future. He'd grown weary of the constant moving from base to base. Stability tempted him far more than repeatedly changing stations. So after months of considering his options, he switched to the reserves while taking on some freelance gigs with chartered flights and even a stint as an instructor for a local flight school. His training and education eventually led him to being recommended for the most dangerous job he'd ever taken: repossessing planes from deadbeat owners for the finance company. Essentially stealing them back but with legal paperwork to back him up.

Repossessing a plane required both stealth and confidence. Taking a plane wasn't as easy as towing away a car. Each job posed unique obstacles and situations. Not always friendly situations. He had to find a way to ensure the plane was airworthy without being seen and then fire it up and fly it away without being caught. Fortunately, he'd only faced irate gun-toting owners a handful of times, but more than enough for his liking.

One case in point was the job he'd just wrapped up. The setup had felt off from the start. Too easy up until the angry delinquent owner sent not only Dobermans—four of them—but also a handful of gun-toting men. He'd barely escaped with the plane let alone his life. His contact had assured him that situation was an anomaly and wouldn't likely happen again. Mitch didn't quite believe him and so had begun searching for another source of employment. Something with flying but no more guns. He'd had enough of facing the wrong end of a weapon.

Strolling casually down one side of the planes on exhibit, he scoured each aircraft for the one he needed to find. The sugary scent of cotton candy assaulted him from one of two food trucks. Breathing out, he hurried past the kid holding a paper cone of the pale pink spun treat, taking several strides before drawing in another breath. Better. He skirted groups of children and their parents to avoid clashing with conflicting smells. He needed to keep his wits about him, not end up sidelined with a perfume-induced headache.

The plane he searched for was a sweet ride. Not a fighter jet, but definitely a comfortable way to travel. The

Beechcraft Bonanza G36 had become one of the most popular of the single-engine, fixed-landing gear aircraft. Given the price tag approached a million dollars, the bank had every right to reclaim it for nonpayment. He scanned the planes as he sauntered past, searching for the distinctive windowed cabin and front propeller with low wing set along with the flashy striping the owner had insisted on adding. Probably out of a misguided boastful pride at flying such a nice plane which he didn't actually own.

Reaching the end of the first row of planes, he paused to get his bearings, to look back over the planes he'd already passed to make sure he hadn't missed the one he sought. Then headed toward the far side of the tarmac to start down the other row. A glance at the sky confirmed a front approached, the shelf of white roiling clouds pushing closer with each passing minute. He picked up the pace, not wanting to seek out both the plane and then housing in the rain. On a motorcycle.

As he approached the first plane—a nice if older Piper Saratoga—a vaguely familiar dark-skinned man turned to approach him. Where did he know him from? A wide smile greeted him and then he knew, as the man quickly closed the distance between them. The smile belonged to his once-close Air Force buddy. Keith Merryman had left the service two years before Mitch had joined the reserves.

Rumors had circulated as to the reasons why Keith resigned his commission so abruptly. Mitch had his own suspicions but he'd never confirmed them. The two men had attended the Squadron Officer School together, and had grown competitive as a result of their individual drive to excel. Despite their friendly competition, they became fast friends. At least until Mitch earned the DG and ended up promoted ahead of him. Keith had stopped pushing for promotion and instead started talking about getting out and building his own airfield. Where he would always be in control? Could that be why? Still, Keith's laughing tawny eyes and extended hand welcomed Mitch.

"You son of a gun, what are you doing out here?" Keith clapped a hand to Mitch's shoulder and then dropped his hands to his sides. "I thought I'd gotten rid of your sorry face years ago."

"No such luck." Mitch swept the airfield with his gaze. He squinted as he spotted an RV with the Bonanza at the other end, surrounded by curious kids and adults. Its distinctive red striping confirmed he'd found his target. He regarded Keith again, searching for changes in his good-natured open expression. "So you did it?"

Keith nodded as his grin widened. "Yep. It's all mine. Along with its challenges."

"It's a nice layout. Lots of people here to enjoy the show, too." A flash of some undefined emotion clouded Keith's eyes for such a brief moment Mitch may have imagined it. "Was it your idea? Or did someone talk you into it?"

"My idea to try and raise awareness of the services I provide." Keith glanced at his watch and then raised his brows at Mitch. "A good turnout, thank goodness. I worried about how much interest there'd be in airplanes so far out in the country. At least my hunch looks like it'll pay off."

"Yeah, if the weather holds." He zipped his leather jacket halfway up.

A gust of chilly air announced the arrival of the cold front, bringing rain and cooler temperatures behind it. Flying would become more difficult in the wind and rain, if not stopped altogether. With the building clouds and increasing wind speed, the show might be grounded in a few short hours.

"Say, how long are you in town?" Keith shifted his weight to the other foot, his gaze flicking away to scan the groups of people moving among the planes and tents.

"I'm not sure. A few days. Why?" As long as it took to figure out a scheme for getting that plane back, that's how long he'd stay. His paycheck from delivering the repo'd plane would pay off the last of his debt and let him put some aside for a down payment on a new house. Somewhere.

"Have you a place to stay?" Keith shoved his hands into his back jeans pockets.

"Not yet. Is there a hotel?"

"No, just B&Bs. But I have a spare room at my place in town, if you don't mind dogs."

"Wow, you really did settle in." Envy flashed in Mitch's chest, burning a hole before subsiding. "It'd be great to catch up. Can I buy you dinner as a thanks?"

"Sure you can. I never turn down free food."

"Great. Just tell me where to go." Too late he realized the huge opening he'd left his friend to fill. If he chose to.

Keith shook his head, a grin lifting one corner of his mouth as his eyes reflected the temptation to take him up on the opening but resisted. "But there's more. I have a favor to ask."

Mitch splayed his hands, palms up, relieved. "Anything."

"I have a boy coming out to take an intro flying lesson for his birthday in a little while. Could you teach him the basics while I take care of an issue?" Keith grinned wider and winked. "For an old buddy?"

"As long as I'm here, sure."

"Cool. I'll hang around and introduce you and then I'll have to go to resolve the snafu at the cargo terminal."

"Sounds like a plan." And the perfect cover story for being at the show and getting to know the ins and outs, who to avoid as well as trust, in order to make a certain plane disappear. Coincidence? Fate? Dumb luck? Didn't matter, he'd take it. "Where and when?"

Chapter Two

A burst of cold air created goosebumps on Beth's bare arms while she waited for Sue and Jeremy to arrive. The temperature had dropped since she'd left the Golden Owl for the drive out to the new airport. She'd left her windbreaker in the car, wrongly assuming she'd be fine. The end of May and the afternoon breeze chilled her through. She hugged herself and coughed as fumes from the planes and golf carts wafted her way. She moved closer to the food truck advertising icy cold lemonade. She shivered but preferred the sweet aroma to the harsh fumes.

She'd never spent much time at an airport. Check that. She hadn't spent *any* time at an airport. She'd never had to travel far enough away from home that she'd even contemplated flying. Nor had she distant relatives arriving at either the Huntsville or Nashville airports she had to go pick up. As a result, she drank in her surroundings with interest. She imagined others attending the show would know what they were seeing, the type and quality of the planes and the airport itself. She could only say they were planes and buildings with a long stretch of asphalt for takeoffs and landings.

A swarthy-skinned man wearing a crisp white shirt and dark jeans sauntered past, tipping his baseball cap at her in greeting. He moved with the assured gait of a military man, or a pilot. Or perhaps both. She'd seen him in the store a time or two, but his future held little interest for her. He seemed destined to remain stuck in the area, too. No way would she settle for the likes of him. He could keep on walking.

The few vendor tents on either side of the runway, behind the planes attracting dozens of people, held a variety of goods. She could see at least two boasting information on planes and the mechanics of flying. Two trucks huddled nearby, the aromas of grilled burgers and popcorn making her mouth water. She'd grab something later, after Jeremy's lesson.

"Afternoon, Miss Golden." A hefty older man, his long dark hair disappearing behind his wide shoulders, practically waddled up to Beth, uneven yellowed teeth revealed against tanned and leathery cheeks. "It's nice to see you."

She had to pause and scramble to recall the over-eager man. Blinking several times, she forced a smile to her lips. "I'm sorry. Do I know you?"

"Nat Bond." He reached out a hand, waiting for her to shake. "I ain't surprised you don't remember me. We met at the fall festival last year and you recommended a book for my wife's birthday."

She hesitantly clasped the man's hand. Her inner eye showed the man and a woman, perhaps of Asian heritage, living along what looked a lot like Coldwater Creek outside of town. A couple of children fished nearby, legs dangling over the edge of a pier. She released his hand and sighed. A peacefully mundane image for sure.

"Did she like it?" At the very least she needn't worry about him having any ideas of continuing a relationship, professional or otherwise. She dropped her shoulders back into place as she regarded the man.

"Oh, yeah. Best knitting book ever. She's been a-clickin' and a-clackin' them long needles nonstop." He chortled, face screwing up into a smiling knot, brows bushed together over merry green eyes. He touched two fingers to his sweaty forehead. "Enjoy the show."

He waddled away, his bulk not hampering his progress for an instant. As he blended into the crowd, she scanned the people milling past. She consulted her watch to reassure herself she'd not been late. Then searched the faces walking by until the piercing cry of a hawk drew her gaze up to the sky. A red-tailed hawk circled above, creating graceful circles above the oblivious people below. She shaded her eyes to see more clearly, focusing on the splayed tail feathers and outstretched wings.

The bird of prey coasted high above, searching the fields surrounding the hangars and various small buildings. She imagined his sharp gaze traveling over the ground, hunting field mice and shrews for his next meal. With all the paving of runways and taxiways, the hunter would have to go farther afield to find food. She dropped her hand as she contemplated the changes in the landscape. The airport construction had cleared acres of land once home to countless animals and insects. Forced to pack their little bags and venture to other fields and streams to start anew. If she were to venture to distant lands, at least she'd come back to where she started. No one-way trips for her. Assuming she ever had any trips.

"Hey, Beth, there you are." Sue hurried toward her, Jeremy close at her side. She'd changed for the occasion into flowered walking shorts and white tee with sturdy tennis shoes. Dark sunglasses perched on top of her head, reflecting the white clouds building above.

"Hi, Miss Beth." The lanky teen nodded in greeting, his

milk-chocolate hair brushing his dark blue polo shirt collar. "Thanks for staying with my grandma to keep her company."

"Are you excited, Jeremy?" Beth moved closer so she could shake hands with him. When their hands met, her inner eye transported her to another time and place. Jeremy in the cockpit wearing a major airline's uniform, a classy billed hat set firmly on his crewcut hair. She grinned as she clasped his hand more firmly. "You never know where these flying lessons might lead."

"I can't wait to be up there." He shot a glance up at the circling hawk and then back to meet Beth's steady gaze.

"Come on, you two, we're going to be late." Sue herded them to the end of the open alley between the two rows of planes toward a small building with a sign in front that claimed flying lesson registration. "Over this way."

Two men waited in front. Both were handsome, tall and muscular, their carriage announcing their military training. The black man smiled warmly, his amber eyes dancing with interest and humor. Attractive with a devilish grin. She returned the greeting as he tapped the other man and they started walking toward Beth and her friends. She sensed his determination and ambition from twenty feet away. The closer he came the more she felt his strong personality. Combined with a thread of competition at odds with compassion. A very complicated man but probably a very interesting person.

The white man hid his eyes behind aviator glasses. His shoulder-length, dark-blond hair was gathered into a ponytail, emphasizing broad, muscular shoulders. She couldn't see his eyes but could feel the weight of his regard. His confident, sexy strides set her pulse soaring like the hawk. He removed his glasses and hung one earpiece into the unbuttoned opening of his open collar shirt, revealing eyes so dark brown they appeared black in the bright sunlight. When their gazes met, the air shimmered and pulsed for a moment, a visual quaking of the atmosphere. Her pulse took off until she couldn't hear anything but the rush in her veins. She blinked several times and tried to steady the tremor in her knees without revealing her unexpected reaction.

He glanced at Sue, then Jeremy, and then aimed those decadently dark chocolate eyes her way and she nearly melted with longing to touch him. To know him. To see his present and his future.

"Are you Jeremy?" Keith flicked his gaze from the boy to Sue and then to Beth before regarding Jeremy again.

"Yes, sir." Jeremy held out his hand to shake with the taller man.

"Great. This is Mitch Sawyer, my friend, who is going to teach you the basic stuff today."

"Howdy, folks." The tall blond looked at each of them.

"I trust your friend is a certified instructor like you are?" Sue nervously fingered the hem of her shirt.

"He's more qualified than I am to teach your grandson, Mrs. Grimwood." Keith glanced at Mitch, a shadow passing through his eyes like a fast moving cloud on a sunny day. "Jeremy will be in very good hands."

Sue aimed her slight frown at Mitch, apparently waiting for him to confirm or deny the statement. Beth noticed when Mitch realized the older woman's silent regard. Smiled to herself when he started and nodded his head.

"Yes, ma'am. I am a licensed pilot with years of teaching experience in the Air Force and beyond. Don't worry."

"Top of his class, that's our Mitch." Tapping the man in question on the shoulder, Keith grinned. "He's got the real right stuff."

Mitch chuckled but looked askance at Keith before shaking his head. "That was a long time ago."

A sudden tension simmered between the two friends. She frowned at the unease that wrapped around her. She mentally reached out to sample Keith's future, seeing him content with his life and his two Labradors. Relaxing on a wraparound front porch of a house and towering shade trees. Where were the other people in his life? Maybe he lived alone for a long time. Or the troublesome past he shared with Mitch would cause a disturbance in his future. A wave of sadness on his behalf flowed through her. But then Keith grinned and the tension dissipated. He regarded her for a beat, aware she'd been staring at him. Her cheeks warmed. The interest in his eyes increased, his grin softening into a question. Unsure what answer he sought, she blinked and turned her attention back to Jeremy. A much safer subject.

"Jeremy has been looking forward to this for a long time, too. Haven't you?" Beth sensed an almost audible sigh of relief from Mitch.

"Yes. Can we begin?" Jeremy pivoted to gaze at the plane, envy plain in his eager expression.

"Let the lesson begin." Keith shifted closer to Beth, shot her a smile, and then glanced at his watch. "I've got to go take care of an issue. Mitch will take it from here."

With a wave of his hand and a wink for Beth, Keith hurried away, his long stride propelling him quickly across the tarmac. She stared after him, feeling a connection forming between them. A tentative sliver of understanding between two people who felt adrift in the world. Searching for meaning among the mundane. He paused to look back at her, then lifted a hand and turned away. Unsettled, she brought her attention back to what Mitch was saying.

"So, we'll begin with the nuts and bolts and then move on to the actual flying." Mitch smiled at Sue and then peered at the teen for a moment or two. "It's not for everyone, and there's no shame in finding out that it's not what you want to do. Hear?"

"Yes, sir." Jeremy nodded slowly and then grinned. "I think I'll like it though. I like going fast."

"That's a good start." He encompassed Jeremy and Sue in a sweep of his gaze. Then he addressed Beth, his dark brown eyes twinkling in the afternoon light. "I'm sorry. We haven't been introduced. What's your name?"

A hint of challenge echoed in his question. She liked the man's mannerism, his direct nature, and the sensual vibe sizzling over her skin. Reserved yet open, relaxed but poised to defend himself. He could be sexy or dangerous, or both. She skimmed over his features, enjoying the masculine strength evident in every aspect of his person. Indeed, there was a lot to enjoy when looking at the man. But she didn't know anything about him. Past, present, or future. Odd, for a person with the ability to see the prospects of others. She'd have to become acquainted the muggle way. She silently chuckled at her joke.

"Beth Golden. A friend." She accepted his hand, eager to see into his future.

When he closed his fingers around hers, something akin to lightning bugs lit up her insides. No mere butterflies with their gentle wings. She flashed a look at the dare in his eyes and waited to see what the path ahead held for him. Instead, she saw a young woman in a ball gown consoling a crying boy. Then nothing. No other hint of what might lie in Mitch's future. Why? How did he manage to shield her vision of what was to come? She'd never experienced such a block to her ability. Suspicions flared inside and she pulled her hand away.

Mitch frowned slightly at her reaction and then pivoted to address Jeremy. "Ready to get started?"

As they walked over to begin the lesson, Beth slowly trailed behind them. Confused and a touch disappointed, she studied him while he began introducing the parts of the plane. The man proved a real enigma, especially since he'd managed to prevent her inner eye from seeing into his future. Who was the woman? Why was the boy crying?

Despite the concerning mystery, she was drawn to his charismatic personality, evident strength, and confidence. Coupled with the hint of daring she'd seen in his eyes, he could be just what she needed to spice up her flat life. Or he could be her downfall. She stopped beside Sue, but kept a close watch on Mitch. Seeing was believing.

The trim single-engine Archer reflected the afternoon sun, sending bright shafts of light into Mitch's eyes. He positioned his sunglasses on his nose as he strode over to the plane. All the while he wondered why the pretty chick had linked up with the kid and his granny. Not that he minded having such a fine specimen of the opposite sex hanging around. He'd noticed her when she'd first arrived, lingering by the food truck. Talk about a stunner. All that long, golden hair surrounding a sweet face, and her curvy figure filling out khakis and a black top to perfection. When she'd shaken his hand, he sensed her surprise as he inhaled her too-floral, too-sweet perfume. Her pale green eyes shot through with gold sparks impaled him with a look he couldn't interpret. Why had she suddenly tensed and practically yanked her hand away? He'd swear she watched his every move since their introduction.

He stopped in front of the propeller and waited until Jeremy stood beside him, the boy's grandmother and eagle-eyed friend a few steps back. That would never do. He motioned for the women to join the group, solely so they wouldn't feel left out. *Yeah, sure. That's the reason.* Couldn't have anything to do with the tempting beauty. He must concentrate on the lesson. He squared his shoulders and addressed Jeremy.

"Let's start with the basics of the plane so you'll know what part I'm talking about as we proceed. Follow me." Mitch led Jeremy and the ladies around the plane, pointing out and naming the various major parts and flight control surfaces, all while demonstrating what he was looking for on a preflight. The entire time Beth's gaze weighed on his shoulders. He stifled a grin, liking her inquisitive yet wary attention. Coming full circle to the front of the aircraft, he stopped. "Now it's time to get in and get to know the controls. Ready?"

Jeremy perked up. "Yes, sir."

"Just a minute." Beth moved closer, concern in her beautiful eyes. "Don't you need to do some kind of"—she waggled one hand helplessly—"ground training before you let him in the cockpit?"

He tilted his head a little to one side and flashed his biggest smile to reassure her. "Nah. This is only an intro flight. The real ground training won't come until the second lesson. Now I'm just introducing the plane and then I'll take him up for a quick flight, but I'll have the controls."

"I don't get to fly?" Jeremy chewed on his lip, disappointment evident in the slight frown.

Mitch shrugged as he gave the boy his hope back. "I didn't say that. You'll get to handle the plane once we're up, just not during the takeoff and landing."

"Is that safe?" Beth crossed her arms over her bosom.

Mitch saw the action with his peripheral vision but forced his gaze to remain fixed on her eyes. His reaction to her presence distracted him in ways he hadn't experienced in—how long? Never. Surprise at the intensity of his awareness of her made him swallow hard.

"I won't put him in danger." Mitch smiled at the pretty yet skeptical blonde, trying to put her at ease and steady his racing heart. "Trust me."

Beth huffed and glanced at Sue. "You okay with this?"

Sue shrugged. "I want Jeremy to have the experience and see if it's what he really wants. Then we'll take it from there."

Beth studied Mitch, concern morphing into determination in her eyes. "Just promise to take care of this guy."

"If you have such reservations, maybe you should just come along." Mitch winced. Why on earth did he say that? Still he'd have complete control. And he'd have Beth close at hand as well. She probably would say no anyway, not wanting to take the risk. In his experience, young, beautiful women didn't frequently dare flying in small aircraft. Passenger jets and commercial planes, sure. But not so much the smaller aircraft. Maybe inviting her would end her questions and concerns. "There's room if you dare to put your life in my hands."

She blinked once, making the gold flecks in her eyes flash. "Fine. But you better know what you're doing."

Know what he was doing? He'd been a pilot for nearly fifteen years. Studied and practiced fighter techniques and tricks and earned honors and awards. She had absolutely no right to question his ability. Her lack of faith in him stung even though he knew it shouldn't. He didn't know her any more than she knew him. If he planned to stay in town he might change that, but his time was limited. Get in, grab the repo plane, and get out. As a result, he'd keep it cool and not do something foolish. His libido simply had to chill.

"Trust me, I know what I'm doing." He peered at her until she glanced away and back to face him. "You're along for the ride, and that's all. Understood?"

"Aye-aye, captain." She mock saluted and then propped her hands on her hips. "I will try to keep my observations to myself."

Mitch hid his mild discomfort with a grin, refraining from correcting her. He hadn't been a captain in years. He glanced at the sky and the approaching clouds. "Time's a-wasting."

"Cool." Jeremy looked at both of them, delight radiating from his entire being. "Let's go."

"After you." He motioned for Beth and Jeremy to clamber into the plane as he slowly followed.

What happened? Mitch clenched his jaw as he took his seat and prepared to take off. He'd probably live to regret his rash challenge, but damn if he didn't love the idea of having the woman close. Even if it were for only the length of a demo ride. Then she'd have to go, move on, leave him alone to take care of business. He started the engine and ended his fruitless musing on the woman sitting so close he couldn't take a breath without inhaling her scent. He eased the plane into motion and turned his attention away from the intriguing and distracting woman behind him. The sooner he finished the boy's lesson, the sooner he'd be free to concentrate on executing and completing his mission.

Chapter Three

$\mathcal{A}$s the runway fell away from view through the side window of the plane, Beth settled back in her seat prepared to try to enjoy the experience. Mitch pointed out the gauges and controls and their uses to Jeremy, sitting in the co-pilot seat. She could see that the teen would take to flying like a bird, so didn't need to worry on that score. She could relax—or attempt to given the vibes flowing off Mitch like hot lava—and watch the scenery glide past. She stared out the window, looking for landmarks.

"I'll use a little more left rudder to stay on course." Mitch's deep voice floated back from the cockpit. "Because of the spin direction of the propeller, you want to use the left, not the right, rudder or you'd keep going farther off course. See how that works?"

"Yep. Can I try?"

"Not yet, but soon."

She half-listened to the lesson, more aware of the instructor than the student. She sensed he monitored her as much as she stayed tuned to him. A certain energy reached her, carrying both his unease with her presence as well as the echo of the vision of the woman and boy. The woman had seemed afraid even as she hugged the boy, wiping away his tears. Who was she? Maybe Mitch's future wife? That would make the boy his son. All of which meant that despite her attraction to the man, she needed to steer clear emotionally. Relief warred with regret at the thought. Another reason to consider finding out more about Keith instead. His future seemed peaceful enough despite the conflicting emotions and goals he harbored. Still, no harm in being friendly with Mitch.

She leaned forward as far as her seatbelt allowed. "Hey, Mitch, do you fly for fun or business?"

He glanced over his shoulder, his dark eyes questioning her, and then focused on the windshield. "More business than pleasure."

"What kind of business?" She kept her hands on her knees to temper the ongoing urge to touch him.

So tempting to reach out and lay her hand on his shoulder. Direct contact being a clearer way of connecting and seeing. What else might his future hold? More than the gist of his hopes and dreams. The brief handshake they'd shared on the ground hinted at the intensity of what she could anticipate the next time. She drew in a deep, hopefully calming breath and pressed her hands harder on her knees.

"This and that." Mitch adjusted a knob, his muscular hand sure and swift in the movement.

"So what brought you to our small town?" His fingers gripped the yoke, the muscles in his arm flexing with every small movement. Swallowing, she forced her gaze to the windshield. She had to keep her mind off his physical characteristics. Concentrate on being friendly and welcoming until she understood him better.

He tilted his head briefly. "A freelance job to pick up a plane."

She stiffened at his curt tone. She simply wanted to make small talk instead of sitting in silence. "I don't mean to pry. I'm just curious by nature."

He half-turned to peer at her over his shoulder. "You know what happened to the cat, right?" He chuckled, his good humor twinkling in his mesmerizing eyes. "Be careful or you might regret it."

When he turned away, she thought again of the woman and child. Her hair was fashioned into an elaborate arrangement Beth would never attempt. Fancy dress, too. All glittering and golden gown. Like something for a ball or prom. So why the tears? The image faded in the blink of an eye. She was left staring through the plane's windshield at the blur of land below. Wondering whether his warning was real or a joke.

Jeremy looked at Beth with his eyes alight with joy. "I want to fly everywhere. It's better than driving a car."

Beth smiled at the eager young man, curious as to how far his flying might take him. If he followed the path that led to being a major airline pilot, he would likely travel all around the world. "Where would you go, Jeremy?"

A sudden thought chilled her. He may leave and never return. Maybe only visit his grandmother for holidays. She wouldn't see him around town, see him mature and make his own home and family. She'd watched other kids grow up and marry, settle down to small-town life. The routine and daily chores of living and working. Jeremy, at least, would be free to explore all his options, even if the idea saddened her.

"Everywhere." He flung his hands wide as he aimed a grin at her. "Want to go with me?"

"Sure I do. I want to go to faraway places and see amazing things. Have a real adventure, live a bit dangerously." She huffed at the idea, knowing she had little chance of making her dreams a reality. "But honestly, you may have to come back and tell me all about yours instead."

Generations of Goldens had lived and worked in Roseville. Her place remained at her sisters' side. Even if she didn't work at the Golden Owl, a nonstarter of an idea, she couldn't imagine living anywhere else. Tara would object to her being gone for long, fearful of her being injured and her not nearby to assist. But a week or so would be refreshing, a vacation from the routine.

"But if you did, where would you go?" The teen shifted back around to focus on the view out the windshield.

Low mountains draped in varying shades of green and lush emerald fields slid beneath the plane. Clusters of white houses with green roofs and red or black sided barns dotted the terrain. The family that farmed the pretty valley were frequent customers at the Golden Owl, popping in for the latest in agriculture research and a cold soda. Their grazing herds of Black Angus and white-and-brown Hereford cows as well as flocks of Suffolk sheep, their distinctive white bodies with black face and legs visible even from such a height, remained oblivious to the people watching them from the sky. The horizon loomed far in the distance, the unknowns of what lay beyond huge in her mind. She'd never been able to see such a long way. Even the gathering clouds to the west couldn't obscure the rounded curve of the planet at the horizon.

"I want to go so many places, Jeremy. To the Mayan ruins in Mexico and the Pyramids in Egypt. Explore the jungles in South America. Maybe even go on a safari in Africa."

Exotic locales all, but ones she'd only ever seen in travel guides. Maybe one day she'd be able to make such a trip, any of them, possible. She suppressed the sigh of frustration in order to keep her disappointment in check. She knew her place and duty. No sense in bringing down Jeremy's happiness.

The atmosphere in the plane changed—cold fog settling over a sunny valley—making her frown. She pondered the change as Mitch resumed the lesson, finally letting Jeremy take the controls. After several minutes lapsed while she probed her senses and their feedback, she pinpointed the difference. Mitch had shut down his thoughts, boxed them in to focus only on Jeremy's handling of the aircraft. No more visions of the woman and boy came in her mind. Nothing but the immediate future of flying and landing the plane.

How had he done that? Perhaps it was a mental technique used to focus in specific situations. Where had he learned to do that? Why had he been so vague with his answer to her questions? Acting all cagey and defensive. She'd never seen him before but she didn't know everybody in Roseville let alone the surrounding county.

The airport had been built far from town to placate the residents as to the noise level and resulting disturbance to the quiet atmosphere. His presence disturbed her in both pleasant and unpleasant ways. She didn't know nearly enough about this enigmatic, alluring male. Not that she knew much about any man. Keith's laughing features popped into her mind, overlaid by the tantalizing man sitting in front of her. Both men raised a swarm of questions. One way or the other, she needed to find answers.

"That's right, hold the yoke steady to keep the plane level." Mitch kept his attention on his student, pleased with how readily he understood the mechanics of flying a plane. "You're a natural."

He'd discovered a certain joy associated with the education and training of new pilots. He relished the opportunity to share what he knew with young airmen to foster their credentials for advancement in the Air Force and beyond. Not every airmen desired to become a general. In fact, many secretly wanted to serve a few years, learn what they could, and then begin a civilian career path. Much like himself.

"Thanks, Mr. Sawyer." Jeremy grinned but kept his focus on the controls and where the plane was heading.

"So the choke controls the mixture of air to fuel of the engine?"

A puff of air on the side of his neck from Beth's question told him how near she was to him. He suppressed a shiver of desire as he swallowed. Her proximity kept his senses on high alert, the too-sweet scent she wore enveloping him. He admitted to having a heightened sense of smell which made perfumes particularly noticeable. The floral scent didn't suit her personality, not the way he thought about her. She needed a soft yet alluring fragrance, a hint of spice blended in. Still, she was more than a beautiful woman. She was obviously very smart and caring. She seemed to grasp the concepts even easier than Jeremy in all his eagerness.

"Right." If only she hadn't mentioned wanting to travel to exotic and, worse, dangerous places. "It's only adjusted before the flight, though."

Up until that point he thought they might have a connection. Had hoped for one. But even if they couldn't be a couple, she might be the right partner for the job. He didn't feel right skirting her questions with evasive answers. On the other hand, he didn't know who she might talk to. Might reveal his intentions if he were to talk about them. The potential for deep roots and connections in her life might work against his need for secrecy until he had the plane. He needed to know more before he could share why he was really in town. If he ever did share it with her.

Beth's voice brought him back to the present. "Why do you—what's it called? Trim the plane?"

"Good question and one not easily answered as there are several factors to consider." Mitch liked her insightful question. Not many first-time students even thought to ask it. Yep. The woman's smarts equaled her beauty. "The short answer is that trimming the plane reduces the amount of effort it takes to control the plane and thus makes it less tiring to fly." He pointed at the mechanism as he glanced over his shoulder to see if she understood. "There's the wheel you turn forward or back, depending on the pitch of the nose, to level out the plane.

A slight frown settled on her brows as she considered his explanation. He turned back to observe Jeremy's handling of the yoke and the flight controls. The boy handled the airplane as if he'd been flying for years. The kid could go far in the world of aviation. Would he end up in the Air Force, a fighter pilot like Mitch had been? A demanding profession but very rewarding, one that could lead to bigger challenges over time. Or would he be a commercial pilot? Flying passengers all around the world? Jeremy might even choose to be a bush pilot, flying hunters into the wilderness of the mountains to hunt big game, like Mitch had once contemplated. Before the adrenaline rush of jets took hold.

The rustle of clothing preceded another breath on his neck. "The pitch causes friction on the outside, so you trim it to level it out and reduce the drag?"

"Not exactly. Pitch is more about direction, not friction. Having the right trim does reduce the friction, though." He shivered and chose to end the discussion of trimming until they were on the ground. And she wasn't literally breathing on his neck. Besides, he needed visual aids to demonstrate the how's and why's of the process. "We'll go over it at a later lesson if Jeremy decides to continue."

"Definitely. I love flying." Jeremy gripped the yoke with both hands, keeping the plane level and on course.

"I know you'll do well." Beth sat back in her seat. "You never know what doors will open once you complete your flight training."

A note of assurance in her voice made Mitch wonder about her statement. While opportunities would present themselves after he had his license, nobody could predict what exactly they might be. Let alone the young woman behind him. Yet her tone hinted at a certain level of confidence in the boy's future.

He paused his thoughts as he realized he knew next to nothing about her. After all, it had only been maybe an hour since he first saw her stroll into view. Why did it seem as if he'd known her forever? As if he had been waiting for her to walk into his life? He blew a burst of air through his nose. Talk about fantasies. She was beautiful and smart and he wouldn't mind discovering she found him attractive. He could envision someone like her calling him husband. He'd started thinking about settling down the day he became a reservist. After all the jetting around the world, it was time. Find a hometown and stay put, then find a woman to love and cherish and start a family.

The son of a career airman, he'd grown up a military brat and all it entailed. A different home every couple of years in a distant place from the last one. He'd attended ten schools in twelve years, including three high schools. His dad retired after thirty years of service, well-respected and decorated accordingly. His mom had thrived on the sense of adventure moving brought with it, and she supported his dad without question. Even led the officers' wives club at some stations, hosting welcome brunches for newly arrived officers and their families. His dad loved his job and the military friends he made. A role model to strive and ultimately fail to live up to. Fifteen years in the service had taught Mitch his limitations. After all the changes of station he'd grown tired of figuring out the rules and laws in a new place, finding the best place to buy groceries, and making friends he'd have to leave behind with the next move.

"Maybe you should try flying, Miss Beth." Jeremy chuckled but kept his attention forward. "You're picking it up easily."

"I don't see the point." Beth chuckled along with the teen. "It won't help me get to work any faster, that's for sure."

He heard regret in her tone. A longing for change and what she called a little bit of danger. An idea niggled into his head. If she wanted to travel, have a touch of danger, then perhaps she'd be interested in helping him. From what he'd seen of her ability to assess a situation and adjust to change, she might find it all thrilling. Why not give her the chance for a little fun with an edge? To dabble briefly in the adrenaline rush of repo. He wouldn't mind getting to know her better, even if they didn't have a future together. Besides, he could take care of her just like he'd taken care of many others in his life.

"That depends on your job, doesn't it?" Mitch waited for her reaction, to see if she might be up for his challenge.

"What do you mean?" Beth's scent wafted closer as she leaned forward. "I work in town."

"For now, maybe." Mitch turned his head to speak over his right shoulder. "I might have a unique opportunity for you, if you're interested."

"A job of some kind?"

"I'll buy you lunch and tell you what I have in mind." Mitch focused on the aircraft's maneuvering instead of succumbing to the temptation to look more closely at her expression. He imagined her green eyes wide open as she considered what his offer might be, what it might mean to her future. "Deal?"

A slight hesitation told him she was mulling over his offer. "Okay."

"Great. Jeremy, it's time to head back. I'll take back the controls to prepare for landing." Mitch kept his gaze aimed out the window, ensuring they stayed within sight of the landing strip. Jeremy's innate sense of the aircraft impressed him. Perhaps Beth had a better grasp of the boy's abilities than he did.

"Like you said, you never know what doors might be opened if you had a pilot's license." Jeremy relaxed in his seat, turning to observe Mitch's handling of the controls.

"You did a fine job of handling the plane, Jeremy." Mitch checked the dials and gauges in one quick sweep. "Like you were born to it. At this point, I need a quiet cockpit to concentrate on landing safely."

Mitch flexed his fingers on the yoke. Nothing felt better than being up in the sky, soaring above the ground like one of the clouds, seeing the patterns of the landscape sliding by below. He lined up the plane with the landing strip and maintained the silence until he'd safely touched down with a perfect landing. He taxied back to where they'd begun the lesson and parked the plane.

Mitch unbuckled his lap and shoulder belts and clambered out of the plane, waiting for Jeremy and then Beth to climb out of the cabin. Jeremy dropped to the tarmac, grinning ear to ear as Sue hurried over to greet them. Mitch turned to make sure Beth descended to the ground safely. Just as he pivoted, her sandal caught on the edge of the last step and she lost her balance. Grabbing for something, anything, she started to fall—straight into Mitch's waiting hands. He caught her at the waist and eased her down to stand in front of him. She lifted those beautiful eyes to meet his gaze, a zinging current of desire coursing through his hands straight into his heart.

He stared into her lovely gaze, searching for some hint of recognition of the shared moment. Her eyes flickered as she blinked, glanced away and then back to meet his impatient gaze. The interest in her expression matched his own. A deep, visceral sensation. Churning his emotions into a need that stole his breath.

"Thanks. I don't know what happened." She lifted a trembling hand to her forehead for a moment.

"No problem. Are you okay?" Mitch realized he still held her waist and reluctantly released her and took a step back. He needed distance to recover. To sort out how to proceed.

"I think so." Beth glanced over his shoulder and smiled. "Hey, Sue, you missed your grandson flying the plane."

"I'm sure he'll tell me all about it on the way home." Sue looked around the group and then shook her head. "We've got to go, but it looks like you all enjoyed yourselves."

"If Jeremy wants to continue—" Mitch stopped as the boy in question burst forward.

"I do." Jeremy nodded vigorously until Mitch chortled at his enthusiasm.

"Then call Keith to set up the next lesson." He addressed Sue with a grin in place. "Jeremy's got a real talent for flying. I hope he'll stick with it."

Sue glanced at Jeremy. "Thank you for showing him the ropes. I'll see about those lessons next week. In the meantime, we need to go."

They said their farewells amid promises of getting together later. Mitch watched the friendly exchange with a touch of envy. They were like family even though not blood relations. He shifted his gaze to land on Beth who lifted her gaze to peer at him.

"I'm both starving and curious." Palms on her hips, she quirked a brow. "You're buying, right?"

He guffawed at her cheek and nodded. She most definitely had the right attitude for the job he had in mind. "Let's go."

Chapter Four

*B*iting into the gyro on pita, Beth savored the mix of spices, hot lamb and beef, topped with tzatziki sauce, shredded lettuce, and tomato. Maybe one day she'd eat a gyro in Greece, but for now the delicious sandwich would have to suffice. Her mother had a cookbook of recipes for foods from around the world. Appetizers, soups, casseroles and much more. Together they had tried many of them, working side-by-side to savor foreign tastes in their small-town home. Sharing the meals and reading about exotic locales had sparked her desire to visit them. See and taste for herself the real places. Yet, either time or money had been lacking. Somehow she'd find a way to make at least a short but fun trip to somewhere she'd never been.

Her gaze drifted over the other people seated around a dozen picnic tables in the welcome shade of large white umbrellas. Men in baseball caps and women in wide-brimmed straw hats sprung up among the bareheaded men and women like colorful mushrooms. Mitch added mustard to his Italian sausage on a bun, a pile of fries surrounding the sandwich.

"I wonder how hard it is to make gyro meat." She examined her sandwich, contemplating how sharp a knife she'd need to cut such thin slices of meat.

"Why would you want to?" He finished squeezing the brown mustard out of the packet.

She'd probably cut herself trying to slice the meat. "No real reason. I enjoy trying recipes from other countries."

"I'm fond of American foods, myself." He took a bite, brushing crumbs from his lips with two fingers.

Beth forced her gaze away from his mouth. "Why American?"

He lifted one shoulder, drawing her gaze to the muscles of his upper body. "Probably because I lived all over the world and so it came to represent home."

He'd seen and done so much. She'd lived all her life in one place. The same house. The same town. Attracted or not, she had no doubt they'd never be a couple. They had nothing in common.

"You wanted to talk about a job?" Beth lifted her bottle of water and took a long drink, cooling her parched throat.

He bit into the sausage and nodded, chewing quickly before swallowing. "I thought you'd want to eat first, but if you're in a hurry then I can get right to it."

"Please. I can't stay out here all day. Work is calling me." Not so much but she really needed to keep her distance from him. Her physical reaction to him when he stopped her from falling had surprised her more than she thought possible. A shiver-worthy rush of desire had left her shaking even more than her close call. With her knowledge of the woman and child she'd seen connected with him, allowing her attraction to him to continue could only be futile. They were not destined to be together.

"Okay, then let me tell you why I'm here." He leaned closer as he made a quick scan of the people seated near them before he continued. "I came to Roseville to steal back a plane from some dude who didn't pay the mortgage on it."

"Steal?" Her heart fell. She wouldn't be involved in anything illegal no matter how challenging.

"From his point of view, yes. But I have the legal paperwork to repossess it." Mitch glanced around again then focused on her. "Not that he's likely to agree. Which is why I have to do this on the sly. That's where you come in."

"You want me to persuade him to let you take it?" She raised both brows at the absurdity of such an idea. "I doubt I have the skills for that."

"I need you to help me make sure the logbook is in the plane while I do the preflight check to make sure the plane is airworthy."

"The logbook?" She frowned at him. "Why do you need it?"

He wiped mustard from the corner of his mouth with a finger, licking it clean. "To prove the flight history and maintenance record. Without it, the value of the plane plummets. It's not unheard of that the delinquent borrower keeps the book with him to prevent the plane from being taken."

"Where would it be?" She took another bite and chewed quickly.

"I don't know yet. I spotted the plane earlier but haven't had chance to reconnoiter further." His dark brown eyes regarded her. "Will you help me?"

"Sounds dangerous." She couldn't help the bubble of excitement expanding in her chest. Finally, something new and thrilling to do. "Is it?"

"Not this time. I don't think, anyway." Mitch took another bite of his sandwich and studied her. "I wouldn't put you in danger."

Well, dang. There went the bubble. "How do you plan to get close to the plane?"

He slowly shook his head and then drank from his bottle of beer. "I haven't figured that out yet. But I need to before the show is over or he'll fly away and I'll miss my chance."

"Why me?" The question burst out of her mouth. Nobody had ever asked her to participate in such an act. Was she even qualified?

He shrugged and glanced away briefly. "Because you're smart and a quick study. But you can't tell anyone." He looked at her, his dark eyes serious. "Can I trust you?"

"I'll have to let my sisters know something if I'm not going to be at the store."

"Sisters?" He held the beer bottle with the fingertips of both hands, slowly spinning it around.

"Tara and Roxie. We own the bookstore in town. They won't say anything to anyone else if I ask them not to."

"You're sure?" He studied her before taking a bite of his sandwich. "I really can't afford for this to fall through."

"I'm sure." She needed to make the chance for some risky fun a reality. Something inside screamed at her to grab the opportunity with both hands and not let go. "I won't lie. I'm intrigued. But we need a plan."

"Let's walk down to where the plane is parked and see what we can come up with." He stood and carried his trash to the large can.

Beth scrabbled up her napkin and followed suit. Her veins hummed with barely suppressed enthusiasm. "Let's go."

Walking beside the tall, muscular man, Beth was very much aware of the admiring glances from other women in the crowd. They couldn't know she and Mitch weren't a couple, but the knowledge burned in her chest. He drew her to him but she must resist, knowing what she did. In spite of her awareness of his future wife and child, she planned to enjoy every minute of his company. Right or wrong. Merely being with him gave her a thrill unlike anything she'd experienced in her life. Partly because she couldn't read much of his future, and partly because he seemed confident in himself and wherever his path led him.

He motioned for her to stop and then pointed to his target. "The logbook should be in the plane but we need to verify that it's there. They run tours before and after the actual air show is on."

A plane with a propeller stood ready on the tarmac in front of a large motor home. She couldn't imagine driving anything as huge as the RV. Two men in slacks and tee shirts relaxed in folding chairs under the awning, keeping an eye on the crowds waiting for their next customer. The plane boasted red stripes down the side and up the tail.

"How do you propose to take the plane when they're sitting right there?" Beth studied the men and the situation, finding no answers to her own question. "Have you done this before?"

"Not in this scenario, but yes, I've repo'd planes for the last several years." He shrugged lightly as he kept his eyes on the target. "It's never the same situation and never easy."

"Why do you do it then?" She looked at him, the steady way he analyzed the situation.

His ponytail draped over one shoulder, tempting her to reach out to touch the dark golden hair. The compulsion to put her fingers on his hair made her flex her hand. Almost of its own volition, her hand lifted toward him. Too soon to act on such an impulse. She shoved her hands into her pockets and forced her gaze back to the two men and the problem they posed.

"The payoff." He swiveled his head, his gaze weighing on her for a moment. "Banks really like getting their planes back when some son of a bitch doesn't live up to his end of the deal."

"So, you paying me, too?" She turned to toss a wink at him, instantly regretting her flirtation when he nodded. "Really?"

"It's a job, remember?"

"Yes, but…"

"No but's. I'll give you ten percent of the take."

"Which is how much?"

He quoted a four-figure number and she blanched. Then flushed red hot. More than a month's pay for a few hours of work. "Oh…"

"We just need to come up with a way to get into that plane without either of those men suspecting what we're going to do."

"Then what?"

"Then we fly it out of here and present it to the bank representative who will take possession."

Beth blinked several times, her mind racing. Then she smiled. "Mitch, you're a genius."

"I am?"

"I have an idea. What if I buy you an intro flight like Sue did for Jeremy? You know, a present? Then you can go through the preflight inspection with the dude to make sure it's safe to fly. I'll go along for the ride and you'll be up in the air with him and can take over the controls."

"While you're getting settled in the back seat you can make sure the logbook is in the cockpit where it should be. We need that, or there's no deal." Mitch studied her, his gaze flicking occasionally over to the two men chatting in the shade.

"Easy peasy." A flush of excitement warmed her cheeks. "We can do this."

He stared at the plane, the men, the RV, and then back to the plane. "It might work. But if it doesn't, our cover is blown and we won't get another chance."

"Then it will have to work." She steeled herself for him to shut down the scheme. Tell her it was too dangerous or silly. Either way she'd miss out on a chance for some fun. She pinned him with her eyes until he looked at her. "Please?"

"Are you sure you want to do this? They're not going to take this well. There is always an element of danger even though fairly low on this repo."

"Without a doubt." She shifted to look up at him, sensing his reluctance and yet knowing he needed her help. "When do you want to do it?"

"We need to do it tomorrow. Schedule the flight as early tomorrow as possible, and we'll meet here in the morning." He pulled out his phone and held it in both hands. "Give me your number so we can coordinate."

A thrill having nothing to do with the adventure on her doorstep shimmied down her spine. He'd asked for her number, something she rarely gave out to strong, handsome men with a penchant for excitement. Breathlessly, she recited her number to him. Then he aimed those dark as night eyes at her with a smile.

"Do you want mine?"

Oh yes, she did. "If you don't mind."

She keyed in the new contact information and then hit save. How long would she keep his info in her phone? That was a very good question. One she wasn't prepared to answer.

With June a few days away, the sweet scents of roses and azalea bushes hung heavy in the evening air. Beth stepped onto the sidewalk leading up to the kitchen door, casting a glance over the backyard as she strolled toward the house she shared with her oldest sister, Roxie. It still seemed strange that Tara no longer lived in the ancestral home with them. She and Grant lived across town since their marriage on New Year's Day. After five months, Beth should be used to just the two of them rattling around in the big old house. Should.

She slowed to a halt when she spotted her sister reading in the conversation pit at the far back corner of the yard.

41

Without making a conscious decision, Beth changed direction and followed the stepping stones to the circular brick patio with its fire pit surrounded by four cushioned chairs. The yard was in full bloom, vines of colorful flowers clung to the slats of the privacy fence. Carefully weeded and pruned beds surrounded the patio and hugged the walkway, bursting with color and scent. She stopped at the edge of the patio, waiting until Roxie, wrapped in an angora crocheted afghan, slowly blinked and looked up from the novel in her hands.

"Did you have a nice time at the air show?" Roxie marked her place with her index finger and lowered the book to rest on her crossed knee.

"Jeremy had a good time and will likely become a fine pilot." Beth sauntered to the closest chair and relaxed on its deep cushion.

"What about you, though?"

Beth shrugged lightly and laid her head back, her gaze on Roxie. How much should she tell her protective sister? "I liked the flying. It looks easy enough once you understand how the plane's mechanics work."

Roxie chuckled as she noted the page number and then laid the book on the wide arm of the chair. "Things aren't as easy to do as they may look on paper, you know."

"Once you have an idea of the theory behind the practice, it makes it much easier to master."

"That may be but not everyone is adept at mastering everything just because they have some book learning on the subject." Roxie brushed her brown hair, shot through with golden strands, back over one shoulder. "Remember my attempt at SCUBA diving? I aced the written tests…"

"You couldn't help being afraid of the waves and dark water." Beth shook her head as she sat up straighter. "You couldn't have known without trying. It's not your fault."

"My point exactly. Just because flying looks easy when you watch someone else, doesn't mean it's the right thing to do."

"Mitch asked Jeremy if he wanted to keep flying, and Jeremy was very eager." Beth caught some flyaway strands of hair tugged by a burst of wind and tucked them behind her ear.

"Who's Mitch? And why did your eyes light up when you mentioned him?"

"What? They did not." Beth shook her head, unwilling to admit any level of attraction to the sexy pilot. "Mitch was the flight instructor."

"And?" Roxie rolled her hand in the air, encouraging Beth to continue. "I can see it in your eyes, you're excited about something."

Roxie knew her far too well. "He's also into repossessing airplanes when somebody defaults on their loan."

Roxie raised one brow and splayed both hands, palms facing the darkening sky. "So what does that have to do with you?"

Everything, if she did a good job. She'd thought about little else all the way home. The sense of expectation and intrigue blended together to set her pulse on high boil. Yet she had to temper her exhilaration because of the uncertainty his apparent ability to block her visions introduced into the situation. She couldn't tell how things would end, whether good or bad. Which of course added to the thrill.

"He's asked me to help him tomorrow."

"Help him do what?" Concern laced Roxie's question.

"Steal back a plane, of course." Beth gripped her knees, leaning forward as a grin stretched across her mouth. "And I thought of how we can do it. Isn't that fun?"

"Slow down, sister. Who is this guy?"

"I told you. Mitch Sawyer is a pilot and he's contracted to do an airplane repo and I'm going to help him pull it off."

"That's all you know about this dude?" Roxie slowly shook her head, keeping her gaze on Beth. "I don't like the sound of this at all."

"I do. It's just what I need." Beth pressed her fingers into her kneecaps, forcing herself to remain seated when she wanted to leap up and do a jig. "It's like something straight out of my suspense novels. The tall, handsome man with grit and determination who needs the fiery, beautiful woman to help save the day."

"By stealing a plane? Are you insane?" Roxie tapped the cover of her book with one finger. "What you read in your books is fiction. What you're planning to get involved in is not."

Beth waggled one hand in the air, brushing aside her sister's worries. "I know that. I'll be careful. But Mitch promised I won't be in any actual danger on this job."

"This Mitch guy can't know the future but you can. What do you see?"

Beth sprung to her feet, her excitement bubbling over inside. "That's the wonderful thing about this whole idea. I have no idea how it will end. Isn't that cool?"

Roxie frowned, slowly blinking as she watched Beth's delighted pacing. "Why can't you see the outcome? I don't like this, Beth…"

"I don't know and don't care. I am dying to experience something surprising and unexpected for a change." She flopped back onto her chair, holding onto the armrests. "Don't be such a worry wart, Roxie. I'll be fine."

"Tell me what he wants you to do and why you think it will be safe." Roxie pulled off the afghan to drape over the back of the chair and then folded her arms across her chest, her entire body tense. "Why exactly shouldn't I worry?"

Beth slowly and carefully outlined the plan. The gift of a flight for Mitch. Her role in locating the logbook. Hopping the plane to a nearby airbase to get it back to the finance company. Easy. Roxie gradually lowered her arms to rest in her lap, fingers relaxing from fists to loosely twine together. Beth relaxed as well. Roxie seemed okay with the plan.

"So it will only be a few minutes until he gets control of the plane. No big deal at all."

Roxie sat silent for several seconds, concern plain on her face. "Do you need anything in particular to pull this off?"

"Not really." Beth suppressed the urge to pump her fist, settling for a smile instead. Her sister had recognized that Beth was adamant about seeing the mission through. Further objection wouldn't change her decision. "I could use your big flowery purse, if you don't mind."

"Do I want to know why?"

Beth wrinkled her nose. "I just have a feeling it might come in handy."

"I suppose if he's done this kind of thing before you can trust him to protect you?" At Beth's nod of agreement, Roxie's eyes clouded for a moment before clearing. "Promise me you'll do exactly what he tells you to do, and not take any unnecessary risks."

"Cross my heart and all that." Beth stood and moved to the edge of the patio. "The next thing I need to do is get online and buy Mitch's gift."

"I hope this doesn't backfire." Roxie pushed to her feet and retrieved her book and afghan before falling in beside Beth.

"Nothing will go wrong." Beth slipped her arm through her sister's as they continued up the path toward the house. "Wait and see."

Business was brisk at the Hideaway Restaurant, the holiday festivities drawing record crowds to the downtown eatery. Mitch had dropped off his gear at Keith's quaint house not far from the square. Met the two dogs briefly before they ventured out to find a place for the dinner Mitch had promised to buy his friend.

"It's amazing to run into you at my place." Keith hefted a beer mug with a wry smirk. "Of all the airports in the area…"

"I'm glad you made your plan work out." He'd tried to mentor Keith after the promotion disappointment. Most airmen could make it to major, but not all qualified. Better to not mention that elephant between them. "How did you decide on the location?"

"A client suggested it to me as a central place in need of an airport that could handle both propeller and jet traffic."

Mitch tossed back a swig of cold beer and then nodded as he swallowed. "That's a good point. I didn't know it existed until a contact told me about it."

"A contact?" Keith lifted one dark brow as he stared at Mitch. "Somebody sent you here?"

Mitch shrugged lightly, choosing to keep his reasons private. "They told me about the show so since I was passing through, I thought I'd check it out."

"Where are you heading?"

"I'm at loose ends for the moment. But starting to think about where I want to land. Permanently."

"Wow. That would be quite a drastic change for you." Keith took a drink and then set the mug on the table. "What do you think of Roseville?"

"I haven't seen much of it yet." The image of Beth Golden arose in his mind. "But I like what I've seen."

Keith studied him and then smirked. "A certain blonde come to mind? I agree. I'm glad I chose to move to this friendly town."

Mitch's heart sank to his knees. Schooling his expression to hide his inner turmoil, he nonchalantly drank his beer. Keith had proven over and over he could have any woman he set his mind on. If only for a single date, he could steal away a guy's gal without even trying. Something about him attracted the female of the species and nothing Mitch had ever done could counteract the impact he had on his conquests.

"So far, so good." Best to keep his true feelings buried deep. Redirect the conversation to neutral topics. "You said a client suggested you build here. What kind of work were you doing?"

Keith lifted one brow and guzzled from his mug, a sly smile matching the laughter in his sparkling eyes. "I was a corporate pilot for a while."

"Was it interesting?" Not sure what exactly a corporate pilot might be, Mitch eagerly waited for details. He had yet to decide which direction his career path should veer. "What did you do?"

"Pretty much everything related to the aircraft. Including keeping the hangar and plane clean and stocked. But I was in charge of the flight I was assigned to. No questions asked." Keith lifted his mug and set it on a round coaster. "The hops were usually short and easy. Basically ferrying corporate bigwigs around the country, or their family on vacation. Whatever assignment the dispatcher sent my way."

More travel. Not of his own choice. Not for him. "Sounds exhausting."

"The pay was great and I made lots of good connections. A few that helped me with designing and building the airport, in fact."

"What do you mean?"

"The client who suggested this location, for instance. He went out of his way to scout the site out and then help me locate the architect." Keith fiddled with the sterling knife lying on the table, angling it one direction then another. "I wouldn't have gotten as far as I have without his prompting and even floating the cash to get the ball moving."

"He must've really wanted an airport here." Warning bells triggered in his gut. "Can you trust this guy?"

"Sure. He's one of the men in charge of the company and has investments all over the world. I know, because I've flown him to many of the cities where he does business."

A pretty waitress stopped at their table, pen poised over a small pad. "Ready to order?"

Mitch rattled off his order then watched Keith in action. Flashing those dark eyes with darker long lashes like a lovesick schoolboy. The lopsided grin that had the girl smiling back, batting her eyes and laughing at the little jokey way the man placed his order. She spun and sashayed away, still shaking her head.

"You're still at it, I see." Mitch chuckled at the surprised expression on his friend's face. "Flirting."

"Oh, that. Why stop?" Keith hefted his mug and took a long drink, wiping the foam from his lips with the back of his hand. "I'm not tied to anybody."

"Do you want to be?" He'd never asked him why he dated so many women but never seriously. Perhaps the man avoided fetters as much as Mitch sought them out.

"Maybe one day but not yet. I've got my dogs, they keep me company without judging me."

"They're quite a pair, Wilbur and Orville. But I'm thinking it's time for me to find a girl and start a family. In one place for a change."

The slow nodding of Keith's head showed his contemplation of the implied meaning behind Mitch's statement. "What about you, then? You're not active?"

"Inactive reserves for now. I need to make some decisions before I figure out my next move."

How much should he reveal to Keith about his repo work? Anything? The man obviously had many connections in his network. Contacts who might help Mitch, but then again they also might tip off the deadbeat and the plane be gone before the sun rose in the morning. Play those cards very close to the vest as a result.

"Settling down requires a steady flow of money, that's for sure. What kind of job are you looking for?"

"That's the question of the month. Something involving flying but not a lot of travel to distant places. I've had my fill." Nothing dangerous either, but he couldn't say as much without tipping his hand.

The waitress brought the platters of food and plunked them quietly down before first Mitch and then more slowly in front of Keith. Her smile was aimed directly at the dark-skinned man who returned it with a wink for good measure as she went on to the next table.

"What are you doing now?" Keith grabbed his cheeseburger and took a big bite, chewing and staring at Mitch.

"A little freelance work." He eyed the grilled ham and cheese sandwich, suddenly not very hungry. Thinking about what might happen the next day to him or worse to Beth made his stomach churn. "I have to do one more freelance job and then I can take a break to make decisions."

Chapter Five

S team rose from the Styrofoam cup, carrying the rich aroma of black coffee. Mitch swallowed and scanned the area. Where was she? The two men had prepped the plane and sat waiting, like him, for Beth to arrive. He glanced at the time. Five minutes. He took another swallow of the hot brew and let his gaze skim the crowd. He noticed a woman strutting toward him, black jeans and a yellow tank top hugging her curves as she drew closer. A floppy straw hat emphasized her movement while a large flowered bag clutched under one arm made her stand out against the landscape. But her lithe cat-woman stride mesmerized him.

He forced his fingers to loosen the death grip he had on his dented cup. Not some woman, but Beth Golden. Wow. He'd appreciated her beauty before. Now he could barely breathe as she sashayed to a halt in front of him, green eyes full of gold fire smiling up at him.

"Ready for your flying lesson, Mitch?" She winked at him, one hand going to her hat to settle it back in place. Already acting the tourist. Patting the purse, she canted her head with a smile. "I've got the paperwork right here."

He nodded, unable to trust his voice for a moment. She'd be a great distraction to the other men if his reaction served as an indicator. For now, their safety depended on him. Later he'd let his imagination out to play. He tamped down his clamoring libido and focused on the task at hand. Time to slip into his own newbie tourist character.

Mitch pasted a goofy smile on his face and made a show of enthusiasm as they turned toward their targets. "I can't believe you'd do this for me, Miss Beth. Thank you so much."

They approached the two men who rose in unison from their folding chairs. Mutt and Jeff looked like they were upstanding citizens but Mitch's file on them proved otherwise.

Mutt, otherwise known as Byron Carter, renowned for his extravagant life style he rarely paid for. Making money on one project to pay off the last flop, only to fail at the new endeavor and having to try yet another. The old rob-Peter-to-pay-Paul merry-go-round of finance. Only the current attempt involved an expensive plane the real owners, the bank, wanted back. Now.

Jeff, or Ned Wright, was not the sharpest pencil in the holder. Some questioned whether there was any lead at all. The man was adept at following orders, though, making him the perfect partner for someone like Carter.

They'd taken the plane but didn't make the payments for the past six months. Time for the good ol' boys to learn a little lesson from a certain pilot. He kept the false smile in place as he stopped in front of the two men. No sign of weapons but they could have them concealed in one of several ways. Like he did.

"Hi, there." Beth started talking, drawing their appreciative looks. "I bought a flying lesson package for me and my friend here to take a little hop in your airplane. Are we too late?"

"No, ma'am, you're right on time." Carter held out a hand to Beth and then to Mitch. "I'll be taking you both for a thirty-minute flight right after we sign the releases and take care of the final flight prep. Follow me."

Mitch grinned at Beth, ensuring for himself that she was still on board with the plan as they'd discussed. She winked at him and hurried after Carter.

"I'm so excited about taking a real airplane ride. It's my first time ever. Same for my friend. Should I be worried?"

Mitch trailed after her, admiring the view almost as much as her performance. Her hips shifted in a tantalizing rhythm. A quick toss of her head revealed her smiling face as she listened to the man's raspy voice.

"No, you've nothing to worry about. I've been flying for a lot of years now." Carter opened the door to the RV and waited until both Beth and Mitch had climbed up the steps and inside. The driver's seat was off to the right. He stood in the cramped living space, trying not to gag on the smell of cigarette smoke. Country music filled the air with twangy guitar. Across from the door, a small table covered in papers was flanked by two anchored captain chairs. To his immediate left a galley kitchen gleamed with stainless steel appliances and marble counters. A short hall to the left led to the bedrooms and bathroom. Very swanky digs. Especially for those two reprobates.

Carter led Beth to the table and showed her where to sign the form. She scrawled her name on the line and then handed the pen back to the erstwhile pilot with a flourish of her hand. Laughing, she pivoted and sashayed away to peruse the rest of the interior of the RV.

Carter turned to place the form in a pouch on the wall, struggling for a little while with sliding it into place among the many others crammed inside. He started muttering, practically cursing under his breath.

Mitch moved toward the back of the open space, his gaze drifting over the contents of the RV. He froze, spotting a logbook on the top of a book shelf on the far wall. The rest of the shelves held a variety of books and notebooks, along with a collection of planes. Carter and Wright only had one plane, so that meant the only logbook lay on the top of the case and not in the damn aircraft. His palms grew damp and he wiped them on his blue jeans. Why wasn't the book in the cockpit where it belonged? If the releases hadn't needed signing inside the RV, they might have failed before they even took off. Been in the air without the needed records for both the plane and his paycheck. Luck was on their side. Not that he believed in luck unless he made it for himself. A chill swept down his back. His gut told him to be extra cautious.

He glanced at Beth, inclining his head to draw her attention. He nodded to the book as he widened his eyes. Praying she'd interpret his message correctly.

She frowned but looked in the direction he'd indicated. Stared at the book, blinked several times, and then raised both brows at him. She lifted the oversize bag on her shoulder. He nodded once and then sidled over to stand by Carter who had turned back around.

"Where do I sign?" Mitch's heart pounded in his chest so loud he'd be surprised if Carter didn't hear it.

"Let me grab a blank." Carter tugged on a sheet of paper stacked on the table.

Beth went over toward the book shelf and then exclaimed over the collection of miniature aircraft gathered immediately beneath the logbook. "These are so cute! How darling."

Mitch glanced at the array of model airplanes. He spotted an airbus A380 beside several passenger planes. A cluster of open cockpit planes took center stage on one shelf. Even a model of the U.S.S. Enterprise spacecraft. He'd laugh if he wasn't so tense. Instead, he aimed his attention on the release form.

Carter harrumphed and shook his head, and then handed a pen to Mitch before pointing out where he needed to sign on the form. "We're about ready to head out to the plane, folks."

"Is there a restroom I could use? All this excitement and everything…" Beth let her voice trail off.

Carter dropped the pen on the table and shoved the last form into the wall pouch. He cut a sharp glance at Mitch and then smiled at Beth. "Sure, hon. Right through that little door on the left. We'll meet you out front when you're done."

Beth hurried down the short hall and into the small bathroom without a backward glance. What exactly did she plan to do? He'd told her not to improvise, but it looked like she had something in mind. It slowly dawned on him that he should maneuver Carter outside quickly. She'd nab the book after they left. He hoped. Mitch squared his shoulders and forced a carefree attitude when his every sense was tuned to Beth. He'd promised to keep her safe and yet he had to leave her alone in order to give her the time needed to swipe the logbook.

"So what happens next?" Mitch joined Carter at the door held open for him. He slipped outside into the bright sunlight, dropping his sunglasses into place.

Carter closed the door and indicated for Mitch to walk with him. He listened while the man described the features of the G36 as he moved around the plane, checking various connections. Pausing, he caught Mitch's attention.

"Your lady friend is taking a long time. Do you think you should check on her?"

"She'll be out in a minute." He hoped. What was taking her so long? "I can poke my head in and see what's what if you'd like."

"No, I'll do it." Carter pivoted and started walking toward the vehicle.

"Wait, I'd prefer to check on her." He waved at the aircraft, scrambling for a reason to detain the frowning pilot. "I wouldn't want her to be afraid."

"Seriously? I'm not going to hurt her." Carter kept walking, his strides quickly carrying him to the RV.

Mitch dogged his steps, catching up to Carter just as a Jeep rolled up to the RV and stopped. Now what? A young man, mid-twenties and blond, leaped out of the driver's side and strode toward the office. Who was he? He had no time to react to the new wrinkle in their plan.

"Alex, there's a lady inside. Check to make sure she's okay. We need to leave."

"Okay." Alex moved to yank on the door to the RV when it opened, pushing him back two steps as Beth emerged into the sunshine, hugging her oversize purse close to her side.

"Oh!" She startled when she noticed the man but recovered quickly, laughing off the close call with a smile. Trotting down the few steps, she smiled at the young man. "Thank you."

"No problem." The young man returned the grin and then went on into the office, the door banging closed behind him.

Mitch suppressed the immense sigh of relief and raised a brow at Beth who nodded slightly. Success.

"Okay, sir, Miss Beth is here so whenever you're ready we can get going." His fingers itched to take the controls and control of the situation. The rest of the plan's success rested on his shoulders. But not until they took off. "What can I do?"

"Let's get you both settled in the plane and then I'll finish the last couple of checks and we'll be off."

Carter opened the side door and helped Beth step inside. Mitch waited his turn before stepping up and easing through the opening. Mitch drooled at the opulent interior of the Beechcraft. Leather seats. Large tinted windows. The avionics in the cockpit were state of the art and arranged for optimum use.

"I never knew a plane could be so pretty." Beth settled into a seat, running her hands over the supple leather. "I'm impressed."

"Thanks. We really enjoy flying her." Carter secured the door Beth had used and then claimed the pilot's seat.

Within a few minutes, everyone was buckled in. Carter described what he'd be doing, then asked for quiet as he taxied down the runway. After they were safely in the air, he reviewed the takeoff procedures with his seemingly rapt audience. After a few minutes, Mitch decided to drop the act.

"Mind if I take the controls for a while?" Mitch looked at the other man, waiting for him to fall into his trap.

"It's easy." Carter toggled the main controls over to Mitch's side of the cockpit. "Keep your turns slow and easy and you'll be fine."

Mitch took control, enjoying the smooth operation of the machine. So much he delayed the reveal of their true intention so he could handle the finely crafted plane. The rolling hills and bright blue sky both seemed endless, welcoming him to where he felt most comfortable. Up in the air and in control. After veering the craft toward where the bank rep waited to take back possession, he decided to end the charade.

"I must confess that I haven't been completely honest with you."

"Oh?" Carter frowned slightly as he glanced at Mitch. "You've flown before, haven't you?"

"Yes, I have."

"I thought so. Why have you turned the plane toward the north?" Carter stared at him, daring him to say the wrong thing as he tensed.

"My name is Mitchell Sawyer and I've just repossessed this aircraft on behalf of the bank holding the mortgage."

Mitch glanced at the man to see how he'd react to the news. His pistol was tucked safely in a concealed holster at his waist, but he didn't want to have to pull it. The close confines of the cockpit would not be the place to start shooting.

"How dare you try to take my plane?" Carter's face flushed an angry red before mottling into an unbecoming mix of white and red blotches. "What right do you think you have?"

Mitch patted his pant pocket where he'd folded the authorization signed by the bank rep to repossess the plane. "I have the documentation right here. It's over. I'm taking this plane to Tullahoma and turning it over. Don't make this any more difficult for yourself."

"Are you kidnapping me along with the plane?" Carter continued to stare at Mitch, the surprise and anger morphing into defeated acceptance.

"Of course not. My job was to retrieve the plane. You're free to go when we land."

Carter shook his head, mouth drooping into a frown.

"You don't seem surprised." Mitch breathed easier seeing the other man back down.

"I'm not. I wondered how long it would take before someone showed up to repo this plane." The older man shrugged and gazed out the windshield. "What happens now?"

"We'll land at the Tullahoma airfield where the bank reps will claim it. Want a ride back to Roseville?"

"Nah. I'll find a way home." Carter sighed and relaxed in his seat. "About time I stopped flying anyway."

Mitch tried to remain professional and not sympathize with the older pilot, but it was tough. Obviously, giving up flying after so many years of the adrenaline high would not be easy. Still, he couldn't let his guard down in case the guy decided to suddenly rebel at the takeover of his plane. Sure didn't want to fight the man for the plane but he'd done it before. How would Beth fare in such a scuffle? That was a bigger question. He didn't know what sort of self-defense experience she might have. She'd probably duck and hide rather than defend herself. Then again, she'd already demonstrated more spunk than he'd given her credit for.

Mitch looked back at Beth and saw her grinning ear to ear. Surprised, he grinned back. But really, what was she so happy about?

A thousand butterflies danced through her entire body. A thousand candles burned inside, lighting up her entire being and world. She wanted to dance, twirl like an out of control child's spinning top. Barely had she closed the rental car's door and snapped her seatbelt in place before she yelled from sheer joy.

Mitch turned to stare at her, a frown drooping his brows. "*What* is the matter with you?"

"Nothing. Nothing at all. I want to go again. I had so much fun." She tapped her hand on the armrest by the open window. Air rushed in to cool her flushed cheeks as Mitch steered the car onto the winding highway. "No wonder you enjoy your job."

"It does have its moments." Mitch focused on the road, his left arm propped on the open window.

"Our plan went so smoothly. Like clockwork."

She'd worried about her small role, verifying the logbook was in the plane and then just riding along as Mitch's friend on his flight lesson. But then to realize she had to not only nab the thing out from under the nose of Carter but also hide it in the big purse. She'd decided to wait until she was certain the men were outside of the RV before leaving the safety of the bathroom. Long, tense moments listening for any sound from the other side of the door to the tiny space. Sitting on the closed lid of the toilet until absolutely sure she heard the front door close behind them. Dredging up every ounce of courage to snatch another's possession, whether he held it legally or not. She'd never stolen anything in her life and worried she'd chicken out when the time arrived to follow through.

Then she sneaked out and made sure nobody could see her movements through the windows while she grabbed the book. She had to wrestle the hardback book into the soft-sided purse, shoving her makeup and wallet out of the way. She'd chosen the flowery bag to add to the carefree tourist she was acting like. Good thing Roxie liked oversized bags or the binder wouldn't have fit inside so easily. She could hide a small dog in the depths of the purse. She chuckled at the image playing in her mind. She glanced at Mitch, aware he remained confused by her glee.

"I should have considered there might be another guy involved." Mitch turned up the volume of the radio, letting the mellow voice of Kenny Chesney fill the silence with a cheery country song. "He almost blew us out of the water."

"But he didn't. That's what's cool about our teamwork." She swung around to smile at him, trying to relay how much she appreciated the thrill he'd shared with her. Make him see her depth of gratitude. "We adapted."

"Improvisation can get you killed." He shot her a wry grin. "Your costume did a great job of distracting the men."

"That was my intention, so yay me." A swell of happiness filled her.

The adrenaline rush hadn't even begun to ease despite having turned over the plane and the logbook to the bank's representative who handed Mitch a check for delivering it safely. Poor Carter had called Wright to come get him in the RV, since they had no reason to hang around the air show with no plane.

She hopped a few times in her seat, despite the belt limiting her joyful movement. "What crazy fun we had. Don't you think?"

"This case ended up much easier than most." He glanced at her, eyes serious. "It's not always crazy fun, as you say. What if he'd fought us? Or pulled a gun? Then what?"

"You're trying to calm me down, but it won't work." She savored feeling useful and energized all rolled into one squealing ball of happiness. "I love this feeling and I want to do it again."

He stared out the windshield as both eyebrows jumped up. "What? Repo a plane?"

"Yep. With you. We're a great team." She squirmed against the back of the seat, anxious to share her day with her sisters.

He shook his head and then aimed his dark eyes at her, no light of amusement evident in their depths. "No way. This was a one-time deal. My last job for that matter."

"Don't say that. I can do this. With you. What would I need to do to prove it to you?"

"It's not safe."

She huffed out an annoyed sigh. Maybe not but the risk fueled the rush of the endeavor. Her blood sang in her veins, pulsing life and joy throughout her frame. She'd never felt so alive and vital. She couldn't imagine never feeling this high again. She'd do whatever it took to make sure she experienced the thrill often.

"So tell me. What training do I need?" She gazed at Mitch, daring him to deny her right for injecting some fun into her life.

"You're not going to let this go, are you?"

"No." She studied his tense profile, letting him process her simple response. "So?"

He drew in a deep breath and let it out slowly. "You'd need to be able to defend yourself if one of these guys gets ugly."

"How?"

"Martial arts to start. But that won't protect you in every situation." He looked at her out of the corner of his eyes. "Do you know how to handle a gun?"

"No, but I bet you could teach me how to shoot, right? Or somebody can. And there's a couple martial arts schools in town. I'll ask around and sign up for a class as soon as we get back home. Does it matter which discipline?"

"Not to me, since you probably will never need to use it." He gripped the steering wheel, flexing his fingers in a tense rhythm. "If I have anything to say about it."

"Which you really don't." She crossed her arms over her stomach and shifted to regard him. "Anything else?"

He shook his head, keeping his eyes on the road. "I can't believe you'd want to continue with this. It's not to be taken on lightly."

"I believe I can do anything when I set my mind to it." She gripped her arms tighter, intent on making him understand. "I'm serious about wanting to do this right. So?"

"In addition to hand-to-hand combat skills and weaponry lessons, it would help if you knew how to fly." He shot her a look that made her insides squirm at the heat in his eyes. "Unless you're with me, I mean. I'd pilot and you'd assist."

She'd love to be with him, if only his destiny didn't lead to the beautiful weeping woman and the boy. The connection struggling between them couldn't be allowed if he were to live the life intended for him. The snippets she could see in her visions. She didn't understand why her inner eye seemed veiled where he was concerned. She'd never experienced the shuttering of her visions before. His ability to block her out only increased the allure of the resulting thrill. She wanted to work with him to satisfy the craving. Nothing more.

Who was she kidding? She'd prefer to be with him as a woman. Period. But that was not possible. Not with the way things seemed to be lining up for his future. She wished again she could see her own, to know whether she was making the right choice for herself. Given that she couldn't, she had to go with what made her happy. Easy choice.

"You could teach me how to fly. You are an instructor, right?" She grinned at him, letting her hands drop to her lap. Willing him to agree. "See, I can do this, if you'll help me. Please?"

Chapter Six

The thick fabric of the borrowed two-piece outfit did nothing to hide her nerves. Beth sat barefooted on the thick mat at the back of the class of ten—all men except her—waiting for her first Brazilian Jiu-Jitsu lesson. Correction. Her first lesson had been the name of the outfit, a Gi, along with a belt that designated to everyone else her experience level. In her case, a white belt since she was at the lowest level. She tried to not tug repeatedly on the lapels of the top to attempt to cover her tee shirt. The borrowed pants fit loosely on her hips and stopped short of her ankles. She might look ridiculous in the eyes of fashionistas but that didn't matter. She needed to know how to protect herself and Jiu-Jitsu appeared to be the best option.

Asking around for recommendations of a good martial arts school led her to the newest place in town run by a black belt instructor. The man who'd given her the phone number told her it would teach her how to defend herself no matter what hand-to-hand situation she might face. No guy could take advantage of her once she knew how to sweep him to the ground and hold him there, even put a choke hold on him to make him pass out. She'd always enjoyed watching the high school wrestling team and how they could get a hold and flip or pin their opponent. Now it was her turn to learn how to control the situation.

The instructor, one Joe Walsh, had apparently moved to Roseville the month before. When he first arrived, there had been a buzz about having a martial arts gym in town but Beth had largely ignored the talk. Then, she had no need to worry about her safety. Nothing ever happened in the small town of Roseville, Tennessee. Ever. Until Mitch rolled into town and showed her a different side of life and living. Now she needed to prepare for the next adventure.

She'd called the number she'd written on the back of a bakery bag and spoke to the instructor's assistant, who eagerly signed her up for the demo class to see if she liked the self-defense school. Glancing at the men chatting together as they stretched in various poses, warming up, her damp palms dried. If they could do it, then so could she. Should she be doing some kind of stretches, too? She bent one leg so her foot touched the other thigh, and leaned forward to touch the straight knee. She'd need to work on flexibility, certainly, but it was a start. She did several stretches and then switched legs to limber up the other side.

Located in temporary quarters at the elementary school for the summer months, the gym was well lit and expansive. She was surprised when a petite woman with black hair pulled into a ponytail that brushed her shoulders strode into the gym. She wore the traditional white Gi with a black belt snugged at her waist. She moved with an air of confidence Beth envied. The woman walked to the front of the class, facing the two rows of students. The men all rose lithely to their feet and Beth scrambled up to stand with them. Once they stood quietly, the woman nodded.

"Welcome to the Phoenix Training Center. I'm Jocasta Walsh, or Jo. For those new to my classes, you may call me Professor." She nodded to the young man who hurried across the gym to join her, stopping a few feet to her side in a royal blue Gi with a brown belt knotted at his waist. "You may call my assistant Rob, Coach. Are you ready to begin?"

The next few minutes flew by as Beth concentrated on keeping up with the pace. First the warmup exercises took their toll, as she floundered doing jumping jacks, unable to do all of them that the rest of the class managed to complete. Hot sweat trickled and burned in her eyes as determination filled her soul. Her failure to meet the level of the others only spurred her to try harder. She must conquer her weakness in order to achieve her goals. Pain and sweat would not hold her back.

The coach showed them how to "shrimp" out of a holding position, a movement made lying on your back and then pushing your hips out first one direction and then the other. Then they were told to shrimp all the way across the mats to practice. She was panting by the time she wiggled her way across the thirty feet of mats. Another area she needed to work harder. She should make a list.

Then the guys started doing something she'd never seen done before and which made her slowly shake her head side to side. They lined up at one end of the mats in two lines, then dropped to do a pushup before jumping their feet up to be outside their braced palms on the mat. Stood and repeated the process. Again and again. All the way across the floor. Too soon it was her turn and she did her best, struggling to do the first pushup, walking her feet up to be near her hands, and then pushing up to stand.

Jo raised a brow in her direction but said nothing. Merely motioned for her to continue.

Taking a deep breath and letting it out quickly, Beth dropped again and repeated the struggle. The hop of her feet up to her hands was closer but still lacked fluidity let alone any hint of grace. Enough improvement for her to try harder to improve her technique. When she finally stood up at the end of the mats, dripping in sweat but cheered at completing the exercise, she turned to see everyone watching her. Tempted to look down, away, she forced herself to keep her gaze steady. Jo nodded once and then strode to stand in the center of the mats.

"All right, gather round. Let me show you this technique for escaping from a hold." Jo dropped easily to the mat and lay on her back while Rob assumed a mock hold on her. "First, take a firm grip of the Gi, like this. Then…"

Beth inched closer for a better view and to hear what the professor said. After several demonstrations of the technique, the instructors got to their feet and set a timer for the students to practice. When they paired off, white belts with higher level students, Beth looked up into the grinning face of a muscular man. Her determination considered making a run for the door. How could she possibly take him down, let alone beat him at anything?

Jo moved over to her and nodded encouragingly. "It's your first night. Don't worry. Let me show you again."

"I need to learn this fast. So I'm all ears." Beth faced the woman and nodded. "My future depends on it."

Jo canted her head to assess the seriousness of Beth's statement. "Let's talk about the future after you finish this class."

Chastened, Beth paid close attention to the professor's instructions, following her directions on hand positions and leg movements. She was surprised when she actually broke the man's grip on her and ended up controlling him. She grinned at him as she stood and they switched places. The grin died when he easily flipped her on her back and held her down in what seemed like one fluid motion. Panting from both the speed and the impact, she accepted his hand to help her stand. She had a lot to learn.

At the end of the class, the professor walked up to her while Beth grabbed a towel to mop the sweat from her brow and nape. "Let's talk in my office."

Feeling like she'd been summoned to the principal's office, Beth trailed after the petite woman. Glancing between the professor, standing a little over five feet, and the average man in the class, reaching at least to nearly six, Beth considered the power of Jo Walsh. She could learn a good deal from her.

"Tell me why your future depends on learning Jiu-Jitsu."

"I need to prove I can defend myself if the occasion arises." How much dare she tell this woman about the secretive job she was preparing for? "Just in case."

Jo nodded, keeping her gaze resting on Beth. "If you're serious, and I think you are, then you may have noticed you have a long way to go to be able to defend yourself from another woman your size, let alone a bigger and stronger man. But you're in the right place to learn how to level the playing field, so to speak."

Relief flowed through Beth's veins. "What do I need to do?"

"First, study up on the general philosophy of Jiu-Jitsu. You'll need to eat and breathe the philosophy over the next month or two. Second, eat wholesome and healthy foods to help your body strengthen. Third, you'll need to train every night, and take both group and private lessons several times a week. Can you do all of that?"

Beth blinked several times, soaking in the enormity of the proposed program and its impact on her work schedule. Roxie had reluctantly given her permission to pursue this second career path, but Beth would have to somehow keep up with the bookstore as well. She didn't know how exactly, but something would shake out. It had to.

"When do I start?"

"Thanks for your help, Mitch." Beth propped her hands on her hips as she surveyed the transformed bedroom.

"You're really going all in, aren't you?" Mitch stood in the open doorway, one hand on the jamb near the top.

He'd been working hard, damp sweat marks darkening his light blue tee shirt. She'd done her best to keep her distance for the last couple of hours while he moved the heavy equipment into the room and gave her a hand with placing furniture where she wanted. All without a grumble or complaint. Instead he whistled the dwarf song from Snow White. The big, strong pilot whistling a Disney song. It made her heart happy.

"I told you, I'm serious." She flashed a smile at him before surveying Tara's old room turned home gym.

The bed and dresser had moved with her sister, leaving only a couple low bookcases holding a smattering of mysteries and poetry books. Mitch had mounted a flat screen TV on the wall above one case in the corner which now held rolled spa towels. The new treadmill stood in front of one of two windows, facing the TV. Rubber mats filled the center of the room with one wall of mirror tiles, cheap ones from the dollar store, positioned so she could ensure she used the proper form during her yoga sessions.

She crossed to the other low case beside the mirrors, crammed with elastic bands and varying weights of medicine balls, to pick up the rolled motivational poster she'd bought. Tapping it lightly on her opposite palm, she contemplated where to hang it. The corner behind the treadmill was occupied by a low net strung across it for the large exercise ball. Kind of like a hammock for the ball to nap in when she wasn't using it. Chuckling, she pivoted to look at the other walls, seeking possibilities. Probably between the other window and the closet in the back right corner of the room.

"If you don't need me to do anything else, I have someplace I need to be." Mitch dropped his hand to slip into his jeans pocket.

"Sure thing. I can take it from here." She dropped the poster back on top of the case and walked toward the tempting man. Avoiding looking directly into his eyes for fear he'd see the hunger she felt each time she thought of him. She must resist. Must stay neutral or her plans would fall apart. "Let me show you out."

She brushed past him into the hallway. Inhaling his masculine scent proved a form of torture. He smelled good enough to eat but she had to refrain from letting herself become attached to him. They couldn't happen.

"I suppose you still insist on learning to shoot?" His deep voice sounded loud in the close confines of the hall.

"Absolutely." She picked up her pace, wanting to reach the kitchen door before her will power failed. "I have time whenever you do. Roxie is being really supportive of my efforts to fit everything in. She's allowing me flexibility with my schedule, at least for a little while."

"I'm still against this idea, but if you're going to do it, do it right." He trailed her into the kitchen and across the small cheery space. "Let me schedule a lane at the range and I'll be in touch."

She laid her hand on the doorknob and pulled open the door. She turned to peer up at the man who had her pulse flying. "Sounds good. I can meet you there."

"I'll text you the time and place, then." He started to leave then hesitated. His gaze flickered between her eyes and her lips before he inclined his head for a moment. "See you later, Beth."

Had he been about to kiss her? She searched his eyes while he studied her in return. A mistake. She shouldn't have met his gaze, seen the matching hunger tempered with caution. A silent question lingered in the air, unanswered. He blinked once and a slow smile spread on his lips. No way.

"See ya." His future apparently didn't include her. She swallowed the urge to throw away her restraints and kiss him anyway. Find out what she was denying herself. She half-turned away, prepared to add space between them instead of giving in to the temptation to lean toward him, to invite his kiss.

He tilted his head briefly, an acknowledgement of her dismissal, and then he walked out, leaving her to gaze after his loose-hipped saunter down the steps and along the sidewalk to the street. The rumble of his bike disturbed the quiet only for a minute before the twitter of birds in the trees and crickets hiding in the grass replaced the sound. She stared at the last spot she'd seen him, where he'd angled the bike around the corner and out of sight, for what felt like a long time before she slowly closed the door.

Taking a cleansing breath, she shook off the tremor in her tummy. Would she have returned the kiss in spite of all of her reservations? Torn between her desires and reality, she didn't want to answer her own question. She needed to work, to do something productive.

Pausing to grab the box of push pins from the junk drawer in the kitchen, she hurried down the hall to her new gym. She stopped in the doorway to peruse the layout, pleased with the arrangement. Everything she needed to increase her strength and flexibility as well as her endurance. Well, almost. Good enough for the moment. Humming a happy tune, she grabbed up the poster and went to work hanging it in the corner.

The distant sound of the kitchen door closing announced Roxie's arrival for lunch. Beth glanced at her watch. Right on time. She took several steps away to make sure the poster hung straight.

"Hey, Beth… What's all this?" Roxie strode into the room, surprise in her wide eyes.

"I told you I was going to make a home gym. What do you think?" She swiped an upturned palm through the air, encompassing her efforts.

"I thought you meant in a corner, not the entire room." She slowly scanned the room, her gaze landing on each of the pieces of equipment and the mats. She blinked when she spotted the TV. "Did you hang that yourself?"

Beth shook her head, chortling at the image of her trying to hang it. "No way. I roped Mitch into helping me."

"Mitch, the pilot?" Roxie shot her a snarky grin. "You talk about this guy but I never see him. Are you sure he's real?"

"Very. You just missed him, actually."

"If I hadn't waited on that one last customer…" Roxie rolled her eyes and then shook her head. "You may be going a bit overboard on this whole fitness thing. You don't want to overdo it."

"My Jiu-Jitsu professor helped me put a progressive but safe training plan together. Don't worry. I'm not going to do anything to hurt myself."

"See that you don't. We need your help at the store." Roxie's smile dimmed. "I need you around for my own selfish sake."

Beth hugged Roxie with one arm around her waist. "I promise to be careful and I appreciate your support. It means a lot to me."

"I won't stand in the way of your happiness." Roxie cast a sideways glance at her. "Unless you get in over your head. Then all bets are off."

"Understood." Beth nodded slowly before looking away to skim the room, satisfaction flooding her chest. "I can't wait to jump in and really begin working out in this space. It feels right."

"You've done a nice job, but something's missing." Roxie let her gaze travel around the room again. "What you need is some flowers in a pretty vase. Add a touch of nature and positive aromas to your experience."

Beth snorted a laugh. "I was thinking a bucket of sand, not a vase of flowers."

Roxie frowned as she angled her head. "Sand?"

"It's one of the ways to strengthen hand muscles, essentially stirring the sand in different directions for an increasing length of time." Beth squeezed Roxie's waist briefly. "But flowers would be nice, too."

Despite the ear muffs, the blast of the handgun reverberated in the range. The target at the far end wavered after the impact of yet another bullet. He leaned slightly forward, rocked up onto his toes, looking over her head. Not quite dead center, but very close.

Mitch studied his student from where he stood outside of the shooter box, dismayed at her natural ability to handle a firearm. He'd helped her select the Glock pistol, checking its weight and balance in her grip. Instructing her on how to handle and load the weapon. She'd listened and followed the safety rules without fail and proved she could hit what she aimed at. He eased a sigh out through his nostrils. She'd never walk away from the danger now.

Beth laid the pistol on the bench, pointed down range as he'd instructed, and spun around to flash a happy grin up to meet his gaze. "How was that? Pretty good, huh?"

"You've got quite a talent with a gun. Remind me to not make you angry." He forced a chuckle, only half kidding.

"I'll protect you." Laughter danced in her eyes.

"I hope there's nothing for you to protect me from." He peered closer at her, and then slowly shook his head. "You don't need to do this. Definitely not on your own yet, if ever."

"I want to." She frowned at him briefly and then glanced back at the gun. "With you. We're a great team. But of course, if you don't want to, I guess I can find somebody else to partner with."

The thought of her with another man sent a spear straight into his heart. Especially after Keith had expressed such interest in her mere days before. He didn't want her to partner with anyone but him, but he didn't have the last word on such a personal question. She'd have to make the choice. He'd rather she choose him, but for the time being she had only one clear objective in mind. A risky, possibly deadly, objective.

"You don't understand." He shook his head and let his gaze hover over the other men and women taking target practice on a rainy afternoon. Guns might equalize but too often led to someone hurt, or killed. He didn't want that someone to be the lovely woman at his side. Pure and simple. "It's dangerous."

"You keep saying that, but I think you're just trying to scare me away." She stared up at him, her steady regard critical. "I don't scare easily."

"Maybe, but you'll need to learn how to shoot with only one hand, not both." He gripped her shoulders, falling victim to the desire to touch her, and turned her to face the target. "Take aim and then I'll show you what I mean."

She lifted the gun with both hands, fingers wrapped around the handle but not on the trigger, and the other hand supporting the weight of the weapon. "Like this?"

He moved to stand close behind her so he could reposition her hands, her fingers. Only when he made contact, a thrill of desire pulsed through him. He shifted his stance but kept his hands steady on hers with an effort. A wave of her sweet scent met his nostrils and he thought again how the perfume didn't suit her. She needed a scent to reflect her personality. Something light with a hint of spice, of warmth and energy. Perhaps a bit of humor blended in. Scents and aromas carried meaning for him. He had a difficult time explaining it to others but every unique smell held hope or memories or peace. Depending on the kind of scent.

"Shift your palm to here..." He pressed on her hand to the new position, aware of her tender yet tough flesh beneath his fingers. He took the other hand away and she countered by lifting more with her grip hand. "Try shooting that way and see how it goes."

He stepped back outside the box, putting distance between them. Giving him a chance to recover while she fired at the paper target, the red circle in the middle boasting several holes.

"Wow. That does make a difference." She unloaded the magazine and laid the gun on the bench. Then spun around to smile up at him. "I guess the training exercises are helping me grow a little stronger every day not only for Jiu-Jitsu but for everything."

"You're on your way, then, I guess." But to where? To confronting an angry pilot when his plane was repo'd? Or being shot for her efforts? The image of her lying on the ground in a pool of blood made his stomach clench.

"I'm so happy. I can't thank you enough for helping me." She smiled up at him, her lips parting slowly to reveal her teeth.

He gazed down at her green eyes speckled with gold dust, wanting with all his being to lower his lips to hers. To claim her as his. This spitfire who saw what she wanted, how to achieve it, and then did whatever necessary to make it happen. How could he spend time with her and not succumb to her tempting person? Yet if she insisted on engaging in activities that put her in danger, or on gallivanting all around the globe in search of a thrill, how could he stay with her?

He craved a quiet, settled life after living all over the world in fits and spurts, moving every year or two, making new contacts and adjusting to new ways of living. He needed a home, a wife, a family that stayed in one town.

He'd turn thirty before long and didn't want to wait much longer to have children.

He wanted to be young enough to enjoy spending time with them, teaching his daughter to play ball, or his son to ride a bike. Wanted his kids to go through one school system, not six to ten in twelve years. Wanted to raise his family and then grow old with his wife, enjoying being together and their eventual grandchildren. Maybe even have a dog of his own for once in his life.

But none of that could happen until he stopped taking jobs which forced him to transplant his home. He was tired, plain and simple, of having to reinvent his life.

She needed to experience more in her life, not less. She'd made it clear how far she was willing to go to become one of the characters straight out of a suspense novel. Tough, fair, determined, fearless. Ready for anything and afraid of nothing. Doing things to satisfy her craving for fun and excitement.

While his head fought for a logical path forward, he firmed his commitment to be true to himself and his needs. Only, could he protect his heart from the woman waiting in front of him? Did he want to?

"Just keep practicing and you'll do fine." Mitch nodded at the gun and she slowly turned around to reload. With her back to him, he could appreciate the beautiful blond hair pulled into a ponytail that fell to between her shoulders. Those shoulders worked over reloading the pistol, shifting and beckoning his hands. He flexed his fingers but kept his hands to himself.

He resisted the temptation to spin her back around, to ask for her kiss, to ask that he be enough to satisfy her cravings. After all, he already knew the answer.

Chapter Seven

*A*ches and pains moved with her as she straightened a stack of bookmarks here, untangled a rounder of beaded necklaces there, then strode to the back room to retrieve another box of new arrivals. Beth had known she'd been shirking her fitness routine up until she started seriously working out in her new gym. The training she'd begun in addition to the grappling sessions over the last four days had underscored how much. Her weak areas like her hand strength and her flexibility indicated how far she had to go. Still, she'd managed to control her opponent every time she'd made the attempt, even if it had been difficult. With time and training, she'd become a fierce adversary like Jo. Her commitment to succeed soared to new heights.

Humming, she carried the partially opened box back to the travel section, plunking it down on a work table near the section of histories of other countries. She pulled the box cutter from her khaki pants pocket and finished slicing the tape holding the cardboard flaps closed. Snapping the blade shut, she slipped the knife away, then pulled the hardback books from the interior. With the ease of long practice, she placed the books where they belonged on the shelves, moving to and fro with a newfound sense of purpose and assurance.

"What's your secret, Beth?"

Beth paused to look behind her and spied her former high school classmate standing with a huge smile on her face. She grinned at Nyssa Clark, the curvaceous woman who'd outgrown the string-bean look of her teen years. They'd been fairly close in school, though gradually lost touch with the business of becoming adults. Nyssa always had a date for the dances, the combination of beauty and brains attracting the boys like no one else.

"Hey. It's been a long time since you've come by the shop." Beth pushed another book onto a shelf and then straightened to address her friend.

"I was out of the country for a while, but now I'm back." Nyssa waved bright blue fingernails in a sweeping motion that included all of Beth from head to toes. "So what have you been up to? You've really changed since the last time we talked."

Years before at the five-year reunion at the high school. Nyssa talked nonstop about her career as a fashion model, of shoots in exotic locales with costumes both elegant and creative. Beth had envied her with all her green-eyed self but no way could she imagine pursuing a similar career path as her classmate. Leaving behind her family to go so far from home for months at a time. Sure, she wanted to travel, but not for a long duration.

Beth glanced down at her plain uniform of khakis and polo. "Same old thing."

Nyssa chuckled deep in her throat and shook her head. "Not your clothes, silly. Your entire attitude is different. You're standing taller and straighter. What gives?"

"I started training in Brazilian Jiu-Jitsu last week. Maybe that has something to do with it."

Nyssa's eyes widened until they couldn't possibly grow any bigger. "Brazilian?"

Beth nodded once, slowly, wondering at her shock. Surely many people did martial arts in a variety of forms. True, she remained the only female student but at some point another woman would want to learn the discipline. Or perhaps Nyssa never expected Beth to be interested in self-defense training in any form.

"Holy smokes, Beth. Why?"

"I wanted to learn how to defend myself. You know…" How much should she reveal of her real motivation, her intentions? She shrugged and glanced away, then back to Nyssa. "Just in case."

"I thought only macho men did that sport."

"Mostly. I'm the only woman in my class. Except for the professor. She's a woman."

"Really? That's interesting. I didn't know women even participated in Brazilian Jiu-Jitsu. Other martial arts, sure."

Her friend's curiosity made Beth uneasy. She'd prefer to keep her plans to herself. She didn't want anyone else to dismiss her efforts or ridicule her reasons for striving to make herself over into what she hoped would be a better person. A change of subject seemed in order. "What can I help you with?"

"Oh, not a thing. I can find what I'm looking for." Nyssa smiled, shrugging lightly. "I see you're busy, so I'll talk to you later."

Beth watched her walk away, slowly browsing among the titles of the sections until she stopped in the classic literature aisle. A little "light" reading seemed to be in store for her. Beth snatched up the empty box and carried it back downstairs and into the work room. All the while she thought over what the woman had said about her change in attitude. She felt different, too.

Jo had taught the class to always be aware of their surroundings, the location of exits and how to position themselves so they could escape or defend themselves depending on the situation. As a result, she worked on staying alert and poised to respond when necessary.

The combination of awareness and readiness to defend herself made her more confident in her ability to effectively protect herself. Even after only a few days of private and group instruction, she had to admit she strutted more than strode. Part of the philosophy behind the sport included the self-confidence to avoid escalation of a conflict knowing she could end the confrontation with her skills. Or would be able to more easily after more training. She added the box to the growing pile at the back and then washed her hands. Drying them on a paper towel, she stepped out to the coffee bar to see what needed to be done.

"There you go." Tara placed a lid on a coffee and handed it to the woman at the counter. "Have a nice day."

"What can I do?" Beth joined Tara as her sister closed the cash drawer with a *ching*.

Tara's hazel eyes crinkled at the corners. "You're really energized this morning. What have you been taking?"

"Nothing. Why?" Beth pursed her lips to the side, pondering the reason for Tara's smirk.

Tara spread her palms outward and then dropped her hands to her sides. "Have you had too much coffee again? Or sugar? Which is it?"

"I've only had one cup of coffee, black. I've cut back, trying to eat a little more healthily. You know, veggies and protein, limiting fats and sugars." Beth reached for an apron and tied it on. "I'll be a lean mean, fighting machine."

Another aspect of the philosophy she'd been learning included eating wholesome foods. Avoiding junk foods entirely. Fresh and whole natural things like salad, fresh veggies, eggs, lean meats and fish. Roxie had grumbled a bit about the change in the dinner menu, at least on the nights Beth fixed dinner. Overall Roxie had realized the diet made her feel better so had stopped her complaints. Beth also noticed a difference in her entire body after only a week of no added sugar and cutting back on bread and pasta. She drew the line at never eating pizza, though. A girl had to have something to look forward to once a month.

Tara tilted her head, regarding her with a quizzical expression. "You don't mean to really fight, do you? Just the stuff you're learning at the training center?"

"I want to be ready in case I ever need to defend myself. I don't want to rely on somebody else to have to come to my rescue. I'll rescue myself."

Tara opened her mouth far enough to start to say something and then closed it again. She picked up a cloth and spray bottle, holding them in front of her as she looked at Beth for several seconds. "I hope you're not deceiving yourself."

"Don't worry, I'm not." Beth and Jo had worked out a sound plan to help Beth ramp up her abilities in the shortest time possible. Not that she'd even earn the next level belt—blue—for a year but she'd know enough that she'd be capable. That's what mattered. She had no way of knowing when Mitch would need her help again. If he'd ever want her to assist in another job.

"I hope you're right." Tara sidled past Beth, heading toward the bakery counter to clean the glass.

The bell over the door announced a new customer, drawing Beth's attention. She welcomed Mitch with an easy smile, which he returned as he sauntered to the coffee bar. He was dressed in blue jeans and a black tee shirt, his work boots thudding across the linoleum until he halted at the bakery counter. His gaze fastened on hers, making her blood simmer throughout her body.

Tara glanced at Beth, a question in her eyes. "Know him?"

"Sure. Hi, Mitch. This is my sister, Tara." Amazingly, her voice sounded nearly normal despite the desire pulsing inside and stealing her breath.

They exchanged greetings, Tara reaching over the case to shake his hand. She shot Beth an enigmatic look she chose not to identify, then started squirting the fluid on the glass, wiping it dry with a towel even as she cast frequent looks at Mitch. Beth waved a hand at her, trying to make her stop the ogling but Tara tossed her head and kept on.

Mitch shook his head at her and then turned back to Beth. "I only have a minute."

"What would you like?" Beth rested her palms on the cool surface, braced to resist the flow of attraction pulling her toward him. Failing to ignore her sister's eavesdropping.

Unbidden, the vision of the strange woman, dark hair pulled into a fancy bun and wearing an evening gown, patted a young boy in shorts and top on the shoulder. She sensed lingering fear and compassion shared between the two. The boy must be the son of the woman, the connection between them proved as much. Was her hunch correct the woman would be Mitch's wife, and the boy his son? Surely the most likely explanation for their image associated so closely to Mitch. Which reinforced her need to keep her distance from him despite her physical response to his presence. Emotional distance since she still wanted to work with him. She'd keep it professional. Easy peasy. She hoped.

The image dissipated and she stared into Mitch's magnetic gaze. She blinked away the shreds of the vision, focusing on the tall, seductive man instead. She drew in a long breath and pasted a small smile on her face. Keep it professional. "Coffee?"

His hair, left loose and flowing, brushed his wide shoulders as he shook his head. "Sweet tea, please. To go."

"In a hurry today..." Beth filled a large cup with ice and the dark amber fluid, snapping a plastic lid on top before placing it on the counter. She pulled her hand away to make sure they didn't make contact. No chance encounters to stir agitation and want inside. Any more than already existed at the urge to run her fingers through his beautiful flowing hair.

"I need to get out to the airfield. Keith is waiting for me." Mitch laid the cash for the drink on the counter and then stripped the wrapper off a straw and inserted it into the lid.

Beth rang up the purchase and handed back the change. Careful to drop the coins in his palm. "That reminds me. You promised flying lessons. When can we start?"

He blew out a breath as he regarded her with a steady look. "You're still going through with your scheme?"

"Absolutely. I get off at three. How about I meet you at the airfield at 3:30 and we can begin." She watched the hesitation slide across his features, bolstering her own resolve all the more. "I really want this, Mitch."

He raked the fingers of one hand over his scalp and down the length of the dark blond tresses. His dark eyes studied her as he took a long breath and pushed it out. He glanced to Tara, waiting in silence. Beth kept her gaze on the man who could make her idea come to life. She didn't want to see her sister's reaction to Mitch's silent query but she saw his shoulders relax.

"I can't today. Tomorrow?"

"No, I've got to train and go to the gym after work. Wednesday?"

Mitch shook his head, hope lighting the depths of his brown eyes. "I've got to do some things that day. I'll be out of town. Maybe we should put this off till next week?"

"Come on, Mitch. Work with me. Thursday afternoon and no excuses." Beth propped her fists on her waist and stared at him. "You agreed to help me. But if not, maybe Keith would be more willing."

Mitch heaved a long-suffering sigh. "Fine. But don't be late." Mitch started to turn to leave, but then pinned her with his gaze. "Unless you're smart and change your mind. Then just send me a text to let me know."

"I'll be there." As he shook his head and strode out of the bookstore, she planned to prove him wrong. A light chill crept down her back. Roxie's caution and Tara's concern echoed in her mind. Could they be right? Was she fooling herself? She didn't want to believe she could possibly deceive herself on something so important. She pushed out a frustrated yet determined sigh. If only her gift allowed her to see her *own* future.

After poking his head into several rooms, Mitch finally located Keith in the kitchen. The dogs, Orville and Wilbur, greeted him with a wag of their tails as they approached. Keith had the cabinet open beneath the sink, kneeling on the floor to peer inside. Bottles and boxes of cleaning supplies crowded the counters on either side of the sink.

"What's wrong?" Mitch petted the dogs on the head with both hands.

Keith twisted to look up at him with a wry twist to his mouth. "No clue. I think I'm going to need a plumber."

"Want me to take a look? I'm not an expert, but I have fixed a few plumbing issues."

"If you want." Keith stood and stepped aside, the dogs moving to stand with him.

"What seems to be the problem?" He got down on his knees to examine the pipes. A slow drip fell from the elbow of the pipe into a strategically positioned saucepan half full of water.

"It's leaking but I can't figure out from where." Keith pulled out a chair at the round kitchen table in the bay window and sat on it.

"Hmm…" Mitch poked around and then wiped away the water with a finger. Waited until the drop formed again. He rocked back on his heels to address Keith. "Looks like the dishwasher feedline. It's an easy fix if you have the tools."

"I probably don't. I'll call the plumber and let him handle it." Keith waved at him to join him at the table. "It's my way of helping the local economy, paying for services to the local guys."

Mitch stood and brushed off the knees of his jeans before sauntering over to take the opposite chair. "That's one way to look at it. If you have the money to pay for it."

"I can afford it upon occasion. Houses always cost money for one thing or the other." Keith petted the two Labs and then looked at Mitch. "Did you need something?"

Mitch nodded once, unsure how to approach the subject without offending his friend. "I have a question."

"Anything."

"I told you I came to town to do a job, but I didn't tell you what kind of job." Mitch shifted in the chair to rest one arm on the table, his hand draped over the edge. "I need to know if you will work with me if I need to ask a favor."

"If I can. What kind of favor are we talking about?" Keith leaned forward to clasp his hands together on the wooden table.

"I may need your help with access to a plane."

"Sure thing. You can take any of mine up anytime you like."

"Not yours. My contact texted me about a possible repo job but didn't have the particulars."

"Repo?" Keith frowned and laid his palms flat on the table. "You didn't tell me you were into that."

"I wanted to get the lay of the land before I told you." He shrugged and let a half smile ease onto his lips. "Make sure you weren't connected to my target. If I take the job, that is."

"Whose plane are you going after?" Keith sat back in his chair, keeping his gaze on Mitch.

"I won't know until the job is a go, and if I decide to take it." Mitch turned to face the table and Keith directly. "I want to stop doing the repo but it's provided a steady source of income so haven't done so yet. But I think soon I will."

Keith raised both brows over his amber eyes. "Then what?"

"I'm still working on that." He sighed as he studied his settled and successful friend. "Find something that satisfies and still pays the bills. Let me know if you find such a dream job, will ya?"

"Open to chapter one and get familiar with the basics." Mitch waved at the thick book waiting on a camp table flanked by matching chairs under a red canopy tent.

The disappointment in Beth's glance made him feel like a heel. Only for a few minutes though. He had to stick to his guns. Pun intended. She may resent his delaying tactics, but he didn't want to encourage her harebrained plan. Pulling her into the one relatively safe repo had made him nervous enough. The idea of taking her on anything like the other jobs he'd done made his insides turn to a quaking mass.

An inner reel of frightening moments flashed past. The night he was sneaking around a seaplane parked near the shore, performing the preflight inspection without triggering any alarms. Until he'd opened the door to climb inside and the place exploded with light and sound, dogs barking, men running toward him with guns drawn. He'd barely got the motor on and maneuvered the plane onto the water so he could taxi away and takeoff, sweating like he'd run a sprint.

Then there was the time he had located the target plane in a hangar a fair distance from the nearest house let alone town. He casually moved around it, checking to make sure everything was in place, fuel in the tank, etc. When a pickup truck tore up the driveway, spitting gravel as it rounded the last curve and skidded to a halt. The man who came out the driver's side had to have been the biggest man he'd ever faced, even without the rifle aimed at his chest. He should have been dead. Would have been if he hadn't planned ahead. He'd notified the police before going to repo the aircraft, and thankfully they pulled in right behind the angry dude, or he wouldn't be standing there asking Beth to read a book.

"Reading about flying is not learning how to control the plane." Beth left no doubt as to her opinion of his lesson plan as she strode over to the canvas chair and sat down.

In a normal situation, he would have assigned the reading ahead of time to get it out of the way for the fun stuff. They wouldn't be sitting on the ground near the training plane, but would actually be in the cockpit putting into action what had been learned from the manual. His gut refused to follow the norm and instead made him drag his heels when it came to giving Beth the information and skills she craved to put herself into harm's way. He didn't understand her desire to be involved in such a risky venture when she led such a perfect life in the quiet and welcoming town of Roseville. On the other hand, if he didn't teach her, she'd turn to Keith. He couldn't stomach the thought.

Opening the book with a thump of the cover on the table, she shook her head as she flipped through the pages. She peered up at him where he stood in the subdued sunlight. "After I read this, you'll take me up, right?"

Habit made him look to the skies, checking the weather conditions. Low gray clouds slid across a pale blue background. The windsock on its tall pole near the control tower flapped listlessly, never fully inflating in the light breeze. Mitch wished the sock was ramrod straight, filled with a strong crosswind, preventing any chance of taking a student pilot into the air. No such luck.

"You should be studying. There will be a test." Mitch improvised a new strategy, a fluid shifting of tactics aimed at keeping her safely on the ground.

He turned to review the clipboard and its signed airfield releases. Lifting first one and then the next sheet of paper, he had no clue what the writing said since his attention remained on the pretty woman a few feet away. He'd stare at his boots if he must. Anything to not have to endure the accusation in Beth's beautiful eyes.

"Hey, bro, what's up?"

Mitch raised his eyes from the page in his fingers to greet Keith. He matched Mitch's height but with broader shoulders and close-cropped black hair, a swagger in his loose-hipped stride. The slanted grin on Keith's mug along with the twinkle in his dark eyes warned of his mood. Playful and sarcastic best described Keith. Unless he was feeling particularly prankster like.

Mitch braced for what might stream from his mouth. "Hey, Keith. What brings you out here?"

At the sound of Mitch's voice, Beth's head popped up from reading the manual to smile at the dark-skinned man in the olive green coveralls. Then she lowered her eyes to return to her reading. Probably thinking the sooner she finished the sooner they'd begin the actual flying part of the lesson. Little did she know. Mitch stuck out a hand to shake Keith's while plotting other delays, other excuses—er, reasons—why they couldn't take off.

"Saw you two and wondered what on earth you were doing sitting out here." He nodded to Beth's bowed head and then shook his head at Mitch. "Seriously?"

Mitch lowered his voice as he took a step toward his friend. "She thinks she wants to do what I do but doesn't appreciate the risks."

"I didn't remember you being such a control freak." Keith lifted a black eyebrow and folded his arms over his muscular chest. "Educate her the right way and she'll be okay. Why would you sabotage her flying lessons?"

"I'm not sabotaging anything." Mitch cringed at the accusation laced through Keith's question. Put so harshly, his tactic sounded cowardly. "I'm merely delaying them."

Keith inclined his head toward Beth and then a conspiratorial grin grew on his lips. "If you don't feel comfortable teaching her what she needs to know, then I'm more than happy to pinch hit for you. You'd have a clear conscience—"

"And you'd steal my girl again." Mitch huffed through his nose. Keith's offer held another form of danger. To his heart. "I don't think so."

"I think that's her decision, not yours." Keith made a show of moistening his lips as he studied Beth's profile. "Let's ask her and let her decide."

A shiver raced down Mitch's back, setting off alarms that tingled through every nerve in his body. Mitch had flown as Keith's wingman on many dangerous missions while they were both active duty. He trusted the black man grinning at him with his life. With his soul. But he'd also proven himself a magnet for women. Something in his devil-may-care attitude served as catnip, intoxicating and mesmerizing the female of the species right into his arms. Usually leaving Mitch out in the cold without a woman to keep him warm. Not again. Not with Beth. He changed his plan to meet the new threat.

"I'd rather not." He chuckled, though it lacked humor. "It never seems to end well."

"For you." Keith tapped a forefinger on Mitch's sternum and then dropped his hands to rub together. "Be a sport."

Without waiting for an answer, Keith spun on one heel and strode over to Beth. Mitch clenched his jaw to keep from cussing the man out and hurried after him. By the time he scuffled to a stop beside Beth, he feared he was too late.

"Hi, Beth. Remember me?" He pumped her hand gently several times.

"Of course. What brings you out here?" Beth glanced between the two men, her expression revealing curiosity.

Keith chortled as he leaned closer to peer at the text. "If you'd rather learn how to fly the plane instead of studying its parts, let me know. I'm sure I could give you some instruction on the finer points."

Beth smiled up at him and leaned back, effectively forcing him to take a step back as well. She raised one brow at him and shook her head. "I appreciate the offer, but Mitch said he would teach me."

"Promises, promises." Keith motioned to the open book, one page lifting and falling back into place in the light breeze. "I've bested him all through his career with the Air Force, so if you really want the best, let me know."

Mitch bristled at the claim. "That's not exactly how I remember it."

"Well, old man, we can't expect your memory to be the best either." Keith winked at him so Beth couldn't see the inside joke. "There's a reason why you walked away from active duty, right?"

"Yeah, to give you a chance at being number one." Mitch bumped his fist into Keith's shoulder, hinting the banter needed to end. "Let Beth finish her reading so we can continue with the plan."

"What plan is that exactly?" Keith aimed his tawny eyes at Mitch, speculation and humor dancing in their depths in equal parts.

He had several hastily formed plans he hoped to carry out in a short period of time. First, despite his prior inclinations he had to admit to a strong desire to make her his own. He liked how she looked at him, the way she carried herself, the intensity with which she lived her life. The martial arts lessons gave her strength and conviction as well as confidence. The shooting lessons underscored that sense of fearlessness developing in her expression. All positive changes.

But his biggest fear was that she'd overstep her abilities and find herself in a precarious situation she couldn't extract herself from. If he wasn't at hand, what might happen to her? So he wanted to keep her close, keep an eye on her, and most of all keep her safe. Being her guy would make that possible.

"To teach her what she needs to know in a structured way. Something you wouldn't understand." Mitch smiled to soften the slight, but saw the understanding dawn in Keith's eyes.

Keith chuckled and shrugged. "Can't hurt to try, right?" He shrugged again, nodded a farewell to Beth, and then saluted Mitch with two fingers at his forehead. "I'll catch you later."

After Keith moved out of earshot, Mitch approached Beth slowly. While he did not want her doing what she intended, she'd find a way with or without him. Keith's offer rankled deep inside Mitch. Not because the other pilot was inferior or incapable of teaching Beth the ropes of flying. No. His fear stemmed from knowing how easily Keith could persuade Beth to care for him, something she seemed to resist from Mitch, truth be told. He saw the attraction in her gaze but sensed an emotional barrier raise every time they were together. How could he possibly dismantle the wall when he didn't know what it was made of or why she built it?

"Okay, Beth, let's get you up and handling the plane." He squared his shoulders, ready to find some answers to his questions. To do so, he'd need to give her what she wanted. "Ready to take control?"

Chapter Eight

A few days later, Beth strode into the temporary quarters of the training center at the elementary school gym. The worst of the muscle aches and pains had eased though had not disappeared, leaving behind stronger hand grip and flexibility. Still, her legs and arms continued to point out where they lacked the necessary strength. The training exercises had begun to reshape her muscles and tone her abs and legs. Working out in her home gym was a daily delight, uplifting and productive time well spent. She'd never felt so energized and powerful. How much more so would she feel the longer she continued training?

She dropped her gym bag on the lowest bleacher snugged up to the wall. Slipping off her sandals and pulling her Gi on over her shorts and tee, she tied the white belt around her waist before moving onto the mats. She warmed up as Jo had taught her, keeping an eye on the door as she waited for the professor to arrive for the private lesson. While she stretched, she reviewed the amazing number of movements and techniques she'd learned over the past two weeks. Despite learning to shrimp and escape from a side control or mount, so much more lay ahead that she would need to learn. Not that she fully comprehended the extent, but Jo had told her it took at least ten years to earn a black belt. One whole year to earn a blue, the next level up. She'd only had a sampling of all the strength and knowledge to come.

She'd convinced Mitch to give her another flying lesson, which he seemed reluctant to do at first but then accepted the concept. His buddy had made no secret of his interest in her, of teaching her how to fly, which warmed her innards. What remained unclear was just what kind of "flying" he meant. He exuded masculinity wrapped in a decadent bad boy attitude which enticed her unlike most every other man she'd met. His amber eyes were nearly as fascinating as Mitch's, but set within a darker toned skin. Keith was handsome and fun-loving, but not her type.

Mitch's dark chocolate brown eyes set against a lighter skin tone created a delicious contrast she couldn't resist. Handsome barely described his appeal to her. Add to that a hint of warrior lurking inside. She chuckled to herself as she changed positions, reaching toward her ankles to stretch the hamstrings. Mitch had practically growled at Keith when he'd suggested he could teach her instead. The two may be buddies but Mitch wasn't prepared to share her instruction with the other man.

Which brought her back around to why Mitch was so hesitant to help her acquire the skills she needed to be a part of the excitement. He poo-pooed the idea of her involvement, saying she'd tire of it or find it too dangerous. If it wasn't too dangerous for him, why would it be for her? She didn't think herself his physical equal, but she could take care of herself in her own ways. Her martial arts and gun education would make that possible. Over time, true. But she was growing stronger every day.

Jo sauntered into the gymnasium, barefooted and wearing her white Gi with black belt knotted at her waist. She padded across the wood floor and onto the thick grappling mats, moving closer with each firm step. She knelt beside Beth and rested her palms on her thighs. "I hope I didn't keep you long."

"I'm nearly finished warming up, so it's fine. Everything okay?"

Jo glanced up to the windows on the wall, late afternoon sunlight struggling to find a way through the dirty panes. "As good as possible anyway."

Beth peered closer at her usually unflappable instructor. Lines at her eyes, and lips pressed flat, revealed some worry lurking behind the calm exterior. Indeed, her entire body seemed tense and poised for flight. Beth reached out mentally to Jo, probing for insight but finding only peace in her future. Whatever was bothering her at the moment would pass. Beth released a breath and shifted to sit cross-legged in front of Jo.

"I'm glad you are here. Since you're new to town, do you think we could be more than professor and student? Could we be friends?"

Jo regarded her for a moment before nodding. "I'd like that. It's important to have friends to do things with."

"Yes, and someone to talk to when things get rough."

"I'd appreciate having a friend to turn to. Sometimes I need to vent."

Curiosity sparked through Beth at the edge in Jo's voice, razor sharp bitterness designed to cut down her opposition. No wonder martial arts came so naturally to Jo. She channeled her worry and perhaps some measure of fear into every defensive move. Fighting to protect herself from the demons haunting her life. Whether Beth could help her or not with any specific problem was beside the point. What Jo really needed was a shoulder, an ear, someone to bolster her courage and stand with her no matter what might happen.

"Maybe we could catch a movie and have dinner sometime." Beth linked her fingers and stretched her arms in front of her chest, relishing the stretch on her upper arms. "Do you like action adventure movies? There's a new one playing in town."

"Sounds good. Then maybe we could go to the Hideaway? I haven't tried their menu yet."

"Sure. It's one of my favorite restaurants."

"Good. Now, before we begin today's technique, I want to tell you how well you're doing. I know it's not always easy."

"Thanks. I've had my doubts." Beth refrained from sharing her rather embarrassing cryfests in the car after a couple of the tougher sessions. Times when she questioned her sanity as well as her ability. Maybe she'd share such a personal moment with her new friend later, but not yet. Not until they knew each other better. Or until she felt more competent. "At least I think I'm making progress."

"You are." Jo studied her before nodding once. "Ready?"

They spent the next little while learning a new way to escape, to counter an arm bar and regain the top position. Then Jo introduced how to sweep an opponent to the mat, a move Beth had longed to learn. They were working on nuances to perfect the move when a blond toddler and a teenaged boy, apparently his sitter, made their way into the gym and stood off to one side of the mats. The two chatted while the teen kept a firm grip on the boy's hand.

"Who's that?" Beth panted her question after defending from Jo's sweep, hands resting at her hips.

"Who?" Jo looked where Beth pointed and a big smile broke onto her face. "Artie!"

The little boy paused only long enough to slip off his shoes before racing across the mats and into Jo's open arms where she knelt. The bear hug lasted a full minute before Jo gently separated them. She glanced to Beth, who remained standing as she waited for an introduction.

"Beth, this is my son, Arthur Walsh." Jo lightly gripped the boy's shoulders. "Say hello to Miss Beth, Artie."

"Hi, Miss Beth." The tow-headed boy stayed close to his mother as he looked up at Beth.

Surprise flashed through her at the realization there must be a father somewhere. Jo hadn't mentioned a husband. So who did the child call dad?

"Nice to meet you, Artie." Beth grinned at the kid, reaching down to shake his hand and then froze as an image formed in her mind's eye. Peering closer, her heart thudded against her ribs. She accepted his small hand in her fingers, dazed.

The boy from the cloudy vision. Then... She cut her glance to stare at Jo, trying to superimpose the vision with the reality. The back of the woman wearing the fancy dress with her hair in an intricate upswept bun, leaning over a crying boy with blond hair. The longer she studied her new friend the more certain she became. Same dark hair, but not in a fancy do, just a simple ponytail. Same lithe but petite frame. Why hadn't she seen the similarity in Jo before?

Obviously Jo wasn't married to Mitch, so that answered one question. The woman and boy in the vision weren't his family. But that raised new questions. What connection did they have with him? Why couldn't she see very much about Mitch's future? Did he have some way to block or interfere with her visions? Could she trust him, if so? Leaving the most difficult question for last... One her heart had grappled with all along. Should she allow her attraction to him to grow after all?

"You're doing good. Drop the nose... A little more." Mitch fought the desire to grab the yoke and take back control of the Piper Archer. "There. Keep it steady."

He enjoyed flying the single-engine aircraft. Designed to be comfortable for the pilot, it also made for a great training plane. The first time he had taken an Archer up he'd been impressed by its stability and its power. Enough to go where he needed to go but not enough to get a student pilot in trouble. It didn't hurt that it was one of the Cherokee family of planes from Piper. A smile eased on his lips even as he kept a close eye on his student. His Indian ancestors surely smiled as well.

"This is not as easy as you make it look. But it's still a blast." Beth flashed a glance at him as she flexed her fingers on the controls. "Will you let me land this time?"

"Only after you demonstrate you have complete control in the air." He nodded once as she kept her eyes ahead but her attention on him. "Focus on keeping the plane trimmed and the wings level."

Beth adjusted the trim with a slow adjustment of the wheel until the plane leveled nose to tail. "Like that?"

"Perfect." Mitch mentally shrugged at his own indecision. One fact was indisputable. He couldn't keep her out of a plane if he tied her to a tree. She handled the aircraft as if she'd been flying for years instead of days. Was there nothing the woman couldn't do? "How's your martial arts coming along?"

She bobbed her head several times, her gaze darting to either side of the windshield. "Jo said I'm on track with our plan. If I keep up the pace she set, I'll be lethal in four more weeks."

"Lethal?" Mitch blurted out his surprise as he contemplated her. "What do you mean?"

"Wait a few weeks and I'll demonstrate it for you." She cut a glance at him, a flirtatious smile on her tempting lips. "I'm learning all kinds of fun ways of grappling an attacker."

"I'd rather you demonstrate it on someone else if you're going to kill somebody." He checked the gauges and dials to reassure himself the plane functioned normally. Kept his mind away from the images of grappling with her in bed. He couldn't go there. Not yet. "I have things I want to do with my life."

Her smile faded as she kept her gaze on him for several seconds. "What sort of things?"

He sensed her withdrawing from him despite the close confines of the cockpit. Had he said something to upset her? "First, I want to settle down with a home of my own."

"I thought you were more of a free spirit than that." Her fingers gripped the yoke until her knuckles gleamed in the sunlight. She kept her attention on her flying despite the suddenly uncomfortable atmosphere. "You said you've traveled all over the world."

"Not anymore." The clawing need to park his bike in his own driveway tore through his soul.

She'd grown up in the small town, so he understood why she wanted to explore. To travel and experience life in other parts of the planet. He'd passed the stage in his life when doing so enticed. If only they could make a relationship work between them. He'd tried to keep her at a distance, but the more time he spent with her the more often she invaded his thoughts, his dreams, his desires. He needed her to understand his priorities in order to discover whether they had anything in common. If they had any hope of acting upon the attraction they seemed to have for each other.

"I've lived all around the world since I was an infant and am tired of starting over."

"How many places have you lived?"

"All told, twenty in my twenty-nine years. Though I don't remember the first five since I was just a baby."

"That's amazing." She shook her ponytail until it draped over her right shoulder. "I've lived in one home all my life. I've never traveled outside of Tennessee. Unless you count popping down to Huntsville, Alabama, on occasion."

"Probably not, since it's so close." He drew in a long breath and let it out slowly. "I guess you're looking for a guy who will take you places?"

"I'd love to find a man who would travel with me, yes." She glanced at him, a glint in her green eyes. "Do you think Keith might be eager to explore with me?"

Mitch swallowed the sharp retort ready to burst from his mouth. Keith best keep his hands off her, steer clear of her. His tendency to love 'em and leave 'em after he stole a woman away from Mitch still curdled his blood. Then again, they were all adults and Mitch hadn't wanted to find a wife and start a family until very recently. Maybe she'd be better off with some flirtation with his buddy instead of being anchored in place by Mitch's druthers. Torn between two conflicting goals, his direction suddenly clouded.

He envisioned the two of them gallivanting around the globe, experimenting with foreign foods and dancing. Thrilling to skydiving over the plains of Africa, or climbing the mountains of Switzerland. Cruising between the Greek islands, laughing together while they sipped cocktails on deck. The film playing in his mind both invited and made his hands tremble.

Time to end the lesson and put some distance between them. Just like he sensed she had attempted to do minutes before. Thinking about her with Keith settled a dark cloud on his mood. Beth was everything he'd dreamed of having in a woman, in a wife, in the mother of his children. Yet she wanted something he wasn't sure he could give. On the other hand, he couldn't hold her back from her dreams simply because they clashed with his.

He cleared his throat and his mind of the painful daydream. "Okay, you seem to be doing well enough to attempt a landing. Ready?"

Chapter Nine

The next morning, Beth hurried into the gym to meet Jo for a private lesson. Lack of sleep dogged her steps. Mitch's mood as she'd landed the plane—a decent landing if she did have to say so herself—left a sour taste in her mouth. What had happened to change the atmosphere from friendly to not so much? Did she do something wrong without realizing it? She'd pondered the answer while counting sheep instead of sleeping.

She lowered herself onto the mat and laid on her back, staring up at the cross-beams of the trusses supporting the gym's roof. Letting her gaze follow one beam to another to another, she breathed deeply. Slowing the inhale and then the exhale until her mind settled. She closed her eyes and focused on the muscles contracting and expanding instead of the angst lingering from the flying lesson. When calm replaced the anxiety, she sat up and began stretching while staying focused on her body and movement. Peace descended on her heart.

After several minutes, she heard footsteps approaching and smiled when Jo came into the gym, ready for the next session.

"Sorry I'm late again." Jo dropped a red gym bag on the floor at the edge of the mats. She toed off her slip-on flats before striding to where Beth waited. "I had to take a phone call after I'd parked."

Tension was back in Jo's expression. Beth sensed the deep-seated concern radiating from the professor's body. "Anything wrong?"

Jo made a dismissive gesture and shook her head. "My soon-to-be ex-husband needed to rail at me again."

"You're getting divorced?" Beth figured there was a father to Artie and thus a husband, but she hadn't anticipated they would break up the family. "I'm sorry."

Family was everything for Beth. Her sisters had to become even closer after their mother died suddenly several years before. Their father Roscoe had been a giant of a man with a matching laugh. Not that she remembered much about him. He died when she was seven years old. All the more reason to cling to her sisters. The idea of wanting to break up a family must come from pain and sadness.

"Don't be. It's my idea." Jo looked away, emotions flashing across her features. "Can't come soon enough." She retied her black belt with a final angry tug.

"When does it become final?" Beth resumed stretching, reaching to loosen her side muscles.

"Actually, my lawyer will file for the divorce in a few weeks, after the one year legal separation is finally over." She pulled the holder out of her hair, slipping it onto her wrist while she brushed her hair back into a ponytail again, wrapping the holder around the shoulder-length strands with a final snap. Then she did some leg stretches while standing. "Whoever decided people who want to divorce have to wait a year before they can even file the paperwork just doesn't understand."

"That's a long time to wait." Beth shifted to a straddle stretch, touching her fingers to the mat between her spread feet.

"Tell me about it. Especially when the man is abusive."

"Your husband beats you?" Beth stared at her strong, capable instructor, trying to process how a woman with a black belt could be physically abused. Sure, she was petite, but with wiry muscles and the ability to take down a man much larger than herself. Something Beth could also do after only weeks, not years, of training.

"He knows better than to lay a hand on me." Jo's brows lowered as her eyes darkened. She sank onto the mat and began her warmup routine. "I wish he would try. That would be some kind of fun. But no, he is verbally abusive. Plays mind games. Trying to convince me of my inferiority to him, to men in general."

Beth stood and bent to one side, enjoying the release of tight muscles on her side. "You're such a strong woman, I can't imagine those games work very well."

"After years, it can be hard to turn off the inner voice that sometimes agrees with him." She shook her head slowly and then drew in a long breath before rolling on her back to stretch her buttock muscles. "I moved here to start over, away from him and all his crap."

"Don't let him bully you into doing anything you don't want to." Beth bent to the opposite side, tension easing the longer she held the pose.

"He's a bully all right. One who is into some shady dealings I don't want him sucking Artie into."

"How shady?"

Jo sat up and stared at Beth and then slowly shook her head, her arms crossed over her chest. "I honestly don't know and do not want to."

"Drugs?"

Jo shrugged, lifting her shoulders close to her ears and then dropping them back into place. She stood and stretched side to side. "Maybe. The less I know the better, I think."

"As long as you're not an accomplice, you should be okay." A shiver racked Beth as she contemplated the risk to Jo and Artie. "Keeping your distance is smart."

"That's why I moved away. He knows I moved to Roseville, but he doesn't live close enough to significantly interfere with my life anymore. I don't have to answer his phone call…"

"No, you don't." Beth stomped on the mat to emphasize her point. The muted thud of her foot on the rubber left her very unsatisfied. "Just like in that movie we went to the other day, you can stand up for yourself."

"You know, some of the moves that blonde woman made, even though choreographed for the movies, we could modify to our purposes." A grin spread slowly onto Jo's face as she demonstrated a particularly unusual sweep with her hand.

"Legal moves?"

Jo huffed, then laughed out loud. "You're not learning how to compete so much as defend yourself. A few surprises never hurt anybody…except your attacker."

Jo laid a hand on Beth's shoulder while standing barefooted on the mat facing her. The contact flashed the image through Beth's mind of Jo arguing with Mitch, her hands on her hips as she leaned toward him, anger in her eyes. Shadows surrounded them, blurring the edges into oblivion. The sense of fear stung Beth, angry bees attacking her skin, making her pull back from the vision until it faded out of view. What did it mean?

"Are you okay, Beth?" Jo angled her body closer, concern on her face for a moment before she grinned. "I promise I won't surprise you."

Beth sighed and then chuckled at the glee on Jo's features even as her heart tightened at the unclear future of her friend and mentor. "As long as you keep away from that man, you can pull whatever surprises you want. Just teach me how to block them first."

Mitch rumbled into the town square on his Harley, snaking through the heavier than expected afternoon traffic until he found a parking space a block from the Golden Owl. Cutting the engine, he removed his helmet and let his gaze wander over the vicinity. Summer brought heat and humidity in equal measure. His tee clung to his back as he dismounted from the bike and placed the helmet on the seat. The quiet weekend would likely soon be shattered by Beth's response to his sound reasoning. It couldn't be helped. Squaring his shoulders, he set off down the sidewalk toward the bookstore.

Reasons for his decision had formed and revolved in his brain for days. The last job had paid well and went surprisingly smoothly. He didn't need or want to keep on with the high-risk repo jobs. He wanted to start his search for a house in a town he could call home. The time felt right to begin the next chapter of his life. With a loving companion. Maybe Beth, if she'd see how much sense his plan made.

Each stride carried him closer to the confrontation he'd hoped to avoid. Deep in his heart he knew he was doing it for Beth's own good. He simply had to convince her to agree. He pushed open the door and strode into the cool store, glad for the respite from the heat outside.

"Hey, Mitch, what are you doing here?" Beth dried her hands on the apron hanging around her neck and tied at the waist.

"I came to see you, of course." He scanned the nearly empty shelves of the case. "And maybe grab a bite to eat?"

"We don't have much left after the breakfast rush." She peered into the case with a rueful grin. "Tara went to resupply from the bakery that provides all the good stuff."

"I guess I'll just have to choose from the options available." If only Beth would receive his decision as the best option. He drew in a shaky breath. "I'll take one of those and a coffee, please. To go." He held no illusions he'd be staying long.

"Sure." She snared a waxed sheet and retrieved the honey dipped doughnut, sliding it into a white bag. "Cream?"

"No, just black." He studied her efficient moves while she poured his coffee and snapped on the lid, aware of an increasing urge to be with her. Yet what he'd come to say would not likely go over well.

Beth rang up the order then looked at him with puzzlement in her eyes. "Okay, spill. You didn't come all the way here for a doughnut."

Caught. The moment had arrived but he hesitated. Reluctant to risk severing a relationship that might mean his happiness. But he must take steps to protect the woman he'd come to love. Even if that meant walking away. "Truth be told, I need to talk to you."

Roxie poked her head out of the back room then walked out to stand by the register. "You must be the pilot I've heard so much about."

Mitch inclined his head a bit and smiled. "Guilty as charged. And you are?"

Beth waved at the woman regarding him with cautious humor. "This is my sister, Roxie."

"Nice to finally meet you, Roxie." Her steady stare ensured that Mitch received her message: don't hurt my sister. She'd certainly be one to contend with. Duly warned, he straightened and turned to address Beth. "Can I speak with you? Privately?"

"Did I forget a lesson or something?" A light lit in Beth's eyes, eagerness and excitement mixed.

"Hold on there, Romeo." Roxie crossed her arms over her chest, her brows raised. "She's got some work to do before you can claim her."

"I don't need to take her away from her work." Mitch shook his head and took a breath as he eased closer to Beth. "Actually, I'm here to talk to you about the lessons."

"Cool. What about them?" Beth rested her hands on the edge of the bakery shelves, her gaze open and yet wary.

All his carefully prepared arguments fled. He'd have to wing it. "I know you had a thrill when we repo'd that plane a few weeks ago."

She bobbed her head enthusiastically. "Absolutely. I can't wait to go out again."

He steeled himself for her reaction but pressed on. "It's not always like that. Sometimes it's downright scary."

"But that's what makes it exciting." She glanced to Roxie and then back to Mitch. "What's wrong?"

Mitch swiped a hand over his head, determined to continue but reluctant to hurt her feelings. "You've got to stop this madness, Beth. You're not up to the challenge."

"I'm working on it, though. A few more weeks…"

"No, you don't get it. I can't let you put yourself in harm's way just to have a bit of spice in your life." He stared at her, willing her to understand. His heart and soul couldn't take it. "Please."

The bell over the front door jangled, drawing their attention to where Tara hurried inside carrying several large bakery boxes. "Hi, all. What's going on?"

Roxie motioned for her to come closer, giving Mitch the chance to fully appreciate the likeness between the three sisters. He hadn't had much time to become acquainted with them, but they were strikingly similar in height and hair color. Their eyes varied between green and hazel, but they really were more alike than different. Would he get to know them after he said what he came to say? He gripped the cup in his hand and crimped the folded edge of the bag with tense fingers.

"Mitch is in the middle of explaining why Beth shouldn't want to get involved in airplane repo." Roxie cleared her throat as she raised a brow in Mitch's direction. "Please continue."

The look she shared with Tara suggested the sisters were in agreement with him. Giving him a bit more courage. "Beth, I know you think it's fun and exciting, but you can't do this. It's crazy."

Beth propped her fists on her hips. "You do it. Why can't I?"

"I'm military and trained in all aspects of flying and self-defense. You're not. Plain and simple as that."

"He does have a point, Beth." Roxie tilted her head as she shrugged. "I wouldn't want you to get hurt."

Tara slowly nodded as she set the boxes on the counter in front of Beth. "You've always wanted to do more but maybe this isn't what you should be doing?"

Beth sighed heavily as she glanced between her sisters and then shot him a glare. "I can't believe you'd all gang up on me like this. I'm learning what I need to know in order to be a good partner to you, Mitch, or to any other repo agent. I realize I'm not there yet, but I'm getting there."

"I can't help you put your life at risk anymore." Mitch crossed his arms and regarded her silently for several moments. Dismay filled him. He had to make her understand, to turn away from her crazy idea of fun. "I'm getting out of the business myself. Like I told you, I have other things I want to do with my life."

"You're just saying that to try to persuade me to walk away, too." Beth's frown deepened the crevasse between her eyes. "I'll find another partner if you're too scared."

"Damn it, Beth. You're the one who should be scared." Mitch glared at her and dropped his arms to his side. She wouldn't listen. Fool woman. His heart ached but he had to do what he thought best. He hadn't meant to lose his temper, to cuss at her. Time to go. Turning to leave, he paused to look back. "Don't say I didn't try to warn you off from risking your fool neck."

She glared back at him over crossed arms. "Don't worry, Mitch. You won't hear one word out of me one way or the other."

"Fine." He strode toward the door, anger and fear burning a hole in his stomach.

So she wasn't talking to him because he dared to voice his concerns. Fury welled inside at both her childish attitude and his failure to make her see reason. He'd done all he could but not enough to protect her from herself. Maybe if he hadn't lost his temper she would have heard his message. Afraid of revealing either his fear or his love for her, he yanked open the door and hurried outside, the bell overhead jangling into silence as the door thumped closed.

Chapter Ten

S trangulation, both her hands wrapped around his neck, was too good for him. A choke hold might prove useful even if temporary. At least he'd not denigrate her abilities while passed out on the cold ground. Two days after Mitch's refusal to teach her, to even consider helping her achieve her goals, she still fumed over his arrogance. He couldn't tell her what she was capable of, nor stop her from pursuing her dreams. She'd find another way. A better way. One without his condescending attitude.

She stood in the open doorway of a utility closet at the school. Gripping the Gi hanging over the chin-up bar braced near the top of the doorway, Beth pulled herself up as far as she could. Not as far as Jo wanted her to be off the ground but at least her toes left the floor. Better than her first attempts. The thick cloth made an already hard exercise more difficult by not having a smooth bar to grab. Jo insisted Beth build up not only arm and leg strength but her hand strength as well. She dropped back to the floor and prepared to pull up again.

"Don't drop like a rock." Jo strode over to watch Beth's next attempt. "Use your muscles to lower yourself back down. Work them in both directions."

"Slave driver." Beth flexed her hands and then wrapped her fingers into the cloth. She grunted as she slowly dragged her body weight off the floor and then eased back down. "Like that?"

"Ten more, then we'll begin." Jo turned away to start her warmups on the mat.

"Ugh." Beth sighed and began the lifts, concentrating on form and height. She had to prove not only to herself but to Mitch that she could succeed. She put all she had into the exercise. By number nine she was panting for air and her arms burned. She struggled through the last lift with a grunt followed by a sigh of relief. Rubbing her arms, she crossed the mat to lower herself to a cross-legged position near Jo. No whining or complaining. She'd make herself over into a stronger woman capable of protecting herself. No man required. Not even Mitch.

"You're looking mighty fierce today." Jo rested her elbows on her crossed legs. "What happened to put such a scowl on your face?"

"Mitch." Beth shook her head, her blonde ponytail whipping her shoulders. "Said I can't do airplane repo like a man."

"Is that what this is all about?" Jo sat up straight. "Some guy?"

"He introduced me to his freelance jobs and now wants to prevent me from getting any more involved." Beth snorted in disgust. "Like he can control what I do."

"Why doesn't he want you to do it?" Jo rocked onto her back, then stretched her legs over her head, toes barely touching the mat. Peeking around her shoulder, she studied Beth. "What makes him think you can't do it?"

"He says it's too dangerous. For me, not him, mind you." Beth copied her instructor's stretch, feeling the release of tension in her back the longer she held the position. Sitting back up straight at the same time as Jo, she huffed out a breath. "Once I'm strong enough, there's no reason why I can't defend myself no matter the situation." She caught a flash of a frown on Jo's face and paused. "Right?"

"Well…not exactly." Jo rested her palms on her knees as she regarded Beth. "Martial arts is great for certain aspects of self-defense, but it won't protect you from every kind of danger."

"But I doubt the job is as dangerous as he seems to think. Maybe he's making it sound worse than it is so he won't have to deal with me."

"Or maybe he's telling you the truth. Keep that in mind." Serious blue-gray eyes regarded her for several moments before Jo pursed her lips. "Let me show you a new way to escape a holding position."

Jo shifted to kneel, indicating for Beth to get in position on her back to prepare to escape from whatever holding position she was about to apply. Talking Beth through the required steps, Jo grasped Beth's Gi lapels with one hand and placed her other hand over Beth's shoulder on the mat. Beth shifted her right hip inward and then leveraged her right leg up and over Jo's back, pushing her onto her back and then controlled her with both hands on Jo's shoulders. At Jo's nod of approval, Beth shifted back to kneel a few feet from her.

"Jiu-Jitsu is great for hand-to-hand fighting and you're making good progress." Jo moved to lay on her back and motioned for Beth to inch forward. "But you have a lot to learn before you can be truly effective in your positions and submissions as well as escapes. Let me demonstrate to you what I mean. Put your right hand there, and the other one there. Brace yourself to keep me from moving, from escaping as best you can. Now…"

Beth took a firm grip as directed, tensed her muscles to resist Jo's attempt to break her hold. Yet in a split second she was flat on her back, with Jo's grinning face above her.

How? The series of moves and lifts blurred past her so fast she couldn't even say what happened. Point taken.

Jo let her sit up and then helped her to her feet. "You have a long way to go before you can feel secure in your defensive let alone your offensive skills. Give yourself time to train, to grow stronger, to learn as much as possible. In the meantime…" Jo rested one hand on a hip. "Think about what Mitch said, not to turn you off from your goal. Rather, to instruct you to take sensible precautions."

"Like what? Not doing it? That's what he wants me to do. Nothing."

"Learn more about what's involved before you get in too deep. After all, even though I have a black belt, I still had to move away from my husband to protect myself and Artie."

A dawning understanding flowed through Beth's defensive thoughts. "Even though he didn't hit you, he still could hurt you."

Jo nodded as she tugged the hem of her Gi down. "Like I said, there are different kinds of danger. Protecting yourself must come in different forms as well."

Her friend made sense as usual. After all, Beth had learned about the exciting job a few weeks before and had barely scratched the surface of the training required to develop the skills and abilities the job demanded. First things first. While she worked on her martial arts, her shooting, and her flying skills, she'd find out more about how a person became a plane repo agent. Or at least co-agent.

What if she couldn't find a partner? He'd said it was a tight but small group of repo agents. If Mitch spread the word among his buddies not to let her play in the same sandbox? She'd always have the Golden Owl, but would that be enough? A shiver of unease rippled down her spine. While she loved her sisters and working among the books, she craved more than what the quiet town could provide.

She must succeed. She squared her shoulders and pinned Jo with her determined stare.

"Like you said, I have a lot to learn. So let's keep going."

The time had come to end it. He'd had enough. He paced slowly across the wide front porch of Keith's house in downtown Roseville, the two black Labradors sprawled on their sides at one end. He'd procrastinated by tossing a ball for them to retrieve until they'd flopped out on him. Wimps. He chuckled to himself and headed for the grouping of wicker chairs around a matching wicker table. Towering oaks and sprawling maples cast shade against the summer sun, cooling the air flowing past his cheeks. The street was quiet and friendly. Few cars cruised past and even fewer people strolled by. Peace and tranquility flowed around him as he eased into a cushioned chair.

He longed for a similar place to call his own. Keith had made a good life for himself. Well-respected and surrounded by friends. Mitch stretched out his legs and crossed his ankles. He could grow accustomed to this kind of neighborhood. If only he had the ability to convince Beth to relinquish her idea of putting her neck at risk, he might well be on the way to making his dreams come true. He'd enjoy sitting with her on a wide porch, talking about their day, their plans, their kids. A shadow of sadness passed over him. He just needed to move on, find a new path forward.

Pulling out his cell phone, Mitch called his contact who arranged the repo assignments.

"Hey, Mitch. Glad to hear from ya. I was about to call you."

"Listen, we need to talk."

"Yep, we do. I've got a job for you. A big one."

"I don't want it."

"You haven't heard what it is."

"I want out."

"Let me tell you about this plum assignment."

"You're not listening. Take me off your list."

A long silence stretched on the phone.

"You still there? Take me off."

"You're the perfect fit for this job, Mitch."

"How so?"

"It's a jet for one thing, your favorite kind."

"Most of them are. I don't think so."

"At least do this one last assignment. I promise it will be the last one I send your way."

He did love to fly jets. He owed the guy for all the work he'd sent him over the last few years. Enough to live on and squirrel away most of it for fulfilling his dream. A dream he was anxious to make reality.

"I'm done." His statement didn't have the ring of conviction it once had.

"I hear you, bud. But the paycheck would set you up real nice no matter where you land."

His bank account and investments were flush already, but the temptation was great to pad them even more. Give him longer to decide his next steps, where he'd settle. A noisy diesel pickup sped down the road, drawing his gaze. Bringing the town front and center in his mind. He could settle in such a pleasant place.

The neat and compact center of town had diners and antique stores among the boutiques and law offices. A drug store served as both pharmacy and general store for the community. He imagined strolling along the sidewalk, peering into the store windows at the variety of goods offered for sale. Tempting passersby into the shop to browse the merchandise.

Then again, Beth lived in Roseville and worked at the heart of the town. The Golden Owl bookstore stood as one of the central hubs. He longed for her, heart and soul.

Feared for her and her crazy scheme. Wished she would be happy with where she lived and worked and not crave the thrill and daring of airplane repo. Wished he were enough for her.

Maybe one last job would let him show her the inherent risks in every assignment. Warn her away for good, while he was there to protect her.

"Tell me what's involved." He listened intently, a grim smile on his face. After a few moments, he nodded to himself. The setup would be just risky enough. "Fine. I'm in. But it's the last time."

Chapter Eleven

The bright sunlight highlighting the tiled floor made her dark mood worse. A lull in the steady stream of customers gave her a minute to catch her breath and wrestle with her thoughts. Beth wiped down the coffee urn while brooding over how to move forward. If Mitch refused to work with her, then she'd need to find another partner. But who? And where did she begin the search? She rinsed the cloth in hot water and hung it to dry. Scanning the area, she pondered her next task along with her next moves.

Roxie rounded the corner of the checkout counter, an open book in her hands. As she came closer, Beth peered at the page she studied but couldn't figure out what the colorful pictures depicted. Roxie lifted her happy gaze to meet Beth's solemn expression, her smile drooping.

"What's the matter?" Roxie slipped a finger between the pages, closing the book while she stared at Beth.

"Mitch."

"Ah." Roxie sighed and opened the book again. "What do you think of this pattern? I thought I might try it now that I have mastered the basic crochet stitches."

Beth crossed her arms and shifted her weight to one hip. "No lecture?"

Roxie looked at Beth instead of the book and then eased a smile back onto her lips. "I think all that needs to be said has been said."

"So you agree with him?"

"He's the one with first-hand experience, not me. In the meantime, what do you think of this one?" Roxie pointed to the picture of an afghan, dozens of colors creating a patchwork quilt type of effect. "This one uses granny squares. Looks easy enough. Don't you think?"

The mundane nature of the conversation with her sister lit a fast-burning fuse inside Beth's core. In the past, she had striven to be patient, understanding of others priorities. Since experiencing the thrill of the chase-and-steal nature of the repo world, her patience had flown away. She didn't want to merely make coffee, or put books on shelves, or sweep the floor. She needed to feel the rush of adrenaline in her veins. She glared at her sister.

"I don't care if you want to crochet an afghan, Roxie. I have more important decisions to make."

Roxie glanced at her once sharply and then shrugged. "Things will work out as they should. Let it go and see what happens."

"I've waited long enough for something to happen." Beth tightened her arms, hugging herself to keep from bursting with frustration. "I'm going to find a way no matter who or what tries to stop me."

"You don't want to force anything, Beth. Just putting the words into the universe ensures they will be acted on, even if takes a little while."

"You believe in the power of words, their ability to hurt or heal depending on how they are strung together." Beth slowly shook her head, sorting her thoughts into coherent sentences. "Words can only carry matters so far before action is needed. The time has come for me to act, not just think or even speak about my goals. I need to make them happen."

Roxie stared over Beth's shoulder, a slow smile creeping into position. "Prepare yourself. I think you're about to have some action."

Beth pivoted to follow her sister's gaze. Walking past the front windows, Mitch Sawyer approached the bookstore entrance. The store was empty for the moment. Damn. No other customers to wait on. The door opened, setting the little bell jangling in panic. She shot a glance back at Roxie, and lifted a brow in question.

"Maybe he changed his mind?" Hope surged in her chest.

"You're about to find out." Roxie tapped the book in her hands, and strolled away, greeting Mitch as she passed him on her way upstairs.

Left alone with the man she desired but who had thwarted her dreams, Beth didn't know what to say or do. The only thing she could do was act normal, calm and cool. If only her hands weren't trembling, and her knees would stay still. She swiped her damp palms down the frilly apron tied around her waist. He stood a few feet away, separated by the pastry display case.

"Hey, Mitch."

"Hi, Beth. Could I have a coffee and one of the custard filled, please?" Mitch kept his serious gaze on her as he placed his order, not even glancing at the donuts.

She grabbed a waxed paper sheet and picked out the donut, putting it in a small paper bag. As she filled a cup with steaming coffee, she looked over her shoulder at him. "Anything else?"

He let out a long sigh, his attention riveted on her. "Are you still bound and determined to get into the repo gig?"

Beth stilled, resting her fingers on the top of the lid she was about to press onto the cup. Her heart raced at his question. The hope inside sparkled through her entire being. She snapped the lid into place and then handed it to

Mitch. His fingers brushed hers, setting off zinging bursts in her veins as she met his gaze with a slight nod.

"Why?"

"I've got another assignment. One I think you could help me with, if you want to."

Joy swept through her, followed quickly by relief that she'd be working with Mitch, not anyone else. "You know I want to."

He *tsked* with his mouth before his eyes darkened into a serious expression. "But you have to do exactly as I say. No improv. Got it?"

"What's the gig?" Beth untied her apron and hung it on its hook behind the counter. She walked to the end of the coffee bar where Mitch met her.

"Keith has agreed to host a much larger air show over Independence Day week at his airfield. One of the invitees is our target. We need to figure out how we'll get hold of the Learjet but we have a few weeks to do that."

"Do I need to dress any certain way for this one?" Beth shifted her weight only to discover the move brought her closer to Mitch. "Another floppy hat?"

"We shouldn't discuss this here. Someone may come in." He swept the store with his glance and then zeroed in on Beth. "I'll do some preliminary probing and then we can talk in a day or so."

Beth needed a clue, just a hint at whether they'd succeed in the proposed mission. She rested a hand on the forearm of the hand holding the cup. The electric current she'd come to expect when she touched him surged through her, lifting her wide-eyed gaze to meet his. His dark eyes studied her, searching her eyes and lingering on her mouth.

She focused on him for a moment, seeing the flash of the vision where Jo and Artie stood on the tarmac at some unknown airport with an executive-type of jet fuzzy in the background. She refrained from gasping aloud as she blinked away the vision. But she still had no more idea of what was to come. A double-edged sword.

Mitch's intense gaze rested on her as his lips parted. She swallowed, the combination of nerves and the desire to taste him making her salivate. Did her longing reflect in her eyes?

"Beth…" He turned to set his purchases on a nearby table, then moistened his lips and gazed into her eyes, seeking reassurance. "I need to ask. I want to kiss you. May I?"

She swallowed again and nodded, intent on the fullness of his lips and the anticipation of feeling them against hers. "Please."

Mitch lowered his head and she parted her lips as her eyes fluttered closed. Firm and polite at first, his kiss slowly deepened. She let him explore her mouth, savoring his unique taste and the embrace of his arms sustaining her for the sweet kiss. Even though questions about him swirled in her mind, she knew she wanted him to be part of her future. His mysterious ability to block her inner eye intrigued her, making surprises a new possibility in her life. After a few moments, he released her as he ended their contact. Opening her eyes, she smiled up at him.

"Thank you, Beth. I needed that." He grinned back at her. "I'll call you as soon as I have an idea of a plan. Then we can work out the details."

"I'll be ready." For more kisses as well as the next adventure. Her heart sang at having both the job and the man.

Snagging a table toward the back of the busy café, Mitch tapped a finger on the blue tablecloth as he waited for Beth to arrive. He'd learned more about the man who had forfeited on the loan for the specially equipped Learjet. A guy with expensive tastes and rumored to engage in some black market dealings. Keith's contacts had made sure the man felt privileged to attend and show off the plane's features. The basic outline of a plan formed easily in his mind with no apparent safety flaws that would imperil anyone involved. A much similar scheme to the previous job. A bit of fine tuning would be necessary to accommodate the changed circumstances. Something he'd discuss with Beth. He shifted on the hard chair, a sigh escaping as he noted Beth making her way toward him.

The woman moved with the grace of a panther, fluid strength evident in each step as she neared him. Graceful and beautiful even in her khakis and polo work uniform. Her long hair was pulled back into a ponytail, swaying with each stride. A smile lit her green cat eyes, warming his insides into a melty pool of desire. Without question, she was one fine woman. Her martial arts training had toned her curves into a succulent temptation he couldn't deny.

He'd much rather she remained safe at the Golden Owl, serving up books and brews to the small town. But the next job needed two people and she'd proven she could handle herself. Still, if his plan seemed so perfect, why did he have a nagging feeling he'd missed something? They had a couple of weeks before the air show, which should provide enough time for him to identify what his gut warned about. Then to adjust accordingly. Before anyone got hurt.

"Sorry, I'm late. Bet you hoped I'd changed my mind." She sat in the chair to his right.

"I can hope, can't I?" Mitch studied her expression, not surprised at the determination he saw in the set of her jaw and in her eyes.

"A futile exercise." She perused the menu resting on the table, flipping through its several pages then laying it aside. "So what's the plan?"

Mitch chuckled deep in his throat. "Aim for the heart of the matter, why don't you."

"Saves time. So?" Beth clasped her hands together on the table.

He laid his menu on top of hers and nodded to the waitress who materialized at his elbow. After they'd placed their orders, he swallowed a gulp of beer from the sweating bottle while forming his thoughts. Still she blinked at him with growing impatience, evidenced by tension in her shoulders and lips pressed together. Her gaze dropped to his mouth and then moved up to meet his steady regard.

"It's pretty much like what we did before but with a bit of a twist. The owner is a former client of Keith's. He likes to be the center of attention so Keith has convinced him that he's been invited because his jet is a featured plane at the show." He tossed back another swallow and plunked the bottle on the table. Wiping his mouth with the back of his hand, he saw her gaze follow his movements. "The Learjet is a sweet plane, with special seating arrangement for passengers and a hidden cargo hold in the belly."

The waitress brought Beth's iced tea, splashing tea and ice on the table as she set it down. With a hurried apology, the young woman mopped up the mess with a rag and left a stack of napkins at the edge of the table before moving on to the next table.

Beth pulled a napkin from the stack and set her glass on top before addressing him again. Her long lashes framed gold-flecked eyes as she quirked one brow. "What's my role?"

"Make sure the logbook is on the plane and keep an eye out for the dude while I do the preflight check. Then strap in for the hop to Denver to deliver the plane to the bank rep." He tapped his forefinger on the table to underscore his next words. "At no time are you to do anything else. Understood?"

He stared at her as he adjusted his chair to a more comfortable angle. Bringing him closer to where she smirked at him. She could confound and tantalize all at the same time. When he was apart from her, he longed to be with her. When they sat together, an invisible thread wound around them. Drawing him inexorably closer to her. The kiss they'd shared had reinforced his attraction to her as a woman. Yet her penchant for putting herself at risk worried him, gave him reason to hesitate to put his own heart in peril. A fate he didn't know he could survive. If he permitted himself to fall in love with the sexy vixen, would he have to give up his dream of a settled life to keep her happy? Could he meet her need for excitement and the thrill of the chase without losing himself in the process?

She canted her head, one brow raised in disbelief. "I can do more than look for a book and keep guard against the owner interfering."

Her desire to be more deeply involved in the risky nab of the plane set off warning bells in his belly. Warnings of what happened if he failed in his primary goal of keeping her secure despite everything. He shook his head, his voice emerging rougher than intended. "No way. I know you've upped your skills but that doesn't mean I want you doing anything unnecessary. Got it?"

"Spoil sport." Beth stripped the wrapper off of a straw and stabbed it into the icy depths of her drink. "Why do you think I've been pushing myself so hard if not to be up for the next challenge?"

"I've warned you it might be all for nothing. At least where I'm concerned."

"Why? That's what I don't get."

"You want to have the thrill of the danger but I want you to be safe. You don't understand just how tricky these jobs can be." He raked a damp hand across the top of his head and down through his hair, arranging it to lay about his shoulders. "Some agents have been killed, shot by the owner. I've faced men with guns more than once and it's no fun. I think this one will be fairly straightforward so not as bad as others."

She smiled sweetly at him, preparing to sip from her straw. "I'll be good as gold, and do as you ask...unless the situation changes, of course."

The smile aimed his way jangled the alarm bells in his gut yet again. What might she be thinking she'd do? "You should be glad I'm letting you go with me. You should take my warning to heart and keep out of harm's way."

Beth batted her lashes at him, relaxing against the back of her chair. "I will do my best to follow your instructions. However, I'm not afraid of whatever may happen. After all, I'm sure we'll be just fine."

"What makes you say that?" He frowned at her, intrigued by her confidence in an assignment that wouldn't go down for two weeks.

Her assured gaze wavered then steadied. "I trust you to cover the bases since you're so concerned about safety."

She kept something from him, but what? What did she know? And how? The bells in his gut clamored for attention. He'd think through the plan carefully, searching for any threats he hadn't accounted for and then fix the plan.

The waitress interrupted them long enough to set his chicken sandwich in front of him, and a Caesar salad with grilled salmon in front of Beth. They dug in to their meals, keeping an eye on each other as they ate in silence for a few minutes.

The silence dragged out until he thought he'd lose his mind. He needed to say something to ease the tension his thoughts had created in his chest. But what? He racked his brain until an idea popped into it. "You'll need an outfit that won't stand out during the show. We can go on my bike, pretend we're into fast no matter what kind of vehicle. So maybe get something a biker chick would wear. Just make sure it's not too revealing." He didn't need the further distraction. But more importantly, his libido couldn't handle much more.

"What does a biker chick wear?"

"I've seen them wear a variety of outfits, but you might want leather pants or blue jeans to protect your legs." He froze as he pictured her in an outfit like the one Olivia Newton John wore in the musical *Grease*. She'd look sexy in skin-tight, shiny black leather, an image that shot desire to all the right parts but at the absolute wrong time.

"I'll see what I can find..." She leaned forward, casting a quick glance around to make sure they weren't overheard. "I've always wanted to ride a motorcycle."

"You've never been on a bike?" Mitch grinned at her, aware of just how sheltered a life she'd lived if she'd never straddled a bike. "We'll have to do something about that before the job so you're comfortable and don't give us away."

"What do you propose?" Her lips parted as she waited for his reply, reminding him of their kiss two days before.

Her too-sweet-for-his-taste perfume scent drifted past his nose, reminding him of a previous idea he'd considered but discarded. Perhaps there was time for him to find the perfect gift.

"We can take a ride up to Winchester, maybe do some shopping."

"Oh? What exactly would we be shopping for?" Her brows lifted over wide eyes. "I don't think there are many big stores out that way."

He couldn't believe he was actually suggesting a shopping trip with a woman but at the same time relished the idea of her arms wrapped around his waist as they rolled up the highway. He also wanted to see how she'd react to his idea. Would she find it too personal or a romantic gesture? He hoped for the latter. "You'll see. How about next week?"

"I'll have time to find a new outfit to wear and can try it out on your bike at the same time."

"Good." He lifted his beer bottle, motioning for her to lift her glass. Tapping the bottle against her glass, he smiled with grim acceptance of what they planned to do in the coming weeks. "To success."

Chapter Twelve

The aroma of popcorn and motorcycles greeted Beth as she stepped into the store. She inhaled deeply, drawing the intoxicating mix inside. Beth scanned the large, bright expanse of merchandise. She detected the pungent aroma of tanned leather which triggered images of adventure and daring. Western saddles used by the rodeo riders when the annual rodeo came to town. English saddles used by the huntsmen chasing after a fox over rolling hills and fences surrounding Roseville. Vests worn by men on motorcycles, like Mitch, as they roared down mountain roads.

One day, very soon, she'd be riding with Mitch on his bike. Her heart soared with eagerness to experience the wind in her hair and the rumble of the motor between her legs. Her hands on Mitch's waist as they navigated the back roads and highway. Warmth flooded her cheeks, making her breath catch as she forced herself to focus on the store's layout and not her wayward thoughts.

Roxie stopped beside her to get her bearings. Round racks of blouses and tops stood shoulder to shoulder with low tables of pants across the right half of the store, women's to the back, men's up front. She spotted wall racks filled with an amazing variety of jackets and helmets. A section in the middle displayed belts and gloves and other small items.

"This should be interesting." Roxie let out a long breath and shook her head. "Never thought I'd be helping you become a biker chick."

"Two weeks ago I'd have to agree with you. But I do think it's fun." Beth chuckled as she moved slowly toward the tops. "I'm thinking a tank top or something similar, to give me freedom of movement should the need arise."

Roxie stopped her with a hand on her forearm. "I thought you said not to worry? That you're just playacting to be a biker chick."

Beth laid her hand on top of her sister's and gave it a squeeze. "I'll be fine."

"You didn't answer my question and you know I hate it when you try to redirect in such an obvious manner." Roxie pursed her lips and propped a hand on one hip. "Tell me straight."

"I am. We've got a solid plan and Mitch won't let me do anything remotely risky."

"Some things are out of our control."

"So I control the things I can and prepare for the things I can't."

"You're selecting a biker outfit based on the assumption you'll need to defend yourself. That doesn't make me feel good about your plan."

Beth turned to pull a red shirt with a plunging neckline from a rack, holding it up against her chest so Roxie could give her opinion. "That's simply part of my training. To always be aware of my surroundings and to be prepared to defend myself. It's not like an attack is planned, right? There's no invitation or announcement. So I have to be ready at all times."

"Sounds exhausting." Roxie shook her head, dismissing the red top, and reached for another shirt, this one a bright yellow with a black skull and crossbones on the front. She held it up until Beth emphatically shook her head, then hung it back on the rack. "But I'm still worried about all the things that might go wrong."

Roxie preferred knowing what might happen on any given day. She made to-do lists and shopping lists, tools for ensuring she managed her time and life to the best of her ability. The power of choosing the right words, especially when used with the proper intent, had always been Roxie's strength. When faced with the unexpected, she might hesitate at first, but then she'd summon the right mix of letters to form the most powerful words needed to protect the people she loved. A talent Beth could only envy and admire.

"You've always been the proverbial mother hen where Tara and I are concerned. You do realize we're adults now, right?" A black halter top caught her eye. Holding it up, she inspected the laced up, low-cut shirt made of a soft, stretchy fabric. For the hot summer days, the bare back and arms would keep her cooler and allow for the optimum range of motion. Besides, it was a cute little number. One Mitch would probably drool over. "What do you think?"

"I think I will always feel the need to protect you both." Roxie joined her in assessing the shirt and slowly nodded. "As for the shirt, I like the cross-strap at the collar bones to give it some structure, too. It's a cool detail."

"It's not too skimpy?" Beth angled the shirt and turned it around then looked at her sister.

Roxie crossed her arms and aimed a sly smile at Beth. "Mitch will love it."

"Hm. That's not why I'm thinking of buying it." Not the main reason. Beth checked the price and then draped the garment over her left arm. "Next, pants."

"If you're going to be a real biker chick, you need tight pants. But not leather. That's such a cliché."

"How would you know?" Beth paused in the act of pivoting toward the pants section.

"I'm a wealth of useless information. Come on. Let's get this over with." Roxie gently pushed Beth onward.

They strode over to the shelves of jeans and pants. Beth dismissed the idea of anything too flashy. She didn't want pockets covered in rhinestones or other bling. She preferred a clean and classic pant, but comfort and flexibility remained top priorities. Sexy was secondary.

"Leggings?" Roxie called from across the space, pointing to a wall of shelves holding pants in black, blue, burgundy, and green.

Beth soon reached the display and flipped through several pairs before finding what she'd had in mind. Stretchy and form-fitting light blue denim. "Perfect."

Imagining the jeans with the flirty top made her smile, especially when she added Mitch's anticipated reaction to seeing her in the revealing outfit. When she'd approached him at the airfield, his jaw had dropped open and his eyes stayed on her every motion. And she wasn't wearing anything nearly as flirtatious and eye-catching as the top in her hands.

"Is that all you need for this gig?" Roxie perused the shop before dropping her gaze on her sister. "I'm famished. Let's go grab a bite."

"I've got the right low boots at home, but I need one more thing. A jacket." Beth added the jeans to her pile and hurried to the back of the store. "Something to protect me in case Mitch crashes the bike."

Roxie trailed behind, her voice distant. "Don't even put that thought out in the world. Especially since I do not want to visualize it."

"I'll keep that in mind." Skimming the selection displayed on the walls, one black leather jacket captured her attention. Drawn to the glistening material and the zippered front, she particularly liked the red stripes on the shoulders and the cascade of white stars down the upper arms. A subtle patriotic jacket that satisfied her soul. She checked the price and winced. Three weeks' pay but she had to have it. She'd regret walking away. She examined the stitching and the overall effect of the beautiful coat. Looking to Roxie she lifted a brow.

"That's awesome." Roxie fingered the leather cuff. "You could wear that anytime, not just for dangerous forays into the world of undercover missions."

Beth chortled at her sister's assessment of the new path she followed. A path that she hoped would include a certain handsome pilot. She envisioned herself making her entrance, sashaying toward him, and relishing Mitch's reaction. Imagined his eyes widening and glinting as he ran his gaze from head to toe and back again. His lips parting in surprise and appreciation. She flushed and smiled. "You had me at dangerous."

"Don't tell me that, sister mine." Roxie shook her head as she followed Beth to the customer service desk to pay for the clothing. "I'll not sleep well until you're home safely again."

"That's a long time from now so you might want to change your mind about that." Beth paid the cashier and then smiled at Roxie. "Mitch is taking me on my first bike ride in a couple of days, but he won't tell me where we're going."

"Why ever not?"

Beth took the bag from the cashier and led the way out of the store. "He says it's a surprise."

Roxie peered at her, delving into Beth's eyes for a span. "Is it? Really?"

Every time she tried to see into Mitch's future she saw Jo and Artie instead. Having never experienced the visual silence of another she didn't understand the cause. But she liked the effect. Mitch must have his own talent, perhaps to suppress those of others as it pertained to him, or something else was dampening her ability to envision his future. The net result being he could do the unexpected.

"Yes. He is the only man who has ever been able to surprise me." She unlocked the car and dropped the bag on the back seat before sliding into the driver seat.

Roxie snapped her seatbelt secure and gazed at Beth. "You must be careful. You don't know what he's capable of or what he's planning."

"You think Mitch means me harm?" A shiver of doubt crept in at Roxie's caution. She didn't get that kind of vibe from him so she either had nothing to fear or was entirely misreading him. "I don't think I need to fear him."

"Just be careful, okay." Roxie settled into her seat and peered at Beth with serious eyes. "One other thing. If he hurts you, he'll answer to me."

"Relax, Roxie. There's nothing for you to worry about." Beth started the car and eased out of the parking space, heading for home. "I've got this."

Dappled sunshine splashed on the sidewalk. The weather couldn't be better for riding to the little perfumery he'd discovered outside of Winchester. A short but pretty ride through the rolling countryside. Mitch parked his bike in a spot near the Golden Owl, leaving his helmet on the seat. A second helmet was strapped in place, waiting for Beth. He strode to the bookstore and pushed inside, the bell announcing his arrival. A hum of conversation from all corners of the store greeted him. The cool air lifted the heat of the summer sun from his shoulders as he unzipped his jacket to help cool himself. He scanned the people in the store, seeking Beth.

"Hi, Mitch. Beth will be out in just a minute." Roxie smirked at him. A little imp seemed to have taken up residence inside the woman as she continued to study him.

"Cool. You're quite busy for mid-week, aren't you?" He returned the steady regard for a beat before making a point of looking away.

"I think it's the air conditioning that has people stopping in." With a chuckle, Roxie straightened a stack of bookmarks near the cash register. "We're selling more sodas than books at the moment."

"It's a beautiful day even if a scorcher." Perfect temp to enjoy the breeze of the ride. "Will she be much longer? I'd like to get going."

"She's putting the finishing touches on, so it won't be long now." Roxie pursed her lips and then spun around as Beth emerged from the back room. "Mitch is growing impatient."

"He'll need to learn to wait for me, won't he?" Beth quirked a brow as she stopped near Roxie.

Mitch blinked several times, stunned by Beth's transformation into the hottest biker chick he'd ever seen. Her honey blonde hair was pulled up in a ponytail that cascaded curls down her back. She carried what looked like a patriotic themed leather jacket over one arm. But the low-cut clingy top and those skin-tight jeans made his mouth water. When she turned to hug Roxie farewell, his jaw slowly dropped open. Her entire upper back was exposed by the halter top. She ended the embrace and slid the jacket onto her shoulders. Every luscious curve was evident as she sauntered toward him in low-heeled, short boots. She had even gone so far as to apply red to her nails and her mouth, completing the enticing transformation.

He couldn't take his eyes off of her until she stopped in front of him and smiled. Flicked her gaze from his eyes down to his lips and back. She lifted a brow, an invitation.

Why yes, ma'am, he'd accept. Without hesitation, he dipped his head and kissed her mouth. She responded in kind, extending the duration until the sound of Roxie clearing her throat had them pulling apart.

"Enough of that." Roxie's grin softened the rebuke as she glanced between them.

Mitch held out a hand to Beth, amazed and delighted by her audacious costume. "Ready?"

"Where are we going?" Beth zipped her jacket and laid her slender hand in his.

He tugged her along with him, heading out the door. "A little place I discovered that I think you'll enjoy."

"Food or fun?"

"Nice try but you'll have to wait and see." He looked over his shoulder at Roxie. "I'll bring her home before dark so you don't need to worry about her."

"Thanks, Mitch." Roxie inclined her head to acknowledge his consideration. "Have fun, you two."

"If I'm not back by dark, send out the search party, will ya?" Beth chuckled as she waved to Roxie and then allowed Mitch to propel her outside as Roxie's laughter faded.

Minutes later Mitch guided the bike out of its spot and onto the street, Beth holding on to his waist with both hands. She learned the knack of riding in moments and soon relaxed as they finally left the town for the open highway winding gently between crop fields and fenced pastures.

The rumble of the motor prevented any serious conversation which gave him time to think about his next moves. Although his family had hoped he'd follow in his grandfather's footsteps and use his sensitive olfactory talents to work in the family's perfumery, he'd wanted to take more control of his life. Do something more meaningful for himself and his country if not his family. His dad understood his need to be in the service and encouraged him to follow his passions and join the Air Force to fly jets. After his dad retired from the force, he had gone back to running the business. Mitch planned to do something different with his life, though he hadn't determined what yet. But he still had a sense of what kind of scent a woman should seek out based on her unique essence and personality.

He parked the bike in front of the quaint, historic house on the edge of town serving as the mecca for people seeking a specific or unique scent. According to the lady he'd spoken to over the phone, they sold a variety of specialized perfumes and colognes but also allowed customers to blend their own. During their conversation he realized her father was friends with his dad. Her family was renowned for the fine fragrances and colognes they bottled and sold worldwide. She'd been eager to meet him and help him select the perfect scent.

Beth set her helmet on the seat of the bike and smoothed her curls as she stared at the sign above the door. "Scent Masters. What is this place?"

"A place where we can choose the right perfume for you." Her slight frown at his statement made him realize he'd implied he didn't like her perfume. "My family runs a perfume business and I noticed your current one is a bit on the floral side."

She bristled and frowned more. "I like that perfume."

"I know and it's a nice blend...for someone else. But I think I have an idea of what will suit you even better. Something that reflects the person you are and want to be. Come on." He led the way up several stone steps and held the door open while Beth stepped cautiously inside.

The foyer of the house appeared typical of the older houses in the area. Hardwood floor. A marble-topped table off to one side displaying a bouquet of flowers. Chandelier softly illuminating the space. When he detected only a light air freshener he relaxed, relieved to not be bombarded by a dozen warring perfumes.

"Hello?" Mitch sauntered into a side room, what once was the living room but now served as an office. "Miss Rivers?"

A glass-topped desk took up the space in front of the cold fireplace, a cloth-covered executive chair pushed back as if the occupant had left hurriedly. An overflowing inbox and an old-fashioned phone occupied opposite corners, with a legal pad and several pens between. Bookcases lined two walls, holding stoppered bottles of various sizes with different colors of liquid inside instead of books or knick-knacks.

"Maybe we should go." Beth appeared at his side, tense and standing on the balls of her feet, prepared for flight.

"Give it a minute." He listened for some indication of the woman's whereabouts.

A thump from another part of the house echoed down the hall, followed shortly by footfalls as the lady in question entered the office.

Mitch smiled at the tall and trim woman in red jeans with a white blouse, short black hair edging her round face. Red-framed glasses perched on her straight nose, highlighting the bright blue eyes that sized him up in one quick glance.

"I'm Mitch Sawyer and this is Beth Golden." He widened his smile and waited for her to stop in front of him. "I phoned earlier about the Vaniglia."

"Right, the Santa Maria Novella. I'm Joan Rivers. No, not the actress." She stuck out a hand to shake with him. "I'm so glad to meet you, Mitch. I phoned my daddy after we chatted and he said to tell you hello."

"That's nice of him. I haven't been home in a while to see everybody." He'd need to make a trip after everything settled down. He winked at Beth. Maybe to introduce his new girlfriend if things worked out as he hoped. "Do you have the Vaniglia? Do you agree with me, now that you've met Beth?"

Joan addressed Beth, sizing her up just as quickly as she'd done him. Nodding, she grinned at Mitch. "I see why you're interested in it."

Beth slowly shook her head but remained quiet. Moistening her lips, she glanced at Mitch with a question in her eyes.

"Some people, Beth, have an innate ability to determine what kind of scents will work best. I have it to a degree. Joan is renowned for her uncanny way of selecting the right mix every time." He took Beth's hand and gave it a squeeze. "Want to experience it for yourself?"

"I've never heard of such a talent." She shrugged and her eyes lit with curiosity. "Bring it on."

Joan studied the shelves, finally crossing to a particular round and squat bottle. She carried it over and stood in front of Beth, easing out the stopper. Joan held the wand aloft for a second before shaking her head and putting it back inside. "Not that one. Not for you."

"Why not?" Beth glanced at Mitch and then back to Joan.

"A little too spicy for you. Let's try…" She wandered over to another shelf, pointing at first one bottle and then another. Finally she grasped a honey colored bottle and opened it. She sniffed delicately before grimacing with a quick shake of her head and put the wand in place.

"You do have the Vaniglia, don't you?" Mitch moved to peruse the shelves himself, growing impatient with the woman's quest.

"Yes, we can try it. I wanted to make sure we had sampled a couple others Beth might also like." Joan ambled to the other side of the room, lifting the decorative bottle with a flair of ceremony. She moved to stand in front of Beth, slowly pulling out the wand. "I think you'll enjoy this one."

Beth leaned slightly forward to inhale the scent and nodded. "That's really nice."

"Let's try it on your skin. But first, I can smell your other perfume. Where did you apply it?"

Beth held out her hands, palms up. "On my wrists."

"That's easy to wipe away with an unscented towelette." Joan set the bottle on the desk before crossing to a set of drawers freestanding beside the fireplace. Retrieving a wet nap, she handed it to Beth to wash her wrists clean. "Once they're dry, we'll try the Vaniglia."

"What is that scent? I don't recognize it."

"The main ingredients are ones you'd know." Joan picked up the small bottle and angled it so the light reflected off the amber fluid. "It's a vanilla based fragrance. This one is good for either sex and is not harsh or too sweet."

"I think you'll find it is a very clean scent with a slight floral tone balanced by a warm spicy fragrance." A combination Mitch particularly enjoyed. The scent evoked fond memories of time spent outdoors with his family. "Try some."

Joan dabbed a small amount on each of Beth's extended wrists and then slipped the wand back into its home. "The top notes of the floral fade pretty quick, don't they?"

Beth sniffed her wrist and nodded. "I see what you mean, and now I can smell more of the vanilla and a hint of smoke. Reminds me of walking through the woods on a sunny day."

"It's perfect for your adventurous nature." Mitch lightly gripped her wrist. "May I?"

Beth lifted her hand so he could better inhale the fragrance. "Does it meet with your approval?"

Holding her strong yet gentle hand and savoring the lush woodsy scent combined to stir the ever smoldering desire he carried inside for Beth. Despite his head warning him away from her devil-may-care risk taking, he still craved her touch and her laugh as well as her heart. She was the complete package of a woman: beautiful, sexy, caring, smart, and fun-loving.

"Are you about done?" Beth aimed laughing eyes at him.

Reluctantly, he released her hand. He was just beginning but one step, one day, at a time. "I'd like a bottle for her. My gift."

Beth pressed her lips together for a moment before a small smile lifted the corners of her mouth. "Thank you."

With luck she'd be thinking of him when she wore the perfume. Hopefully every day. "I'm glad you're happy with it and didn't take offense. I was worried about that."

"At first, I was somewhat offended but I don't know much about perfumes. That other one I received at a Dirty Santa gift exchange last year so I didn't have any strong feelings about wearing it." She regarded him with a slight smile resting on her luscious lips. "Unlike this one."

Joan turned away to box up the bottle and put into a gift bag. While she was busy, Mitch took advantage of the moment to take Beth's hands and pull her closer to him.

He pressed a kiss to her red lips and squeezed her fingers. Savored her taste and scent along with the desire shooting through him. Slowly breaking off the kiss he gazed into her gold-flecked eyes and smiled. "What do you want to do next?"

He had ideas of what he'd like to do but would leave it up to her. Perhaps dinner. Perhaps a leisurely drive back to town. He wouldn't mind continuing the kissing on some quiet byway. She smiled up at him, laughter sparkling in her eyes.

"Let's meander our way back to town. I like riding with you."

The light in her eyes as she regarded him lit up his insides, warm and soft and happy. "You're an amazing woman, Beth Golden."

"How so?" She tilted her head to one side as she waited for his reply.

"You seem to have it all together. Ready and able to do anything."

"I've been trying to tell you that for weeks." She smirked at him and then straightened.

"Yes, but you must admit you've made some huge changes in your lifestyle." He searched her eyes, the gold flecks glinting. Mesmerizing. "I couldn't help but worry about you."

She pressed her hands on his chest. "Teaching me how to fly and shoot well both were far more useful than worrying. Besides, you owe me."

He gripped her hands where they lay on his chest, pulling his head back to look down at her with surprise. "I do?"

"Yes. You owe me a shooting lesson before next week's job. When do you want to schedule it?"

Not where he thought she'd go. But she was right. She needed more practice before she faced another risky venture. Concern hovered in the back of his mind despite the evident physical changes and emotional readiness he detected in the way she moved. "Tomorrow morning?"

"Fine. We should head back." Beth accepted the gold velvet bag from Joan and stuffed it into her jacket pocket. She grinned and pecked his lips with a light kiss. "I don't want Roxie to fret."

As they thanked Joan and left the house, Mitch remained certain of one thing: Roxie wasn't the only one who worried.

Chapter Thirteen

The ride along the interstate and then the highway to the state-of-the-art shooting range in the larger town of Pulaski proved uneventful. Nonetheless, he couldn't wait to stop the bike. Exhausted after two nights tossing and turning, or staring at the ceiling imagining one disaster after another, left Mitch ready to snap. He'd given his word, though, so would see the job done. He'd also given his word to Beth that she wouldn't be hurt while she dabbled in repo. That one may prove far more difficult to keep. Still he relished the time spent with her.

"Ready to shoot something?" Mitch waited while Beth secured her helmet, appreciating the view as she leaned over the bike. Though sadly not dressed in her sexy biker chick getup, she filled out her blue jeans and white tee in all the right places.

She straightened and moved a few steps closer, pulling her hair into a ponytail as she neared. A slight frown marred her pretty face as she regarded him. The hair tie snapped into place as she dropped her hands to her sides. "We're shooting targets, right?"

"Right. Why?"

She tossed her head to flip the end of her ponytail behind her. "I know I need to start with targets, but that makes me wonder."

He lifted his brows, waiting for her to continue. "What?"

"How different is it to aim at a person, someone attacking or threatening me?"

His thoughts veered off to form a hard lump in his throat. He tried swallowing down the remembered horror after his first kill, but it refused to budge. Reliving the sound of the rifle bullet impacting another man's body. Mitch's plane had been shot down, forcing him to parachute into enemy territory. He'd nearly crept back to his side when confronted by a man with hate in his eyes, aiming an assault rifle at him. Mitch had hesitated but recovered his wits fast enough to fire once, straight through the enemy's heart. The sound of the shot followed by that of the bullet ripping through the man haunted his nightmares. Mitch had fled back to safety and pretended the incident hadn't rattled his nerves. But he knew that it had and would forever underlie his decisions for the rest of his life. Always there though ignored with an effort. One of the reasons why he'd transitioned to the reserves.

He inhaled slowly and let out a sigh. "Let's just hope you never have to find out. Come on."

The familiar scents of metal, gunpowder, and fresh coffee met his nose as he held the front door open for Beth to walk inside ahead of him. A combination sure to kick start his senses. She glanced up at him as she passed, lips parted as if to say something while her special perfume overlaid the store's unique aroma, but he gave her a quick shake of his head. He really didn't want to talk about the differences. They were few but substantial.

"Hey, Major Sawyer, welcome back." The owner, Jake Smith, stuck out a hand as he hurried to greet them. "Who do we have here?"

Mitch accepted the man's firm grasp, then inclined his head toward Beth. "My friend, Beth Golden. I reserved a lane for us on the range."

"I don't see your guns. Do you need to rent some?" Jake glanced between Mitch and Beth.

Mitch lifted the hem of his shirt to reveal the holster with his Glock 43 secured inside at his waistband. "I've got mine, but I'd like for Beth to try something a bit smaller."

Jake considered Beth with a questioning smile. "Why would you want to learn to shoot? To fend off the guys?"

Beth chuckled as she slid her gaze across the store and back to meet Jake's curiosity. "Something like that."

Mitch liked her cagey response, not revealing her true motives and yet providing a reasonable answer to the question.

"Let's see. Maybe a Glock 19?" Jake motioned for them to follow him to the gun display. Pulling out a key ring with a bundle of metal keys, he selected one and unlocked the pistol case. Lifting the black pistol, Jake checked to make sure it wasn't loaded, no magazine and nothing in the chamber when he pulled it open, before handing it to Beth. "Try this one."

Beth accepted the gun, hefting the empty gun easily. "That's about the right weight for me to handle."

"Wait til we put the single-stack magazine in place." Mitch addressed Jake as the man locked up the display case. "Which lane do we have?"

Ten minutes later, wearing their "ears and eyes" otherwise known as ear and eye protection, they stood in the firing end of the lane. Mitch put the basket containing the smaller pistol and ammunition on the raised bench separating them from the target range. He taught her how to inspect, load, and aim the gun while hoping she would never need to pull it out of her special purse. One he'd help her choose after she passed her certification, a small purse with a section specifically for safely carrying a pistol. She listened and followed his directions without hesitation. Part of him wished she'd question or at least fumble. At the same time, her self-assurance gave him confidence she'd rise to whatever challenge or threat she might confront.

Beth gripped the handle and lifted the weapon, pointing it away from them as she examined it. She hefted it several times and then grinned. "Feels good in my hand."

"You'll be able to carry that in your purse so it's at hand when you need it." Mitch covered her hand with his, drawing her green-eyed gaze up to look at him. "After you pass the gun safety class and receive approval from Homeland Security, you'll be certified to carry a weapon. It takes time but that gives you the chance to seriously consider whether you want to follow through with carrying a gun. Do not take that responsibility lightly."

Her grin flattened to a straight line. She slowly nodded twice and then dropped her gaze to the gun encased by their joined hands. "I promise."

He must make her understand the very serious nature of the path she'd chosen. The knowledge she'd gained and the skills she'd developed could lead her to take chances she wouldn't even have considered a few months ago. The resulting choices then might lead to additional risks and consequences. But how to do so without scaring her and making her doubt herself in a crisis?

He squeezed her fingers and then released her hand. Placing a forefinger under her chin, he regarded her in silence for several moments. "What I want you to remember is that you should only draw your gun when you definitely intend to use it. It's not a gut reaction but a decision you need to make when the situation warrants."

"Of course, I wouldn't want to shoot anyone accidentally."

"Be aware that if you ever do shoot somebody, the police will question you. If they determine you were in the wrong, then you could face charges of manslaughter or even murder. Shooting is a last resort. I carry but I rarely need to touch my gun let alone draw to aim at somebody. It's not to be done lightly. Clear?"

"I understand…" She swallowed and dropped her gaze back to the pistol. "Only use it when I need to protect myself or someone else."

"Exactly." Mitch released the breath he'd kept inside and then pressed the button to reset the target and adjust the distance. "Let's see how well you handle this gun."

She slid the earmuffs over her ears and he followed her lead. She assumed the stance he'd taught her. Before she fired, he laid a hand on her forearm to get her attention and then moved behind her to shadow her position, adjusting the elevation of her arms and the angle of her intended shot. When he was satisfied, he dropped his guiding hands to step back and watch her squeeze off three rounds, dead center on the bright red circle fifteen feet away.

She peered over her shoulder with a huge smile, her twinkling eyes sharing how pleased she was with her success. After unloading and laying the gun on the table, she reached up to press her smiling lips to his. Surprised but willing to accommodate her little celebration, he kissed her back. He placed his hands on her shoulders to pull her snug against his chest before he wrapped his arms around her and deepened the kiss. Her hands walked around his waist to link behind his back, pulling him closer as she opened to his exploration. He savored her light scent and sweet taste for several moments before breaking the contact with a series of light kisses on her lips.

She flicked her tongue over her reddened lips and then kissed him once more. "How was that?"

"Perfect." He shifted his weight to one hip as he indicated the target. "The shooting as well as the kiss."

She chortled and smirked up at him. "I learned from the best."

"I didn't teach you to kiss like that."

"Perhaps." Beth studied him as a slow smile eased into place. "You refined my technique though."

He gazed into those laughing eyes and felt his heart meld ever closer to the beautiful woman standing within reach. Drawn to her in a way he'd never thought possible. He wanted her at his side through thick and thin. Longed to protect her. Yet there she stood pleased as punch to have hit the bull's eye three times in three shots. Ready to put her new skills to the test.

He swallowed the dismay simmering in his gut. He couldn't take away what made her smile so broadly but he didn't have to like it. He just needed to do all in his power to ensure that her fun didn't get her killed.

The smell of sweat and rubber mats made euphoria bloom inside Beth as she moved into position. Each step toward achieving her overarching goal of being able to protect herself should the need arise reinforced her self-confidence. Within the week her new skills would be used as she helped Mitch repossess a plane from some dirt bag who had not paid the loan payments as promised. Lying on her back, knees bent and gripping her classmate's Gi as Jo had instructed, she waited for the signal to escape his mount and attempt to flip him into a submission position. The large man seemed even larger, hovering above her as she held still, replaying the sequence of moves intended to free her and capture her attacker. His hands braced on either side of her shoulders and his knees kept her legs apart. Still she had the ability to dominate him with just a few quick movements. She sensed he wouldn't hesitate to use his brute strength to best her. All the more reason to take him out and prove him wrong.

Jo strolled among the pairs of students, her slight weight barely indenting the firm mat surface as she passed. "Ready? Begin."

With a grunt, Beth gripped tighter. Shrimp. Arm bar. Shift. Rotate. Sweep. Submission. She held him for a moment and then pushed back to let him huff into a sitting position.

"Next time, use more of a shift to put him off balance quicker." Jo halted beside Beth as the class waited for the rest of her critique before being dismissed. "Otherwise, not bad. Alright, guys. That's enough for today."

The other half dozen students began getting to their feet, grabbing their gym bags, and making their way slowly, chatting, out of the gymnasium.

"I'll take him down faster next time." Beth nodded to her glaring partner, struggling to recall his name. He'd been coming for a week and she'd only been paired with him once before.

"You can try." The young man gained his feet and trudged away without looking back.

Jo slowly shook her head. "I don't think he quite grasps the intent of our training."

"What do you mean?" Beth scrabbled to her feet and sauntered beside Jo to the edge of the mat where her duffle bag sat open.

"He's too aggressive, too…" Jo slipped out of her Gi and belt and folded them into an open gym bag. She looked at Beth before pushing down the pants covering her shorts. "Angry, I think."

"He wasn't very pleased that I could break his grip that easily." Beth untied her belt and put it and her Gi in the duffle bag, followed soon by the pants. Left dressed in a loose-fitting tee and mid-thigh shorts, she zipped closed the bag and slung the strap over one shoulder. "What happens next?"

Jo shrugged and slipped her feet into loafers before putting the backpack on her shoulders, her hands gripping the straps as she contemplated Beth. "I'll give him a little while to sort it out, but if he doesn't…" She shrugged again and shook her head. "I may have to ask him to find another training center where he'll fit in better."

"You're the best one in Roseville." Beth worked her feet into her sandals and then paced beside Jo as they left the gym. "Where would he go?"

"Not my problem." Jo cast a glance at Beth as they stepped out into the late morning sunshine. "My real problem is about to be over, or at least I hope so. My lawyer called this morning to tell me he plans to file the divorce papers after the Fourth of July."

"Next week. That's wonderful." Beth paused on the hot sidewalk near where her car was parked. "Soon you'll be free of any direct ties to him."

"I wish. There's always Artie to consider." Jo's eyes went a shade darker despite the bright sunlight. "As long as Todd stays away from him, we should be okay."

Beth looked sharply at Jo, hearing an edge to her voice. "Has he threatened Artie?"

Jo pursed her lips before flattening them into a hard line. "Todd wants our son to follow in his footsteps, learn the business. Only, it's not any business I want our son to even know about."

"What kind of business?" Beth noticed worry lines on her friend's face as she searched her expression for clues to what concerned Jo. "Surely Todd isn't into anything illegal."

Jo lifted a brow and looked away.

Beth froze and drew in a shaky breath. "Jo?"

Jo stared at her, worry shadows in her eyes. "I'm not entirely sure. I know it's dangerous and takes him away from home frequently. That's what worries me most. Where's he going? What's he up to?"

"Why doesn't he tell you what he does?" Beth hoped against hope that nothing bad would happen to her friend or son.

"Honestly, Beth, I'm to the point that the less I know, the safer I probably am. If it weren't for Todd's casual remark about training Artie to take over, I wouldn't think twice about it since I'm divorcing the man."

Beth slowly shook her head, searching for some reassurance to offer. "I'm here if you need me."

Jo stilled, her gaze fixed on a distant point as a frown deepened between her eyes. Beth perused the area, noting the sunshine dappling through the few trees lining the sidewalk. Cars coming and going on the streets while a gaggle of cyclists cruised by. Heat shimmered the air surrounding them, waves of moisture floating skyward. Several minutes passed before Jo fixed her gaze on Beth again.

"What if it really is something criminal he's up to?" Jo shifted the backpack and then stared up the street toward the square where several clusters of people hurried about their errands. She slowly turned back to frown at Beth. "What if Artie decides to follow that dark path?"

"I doubt that could happen." Beth dropped her duffle to the ground with a thud and pulled Jo into a hug. After a couple of moments, she released her to grasp each upper arm and focus on her friend. "You've raised a fine boy and I'm sure your husband won't do anything to hurt you. You must keep the faith. You'll both be fine."

The flash of a vision of Jo patting Artie as he cried challenged her upbeat forecast. They'd survived some sad event, but was that the end or the beginning of their troubles? Despite her own doubts, Beth would do all in her power to make sure her belief in Jo's future would come to pass. But how?

"Hello? Beth?"

"In here." Beth continued reps with blue hand weights as she pivoted away from looking out the window to face the open door. "In your old room."

Her sister hadn't been to the house since Beth had redecorated the bedroom. She trailed her eye over the home gym, pleased with the neat and orderly arrangement. Having a place for each item helped maintain a sense of calm inside. Clutter tended to make her uneasy, as if her environment had become jumbled and messy. Soon she'd find out Tara's reaction to the new look.

Tara, dressed in tan shorts and a red top, appeared in the doorway, her smile quickly replaced with open mouthed surprise. "You're serious, aren't you?"

"Absolutely." Finished with the last set of reps, Beth crossed to place the weights on the shelf. "What brings you here?"

"Roxie mentioned you'd taken over my room so I wanted to see it for myself." Tara gave Beth a brief hug before taking the time to peruse the changes.

Beth's phone buzzed where it lay on top of the bookcase. A text from Mitch suggesting they go to the first day of the airshow to familiarize themselves with the layout and the situation. Prepare for the actual taking back of the aircraft. She texted a quick reply that she'd be ready and then dropped her phone back on the bookcase. Yet again, Mitch had managed to surprise her. She smiled when Tara pointed at the cheerful vase of flowers on the shelves under the TV.

"Roxie's idea." Beth touched her forehead, finding it damp with sweat from her exercises.

"I like what you've done. Very efficient and welcoming." Tara lifted both brows and then grinned as she continued her exploration.

"It's the perfect place for me to train." Beth shifted to snatch a clean towel to mop her face. A small smile flitted onto her lips at the surprise evident in her sister's expression. "I really enjoy working out in here."

"I see that." Tara paused in front of the poster, reading its encouraging words silently. "Good advice. I like how it can be read either 'do it' or 'don't quit.' But I can't imagine you'd back down from the challenge you've set for yourself. You never have."

Beth draped the towel around her neck, tugging on the ends. "I have no intention of stopping. Even though I don't know how it will all come to pass."

"Why would you say that?" Tara stopped her investigation of the gym to stand in front of Beth beside the treadmill.

Beth shrugged lightly. "It's the strangest thing, sis. This guy, Mitch Sawyer, he's a mystery to me."

"I thought you liked mysteries." Tara chuckled at her little joke, pulling her long blonde hair over one shoulder. "A little suspense thrown in?"

"In books." Beth shook her head as she removed the towel and dropped it into a wicker basket beside the bookcase. "This is different."

Mitch intrigued her in many ways. Compelled her to do and say things she'd never done before. Tall, strong, handsome, kind, and caring. All the right characteristics she wanted in a man. When she was with him, she had no fear. In fact, his presence completed her in some undefined way. Her discovery of the unexpected, of surprise, when with him added to his allure.

"Let's grab something to drink and you can tell me about it. Come on." Tara shooed Beth out the door and down the hall to the kitchen.

A welcoming cozy space where the three sisters and their mother had prepared all kinds of meals and treats for decades. The compact area included a central island where the girls had stood on one side talking to their mom about their day while she prepped a salad or chopped veggies. Memories that filled Beth with a sense of security and grounding, of belonging.

Her family meant the world to her. Her sisters, Grant, and their cousins all joined together to support and console. What they didn't understand was how it burdened to know more about their future than they did. She could filter the visions but not completely stop them. Though she'd tried more than once. Stifling a huff, Beth retrieved two tall glasses while Tara pulled the pitcher of lemonade out of the fridge.

"Go on." Tara filled the glasses, handing one to Beth. "Tell me what's the matter."

"I can't explain it." Beth walked over and sank onto one of the chairs at the square wooden table, years of use leaving it scarred but sturdy. "It's just...I can't see his future."

Tara joined her, scraping a chair out to plunk onto it. "Nothing? That's odd."

"Right?" Beth sipped from her glass as a frown tugged on her brows. "All I can see when I'm with him is a flash of a vision of my instructor and her son. What do they have to do with him?"

"Do they even know each other?" Tara inclined her head as she regarded her sister.

"I don't think so, which is why it's all the more confusing to me." Beth leaned back in her chair, dragging her glass to the edge of the table. "Why can I see them in his future but nothing else?"

"You never have been able to see all of a person's future, right?"

Beth rocked her glass back and forth in her hands, images from her inner eye flickering past. Snippets of others' lives yet to be lived, of people and places and emotions yet to be experienced. How much of any of it had happened? She had no way of knowing and didn't want to pry into her neighbors' lives in order to try to find out. Doing so would mean revealing her secret talent. She held no illusions as to how people would react to the news. Avoiding her and possibly her sisters as a result of their insecurities around people with different abilities. None of the sisters shared their hidden talents unless forced to, one on one.

She looked up from her glass to meet Tara's patient gaze. "I only see bits and pieces. More if I actually touch the person. But with Mitch, I see nothing except that one blip of Jo and Artie."

"Then that must be an important event in his life." Tara sipped her drink and set the tumbler back on the table.

"I sense more than see her fear for the boy. From what she's told me, the father is into some shady stuff." Beth tapped the sweating glass with her forefinger.

"Can you tell when that vision might happen?" Tara leaned forward, clasping her hands on the table. "I mean, any details of time and place?"

"At night, but that's all." Beth stared at her sister before shaking her head, pressing her palms flat on the table. "I just don't know anything more."

"You know more than they do." Tara laid her hand on top of Beth's and squeezed once. "I trust that you'll be there to help if needed."

Beth nodded slowly, her mind racing. "Yet another reason to not quit my training." So she'd be ready.

Chapter Fourteen

The Independence Day airshow started with a bang. Mitch shaded his eyes to stare up at the passing Blue Angels flying in formation overhead. He appreciated the extent of the training and teamwork the pilots demonstrated with their precision maneuvers.

He glanced at Beth, standing beside him wearing dark blue shorts that revealed shapely legs, and a patriotic striped top in honor of the holiday. "What do you think?"

"They're very close for going so fast, aren't they?" She flashed a glance at him and then focused on the show in the sky.

"They won't take any unnecessary risks. They're highly trained and skilled pilots." Mitch let his gaze drift over the growing crowd of people of all ages.

Knots of family groupings, much like very young soccer players following the ball on the field, moved across the field a safe distance from the tarmac. The center of the airfield between the two runways as well as the ends had been designated parking for the planes in the show. The next set of planes waited at the end of the runway for the clearance to take off. The sound of the planes roaring past overhead frequently made speech difficult. A man approached with a turkey leg, biting off chunks of the roasted meat as he passed surrounded by several kids of varying ages and their mother. His stomach growled in response to the savory aroma from the turkey, his gaze steady on the happy family until they disappeared into the shifting crowds. Soon, he'd take the necessary steps to make his own dream come true.

He'd hoped to spot the Learjet before too many people arrived but had failed. With the crowds milling and shifting he couldn't stand in one place and hope to find it. He tapped Beth's arm once lightly, drawing her attention. "Let's walk around a bit. See if we can find our target."

"Can we grab a bite? I'm starving." Beth fell into step beside him.

He took hold of her hand so they wouldn't be separated by the mass of people around them. And because he needed to touch her, connect with her. "My thinking exactly. The food's over that way."

He made a path for them until they reached the roped off food court with a dozen options for all kinds of food. Fried anything from cheese to fruit pies to Twinkies, Chinese, burgers and hot dogs, roasted turkey legs and corn on the cob, barbecue, and more. His stomach growled louder at the combined aromas assailing his nostrils.

Halting at the edge of the court, he motioned to the choices as he looked at Beth. "Barbecue?"

At her nod, he tugged her with him to stand in line. "My treat since we're officially on a date today."

Beth aimed a raised brow at him, a smile spreading onto her tempting lips. "I like the sound of that, Mitch Sawyer."

He squeezed her hand to pull her closer and planted a kiss on her upturned mouth. "We'll have more pleasure than work today, but we'll still need to reconnoiter the situation." He kissed her again and then winked. "After we eat."

"I wouldn't be any good to you without food first." Beth chuckled as she scanned the people around them. "All I can think about right now is a pulled pork sandwich with spicy barbecue sauce."

"With a sweet tea." Mitch gently pulled her along with him as the line shortened until he could step up and place their order.

Once they had their sandwiches and drinks in hand, he led the way to the immense tent shading rows of long tables and benches. He found open seats at a table near the edge. Biting into his sandwich, he relished the spicy and smoky flavor of the sauce. He washed it down with a swallow of tea and sighed with pleasure.

"That tastes really good." Beth dabbed at a drop of sauce on the corner of her mouth with a paper napkin.

"Yes... Don't look now, but we're about to have company." Mitch liked Keith but didn't need him horning in on his date with Beth. He'd hoped to have her all to himself for a while. Brushing his displeasure aside for the sake of his friendship, Mitch smiled a greeting. "The show seems a success."

Keith squeezed in beside Beth, placing a cold drink on the table, and grinned at him. "A few bumps and issues, but yes. Everyone seems to be having a good time."

"The food's great." Beth took a bite and laid her sandwich on the paper tray.

"I came to find you guys because I found out something you need to know." Keith peered at Mitch, his smile drooping. "It's about your job."

The look in Keith's eyes alarmed Mitch, a sliver of unease wedging into his gut. "The Learjet I told you about? What about it?"

"The owner...he's the man who helped me build this place." Keith shook his head as his smile disappeared. "He's known to be ruthless and has armed bodyguards. You'll need to be very careful."

The danger level jumped sky high with Keith's revelation. "How well do you know this Todd Walsh?"

"Walsh?" Beth shot him a look of surprise laced with horror.

"Yeah, Todd Walsh. Why?" Mitch laid a hand on her arm, trying to calm her down to no avail.

"I don't believe it. Why is he here?" Beth glanced between Mitch and Keith, her eyes wide and glittering.

"We invited him, remember?" Mitch frowned at Beth, puzzled. "What's the matter?"

Beth's entire body sat rigid and trembling as she continued to slowly shake her head. "He's the man my Jiu-Jitsu instructor is divorcing soon."

Keith sipped his drink, then replaced it on the watery ring on the bare wood table. "That's quite a coincidence."

"Jo said he had suggested she move to Roseville." Beth gripped the edge of the table, fingertips white against the dark surface. She stared at Keith for a long moment. "He suggested you build this airport here, too?"

A chill swept through Mitch at the implication of her words. "So he could keep an eye on her, you mean."

"Damn." Keith took a long drink of his beverage. "What do we do now? Tell the wife?"

"We have only suspicions at this point. We don't say anything to anyone, understood?" Mitch looked at Beth and then Keith. "We'll adjust our plans. Find a time when Walsh isn't around with his bodyguards to get hold of the plane."

"You're going through with it? Despite the risk?" Keith drummed his fingers on the table in a steady rhythm. "I'm not sure that's a good idea. I've heard rumors about this Walsh dude."

The way Keith said "rumors" sent tentacles of concern crawling down his back. Goosebumps rose on his forearms despite the afternoon heat. He'd agreed to do just one more repo before he quit. Before he moved on to the next phase of his life and his plans. More importantly, he'd promised Beth she could help and he'd keep her safe. That was a promise he'd keep or die trying.

"I don't have a choice. I've agreed to nab that plane." He pinned Beth with a stern look. "You will follow my orders, young lady. I'm not joking."

"But what if—"

He shook his finger at her as he stared at her. "Exactly what I say and nothing more. Got it?"

She glanced at Keith and then smiled at him. "Unless something—"

He huffed a sigh and quirked one brow. "Tell me you understand my conditions or you won't be going."

She nodded obediently, a light in her eyes that gave him qualms all over again.

"Now, let's go locate the plane and figure out exactly how we're going to do this." He rose to his feet and waited for Beth and Keith to follow suit. "We're not going to do this in a way that might get us caught." He swallowed the rising fear in his throat. Or killed.

Every cell in her body vibrated with nervous excitement. A simmering tension heightened her awareness of everything from the dwindling crowds flowing around the exhibits to the darkening sky. The second day of the immense air show wound down as Beth's anticipation of the fun and games to come skyrocketed.

They'd scoped the area until they'd found where the plane had been parked to allow for guided tours during very limited hours. No sign of Todd Walsh or his bodyguards, only the pilot parked in a chair under a small square tent between tours. They'd revised their plans accordingly and the time had arrived to execute them. Starting with acting like the lady of a biker.

She unzipped her leather jacket and slipped it off, permitting the cooling breeze to waft over her heated skin as she draped the jacket over one arm. Mitch finished parking the bike and securing their helmets while she scanned the airfield before turning to look at the sleek Learjet gleaming under the fading sunset.

"There you guys are." Keith sauntered toward her as Mitch straightened and stepped to her side. "I've been looking for you."

Mitch nonchalantly laid one arm around Beth's shoulders, a silent "she's mine" ghosting in the air. "Something up?"

Keith grinned and slowly shook his head. "The pilot who flew this baby in the other day asked me to keep an eye on it while he grabbed a bite to eat. Walsh is apparently due soon to take off for parts unknown. You don't have much time."

"Why the hurry?" Beth's stomach flipped at the unexpected news. She pressed the leather against her fluttering tummy. "I thought they were supposed to stay through the end of the show."

Keith jammed his hands into the front pockets of his jeans. "Some special last minute cargo that needs to get south quick."

Beth didn't like the sound of such a sudden change in plans. What did it mean? If Walsh arrived too soon, they wouldn't have enough time. She didn't want anyone hurt but she did want to see their mission accomplished. She was ready, willing, and able. She glanced up at Mitch, worry bright in his eyes.

Mitch frowned and his arm tightened around Beth's shoulders. "Guess we need to scrap our plan and make a new one."

Beth looked up at him, dismayed at not having the chance to nab the plane. Surely there was a way. "Why can't we do it now? Before he arrives?"

Mitch pressed his lips together as he glanced away and then gazed down at her upturned face. "It's too risky."

She stared at Keith, who shook his head slowly, and then flicked her gaze around the immediate vicinity. Nobody approached or even seemed to notice their little group. "Not if we act quickly. Keith, help me locate the logbook while Mitch checks the plane. We can be out of here in minutes."

"And the pilot could catch us in the act. Did you think about that?" Mitch dropped his one arm to cross both over his powerful chest. "No way."

Beth huffed in exasperation. Again with the risk, blah blah blah. She scowled at him before smiling at Keith. "So…"

Keith raised his hands to ward off her next words. "Don't look at me like that, Beth."

She couldn't give up so easily. Nobody would be hurt if they jumped at their one chance. Before anyone else arrived to spoil the fun for good. She batted her lashes several times with a sly grin. "Look at you like what?"

"You know very well." Keith mimicked Mitch's severe stance and attitude. "He's my friend and I do what is best for him. And you, of course."

"Great." She slipped the long purse strap over her head and moved to grasp his hand to tug him along with her, albeit reluctantly. "Then show me the plane. I'm playing tourist while my guy inspects the exterior."

"Mitch?" Keith dragged along behind her as his weighted question floated on the air.

"Damn it." Several seconds passed while Mitch spluttered and Beth coaxed Keith toward the jet. "Fine, but make it fast."

"You've got it." Joy tempered with caution surged inside her. Beth shot him a victorious look over her shoulder then fixed her happy gaze on Keith. "Open her up."

"I really don't think this is a good idea." Keith pulled free of her grasp. "You don't know these people."

"We don't have time to argue if we're going to make this happen." Beth regarded him, forcing herself to stay calm and focused. She wouldn't jeopardize the mission—she needed to do what they had intended. Sticking to the script as she agreed. "Please, Keith."

Keith slowly shook his head, eyes steady on her. "Are you sure? Really, really sure?"

The caution she'd sensed earlier flared in her mind. If they dawdled, things might go south very quickly. So they'd better hurry. She firmed her lips and nodded once. "I've got this."

"Fine." He heaved a sigh and shrugged. "Just be careful."

Once the steps had been lowered, Beth clambered inside the posh plane. She let out an appreciative sigh at the luxury aircraft's interior. Suitable for transporting if not royalty then millionaires and company executives. The open space she stood in featured a small table flanked by cushy chairs. A glance to the left revealed the cockpit, compact and convenient with what looked like easy to use controls and easy to read gauges. Even her little bit of knowledge about flying made her hands itch to take her for a spin. Chuckling at her flash of impatience, she perused the rest of the interior. At the back, beside the door to the bathroom was a set of double doors with a padlock linked through the handles. She pointed to the doors as Keith came to a stop at her side.

"Another exit?"

He shook his head. "Some kind of a storage closet, but I can't imagine why it would need to be locked up like that." Keith strode closer and tested the lock. "Strange."

"How so?" Beth stared at the doors, wondering what secrets hid behind them.

"It's unusual to have that kind of storage inside the plane." Keith slowly shook his head, a bark of laughter shattering the silence. "Maybe Walsh's wife needed space for her jewelry."

"No way would Jo be on a plane with him, so that's not it." She moved closer, curious about the good-looking man. "Hey, what about you? Any wedding plans?"

"Why are you asking?" Keith winked at her as she sidled closer.

Beth tapped him on the shoulder with her fingers. A vision flashed past her inner eye. Keith fishing, a couple of kids playing on the river bank nearby. An open picnic basket on a checkered cloth under a shade tree, where a brunette woman relaxed with a book. Beth smiled to herself at the pastoral scene. He had a pleasant future waiting for him.

"Curious. I'd still like to know what's so important it has to be locked up."

"Maybe he's got Cuban cigars in there."

She gripped the long strap to still the swinging purse. "Don't be silly. It's probably his clandestine collection of smut magazines he doesn't want anyone to know he has."

"If so, then he needs a beautiful wife instead." Keith winked at her. "A woman like you who has it all pulled together. Smart and beautiful. A man could do far worse."

Beth blew out a breath and rolled her eyes. "Pathetic. Does that line work on your other would-be dates?"

He inclined his head, laughter twinkling in his eyes. "So you want to go on a date? Is that your way of asking me out?"

She punched Keith lightly with her closed fist. "Hardly. You'd have to fight off your best friend if I were to be so foolish as that."

Keith rubbed his chin, the sparkle in his eyes increasing the longer he contemplated her. "You have a point. I suppose we should deny our true feelings for each other when he's around."

"You're incorrigible. We only have a couple minutes. Is the logbook in that closet?" She looked around the rest of

161

the interior but didn't see a place to store the book. "Or is it up front?"

"It has to be accessible." Keith stood in front of her, poised to move at a moment's notice. "Should be in the cockpit. Somewhere close at hand but the exact spot depends on the aircraft. Come on."

They hurried to the nose of the plane and he slid into the pilot's seat. While Keith adjusted his position in the seat, Beth rapidly scoured the small yet surprisingly roomy space, finally spotting what they searched for. She nudged Keith's shoulder just as he looked up at her.

"Is that it?" She pointed to the pouch mounted on the wall above and beside the pilot's seat.

He swiveled to look to his left and nodded. "Right where it ought to be. Good job."

"Leave it there then so we know where it is." Beth rested her fists on her hips and nodded. "See, this will be easy."

"I hope so, for both of your sakes." He motioned for her to step back and then joined her behind the cockpit. "Mitch should be here any minute."

"I hope so. Time is wasting." She pursed her lips, her nerves ratcheting into a firestorm inside. Too many minutes had passed while under such an uncertain deadline. "What's taking him so long?"

"I'll go find out." Keith waved a hand in the direction of the plush seats. "Make yourself comfortable."

"Will do." She scanned the compact yet elegant interior, her gaze zeroing in on the leather chairs. Supple and inviting. "May as well make myself at home."

No way. Mitch had nearly finished the preflight inspection, bent over to check the undercarriage, when boots appeared in his line of vision. Three sets of shined black leather beneath black slacks with traces of dust at the cuffs.

"Hey you! What the hell do you think you're doing with that private plane?"

Mitch straightened to assess the gruff man's demeanor and intentions. Hoping to avoid a confrontation if at all possible. About the same height as Mitch, but definitely more of a bodybuilder. Not good. Mitch didn't want to find out who would win in a contest. Didn't want to jeopardize his team or the mission.

He needed to buy some time. Figure a strategy. The threesome dressed in matching uniforms of black trousers and crisp white shirts. They stared at him with nothing but malice in their eyes. Still, he could playact the reverent pilot until Keith returned any time now to diffuse the tense situation. Sooner being Mitch's preference. One thing the man excelled at was gabbing and talking his way out of a tight spot. He'd done so on more than a handful of occasions Mitch could recall.

"This your plane?" He forced an appreciative grin to his lips, bobbing his head quickly. "It's quite a beauty. I'm jealous."

The hulk lifted a bushy brow as he took a step closer, threatening by his sheer size. "Answer my question."

Not taking the bait apparently. Mitch eased away from the aircraft, careful to stay facing the men to avoid being jumped. "Just looking. No harm in that, is there?"

The big man crossed his arms over his massive chest and then snorted once through his wide nose. "It's not open for tours, so yeah. There's a problem. Move on."

Not yet. Mitch stared at the three men, racking his brain for an excuse to hang around. Until he could get his friend and woman safely off that damn plane. He should never have agreed to this harebrained scheme. His gut had been right all along. He shouldn't have agreed to follow through with their initial plan when too many aspects had changed.

"Hey, no worries. I was just admiring her." Keep them talking. Maybe he'd get more info as to where they intended to fly next. He'd have to try again since the present plan was a definite bust. He had signed the contract to repo the plane no matter what it took to lay his hands on it. A decision he hoped he wouldn't regret. Though the whole thing was looking dicey already. Still, worth a try.

He frowned and angled his head slightly to one side. "Why isn't it open for tours? It was earlier. You guys on your way somewhere?"

"Now, see, that's none of your business." The wheat-haired man who'd been scowling at him the entire time took two steps toward Mitch. Pushing the intimidation bubble closer. "Do what Zeke says and get on with ya."

Mitch raised both hands to shoulder height, palms facing the trio, and backed off two steps, striving to put the goons at ease. Maybe give Keith and Beth time to realize what was happening and stay on the plane until things cooled down. *If* they cooled down.

His stomach knotted at the thought. How could he provide an opportunity for them to slip off the plane undetected? Draw the men away from the steps. "No skin off my nose if you want to keep your secrets. I'm just a curious guy by nature."

The third man, a touch less intimidating but by no means a pussycat, shooed him with one large paw. "Then go poke your nose into somebody else's business."

"Fine, fine." Mitch lowered his hands to slide them into the front pockets of his jeans. "Don't get—"

The sound of shoes thumping down the metal steps from the jet drew everyone's attention to Keith's sudden appearance. Halting on the last step, his mouth dropped open and then snapped shut.

The lead thug, Zeke, growled, an angry guttural noise. "What the hell are you doing on that plane?"

Keith reached the ground as a smirk found its way into place. He slowly shook his head and strolled nonchalantly toward Mitch. He tilted his head briefly, a flash of an exchange between the two friends. "Taking a look. No harm, no foul."

Zeke moved like a cobra striking its prey, grabbing hold of Keith and shoving him into Mitch, who scrabbled to catch his balance and steady his friend. Suddenly the two faced three muzzles.

"Hey! We're just tourists." Mitch tried again to persuade the men to trust him. He must defuse the situation so everyone could walk away safely. At least Keith was safe, for the moment. But what about Beth?

"Something stinks. Cam, check the plane. Make sure it's secure." Zeke motioned with his free hand for Mitch and Keith to move away from the plane. His piercing blue eyes aimed at the captives. "You two stay put or you'll regret ever sniffing around my boss' plane."

Without a doubt Mitch already wished he'd been doing anything else. He briefly considered pulling his gun but squashed the idea as impractical and likely to escalate rather than defuse the confrontation. His heart fluttered somewhere up around his throat as Cam clambered up the steps and disappeared into the target plane. Beth would be surprised and cornered while he and Keith were trapped outside, unable to assist. He cut a glance at his friend. No help there either. The situation couldn't be any worse.

"Mr. Walsh is coming." The third man indicated with a toss of his auburn head the approach of a sleek, dark gray limousine, a cloud of dust churning up behind as it hurried toward the tense group.

Mitch shifted his weight to rest evenly on the balls of his feet. He needed to be ready to move, to board that plane and rescue Beth. He had some hope Cam wouldn't harm a girl.

Slim hope, it was true... But with the boss man arriving, all bets were off.

He caught Keith's attention and mouthed, "Be ready." Then he trained his gaze on the car and whatever threat it contained.

Chapter Fifteen

$\mathscr{A}$s Keith had ducked to scramble down the steps, Beth spun away to take another look around the cabin. She'd love to take a vacation on such a plane. Elegant and sleek as well as comfortable. Not having to deal with the crowds and lines at the airport. Yet still having the thrill of going to other countries, visiting different cultures. She tossed her jacket on the seat of one chair and then settled into one of the closest chairs, running her hands over the buttery leather armrests. The seat welcomed her, gently embracing her body.

Her imagination took flight, images of daring snatches of other expensive planes before the owner had time to react let alone offer any objection or obstacle. Just her and Mitch, jetting from airport to airport, together. Her training gave her the self-confidence and strength to make her fantasies become realities. She flexed her hands, pleased by the increased strength in her grasp and her overall flexibility and resiliency. Between that and her newfound knowledge of planes and her sharpshooter skills, she could handle anything.

She peered out the window at the fading sunlight, the first few stars braving the night sky. Leaning her head back, she closed her eyes. Imagined all the faraway places they could go. As successful repo agents, they'd have plenty of money to afford the best of everything. They could hire a pilot and crew and really enjoy the lap of luxury in style. She let the daydream play out for several minutes then frowned. She opened her eyes to stare about the quiet cabin. Too much time had elapsed without any sign of departure happening. Where was Mitch?

She tensed and jumped to her feet. She tilted her head, straining to hear what might be happening outside but no sounds filtered through the open door. Maybe she should go check to make sure he was all right. But Keith had told her to stay put. Still, if something had gone wrong... She started toward the door.

A large swarthy-skinned man burst into the cabin, his gaze searching and then landing on her with an angry frown. "Who are you?"

How to respond? Beth forced herself into character, made her tense frame relax as she smiled coyly at him. She'd dressed to be sexy, so she would act the part. If he thought she wasn't a threat, then she'd have a better chance of mitigating his accusatory glare. "My name's Beth. What's yours?"

The only exit stood behind her adversary. She darted a glance around her, not finding anything suitable to use as a weapon. Nothing presented itself as even remotely acting like a weapon. She had her gun, of course, but Mitch had warned her about using it within the airplane. Something vital could be damaged, if not some part of the plane then some part of a person. If he came close enough, she could use her martial arts. She inhaled, preparing to do whatever necessary to protect herself.

"Never you mind." He took two steps toward her, the muzzle of a silver gun glinting in the small space between them. "Put your hands where I can see them."

The presence of his gun changed her options. Made her glad she hadn't pulled her own, alerting him to the fact she had one. If she could grab his gun away, she might have a chance hand to hand. She assessed his wide shoulders, the firm grip he had on the gun, and swallowed hard. Maybe not. Staring down the barrel of the weapon unnerved her. One slip of his finger and she could be injured. Or dead.

Waves of fear and uncertainty crashed through her, rattling her confidence into doubt. She'd been training for action but when confronted, her self-preservation instincts kicked in. Mitch had been right to warn her away from trying to live the life of a heroine from a novel. *Be careful what you wish for...you just might get it.*

She slowly raised her hands to ear height. "What do you want?"

"For you to go back there and sit down." He pointed with his free hand, the gun aimed steadily at her heart. "The boss will be here in a minute and he can decide what to do with you."

Todd Walsh, the abuser? More thugs like the one in front of her would also likely accompany the man. She needed to escape, to get off the plane before someone—like her—got hurt. Maybe she could talk her way out of the situation. Her fighting skills might suffice but her courage didn't measure up to the threat she faced. Tears pressed for release. All her efforts to be better, stronger, had worked to make her fully capable of protecting herself. Only to lack the bravery to meet the deadly challenge.

"Let me get out of your way then." She tried to smile but feared she'd failed at that as well. "I'll mosey on out of here..."

"Nice try. Get to that back seat and buckle up. We'll be taking off in a few minutes. The boss is in a hurry." The big guy indicated with his head for her to move as he'd said.

"But really, I don't—" What had happened to Mitch and Keith? Her heart fell with the sudden realization they must be hurt and unable to reach her as a result. "My friends?"

"They're a bit tied up at the moment."

The deep rumble of ironic laughter unsettled her even more. "You better not have hurt them, or I'll—"

"You'll what?" He sneered and spun her around with a hard push toward the back seat. "Sit down and shut up."

She caught her balance on the back of the chair, her fingers clawing at the leather to steady herself. The threat to her life was real. Beyond the chair only a few feet of open space stretched before running into the padlocked storage cabinet. No chance of escape or even to fight back. She'd asked for the excitement and daring of the job but never thought she'd end up a prisoner. She glanced at the man, who glared at her and motioned to the seat again. Sinking onto the soft seat, she clicked the seatbelt home. He tossed her jacket at her which she caught and laid across her lap. Then could only stare at the man with the gun, and forlornly hope for someone, anyone, to save her.

The limo halted and the driver hopped out to open the rear door. Mitch tried to see into the car's dark interior before Zeke stepped in front of him. He wanted to see who he was up against, size up the Todd Walsh character for himself. With Zeke blocking his view, Mitch focused on the bodyguard who smirked at him and then Keith.

"Okay, you two. On your stomach, hands behind your head. Now." He took one threatening stride closer as the other man, a serious weightlifter by his physique, forced them to the ground with a sharp shove in the middle of their backs.

Possible scenarios raced through Mitch's mind as he reluctantly did as directed. With only the two men, perhaps he and Keith could overcome them. He judged the driver, another exceptionally powerful man, and figured their odds weren't good of winning against the men. The driver nodded to a tall, wiry man who emerged from the car and waited while the driver reached inside and dragged a young boy out of the back seat. Artie. Had to be. Where was the mother then? The situation worsened with each passing second.

The trio hurried to the plane, the boy dragging his shoes in the dust as he was marched over to and inside the aircraft. The driver suddenly appeared at the doorway and then descended to the ground. Beth nowhere in sight.

"I'll take care of these two until you takeoff. The boss wants you guys on board. Takeoff in two minutes." The driver pulled a gun from a holster at his waist and leveled it on Mitch and Keith.

"Right. Come on, Zeke." The two thugs trotted to the plane and disappeared up the steps.

Mitch glanced at his buddy, trying to sort out a plan whereby they could take out the driver. But lying on the ground on his stomach was not a defensible position. They'd have to gain their feet before they could be effective. Keith aimed worried eyes at him, a slight shrug indicating a lack of a plan from his view.

He had to do something. Mitch pivoted to look up at the man holding them in place with his pistol. "What's with the boy?"

"Don't worry about it." The driver kept the gun steady on him, and shifted his weight to balance between his feet. "It's none of your business anyway."

The roar of the plane engine stopped any further conversation. Slowly the plane taxied away, turning onto a runway and then gaining speed.

"Okay, let us up. They're gone." Mitch started to lower his hands, desperate to restore circulation in his tingling arms and take down the SOB with the gun.

"Hold still. They haven't taken off yet."

"I can't feel my arms." Keith caught on to the idea of distracting the driver. "Come on, man. Let us up you piece of dog—."

The driver took two long strides closer to take a swipe at Keith before he could finish his sentence.

Fear and anger merged to propel Mitch to his feet and lunge at the man. He yelled as his shoulder hit him in the chest, the gun clattering to the ground. Mitch wrestled with him, his equal to say the least. He lost count of the punches and knee jabs, only conscious of the need to disable the man so he could go after Beth. If Mitch could only grab his Glock, he'd gain the advantage. But it took both hands to defend himself between his own offensive strikes.

The sharp report of a pistol made him look over his shoulder, his right fist cocked to punch the driver in the face.

"That's enough." Keith aimed the gun at the other man. "Get up."

Mitch grabbed the collar of the man's shirt and hauled him up with him, panting and aching head to toe. Mitch glanced at the man, whose right eye was beginning to turn interesting shades of purple and yellow.

"What do we do about him?" Mitch slipped his gun from its holster, ensured the magazine was seated properly, and then leveled it at his captive.

"I've got it." Keith pulled out his cell phone. "The police can sort out what to do with him." He spoke into the phone and then ended the call. "On their way."

"In the meantime, find something to tie this dude up." Mitch glanced after the departing plane, worried about what his girl might be facing. Where were they going? His biggest fears played out before him and there was nothing he could do.

After they'd secured the cussing man with zip ties, Mitch let out an angry breath.

In the distance, the plane sped down the runway and gracefully lifted off the ground. Mitch kept his eyes on the trajectory, trying to decipher the destination from which direction it turned after takeoff. Unfortunately, the plane disappeared into the night sky before he could ascertain where the aircraft might be headed.

"Damn it all. What now?"

Keith started to reply and then paused to stare over Mitch's shoulder. "We see who is in such a hurry."

Mitch spun around, a crossover SUV speeding toward them. The vehicle squealed to a stop mere feet away. A petite woman popped out of the driver's seat and ran to them, overdressed for the occasion in a long, sparkly gown and upswept hairdo.

"Where's my son? Where's Artie?" She bristled with anger and fear as she confronted the friends.

"Who are you?" Mitch made himself stand still in the face of the woman's assault.

"Jo Walsh. My husband, Todd, kidnapped my son from his babysitter's house while I was at a Chamber fundraiser. Where is my son?"

Keith frowned at the frantic woman. "Since he's the father, it's not kidnapping."

She huffed out a breath. "It is when he's about to be my ex-husband and I'm to have full custody."

Mitch's heart stopped for a moment and then resumed at breakneck speed. "I'm sorry, but they took off a few minutes ago."

"Oh no!" Jo looked up into the night sky, tears shimmering in her eyes. "I'm too late."

"He's also taken my girlfriend, Beth Golden, with him."

"Oh my god. Beth is on the plane, too?" Jo turned horrified eyes to stare at Mitch. "He's gone too far."

"Beth told me about you and something about your situation." Mitch peered closer at the distraught woman. "I'm Mitch Sawyer."

"Nice to finally meet you. She's told me about you, too. She's been taking Jiu-Jitsu with me for the last few weeks."

Mitch nodded once and crossed his arms. "At least she's not defenseless. She'll look out for your son."

"Where do you think they're going?" Keith glanced between Mitch and Jo as they stood surrounded by indecision.

"Mexico. So he can get Artie away from me where I can't reach him." She rubbed a trembling hand over her brow before taking a deep breath and squaring her shoulders. "It's my worst nightmare come to pass. Now what do we do?"

"Only one thing to do." Beth and the boy were both in grave danger. He glanced at Keith, who hitched a shoulder and smirked at him. Mitch nodded once, recognizing the "let's go" gesture, and then addressed Jo with his determined gaze. "We're going after them."

Chapter Sixteen

The elegant jet had become a crowded bus with all the large men crammed onboard. Beth sat with Artie on her lap since the others had been claimed by the men. He'd boarded with an uncaring man who practically dragged him into the cabin and pushed him toward her. Luckily, Artie recognized her and came to her outstretched arms.

She was glad for his company. She didn't know what to expect but would protect him as best she could. The poor kid tried to put on a brave face but his lower lip quivered each time his father looked at him. She snugged her arms a smidge closer around his soft toddler body, silently reassuring him. Somehow she'd keep him safe.

"Are you okay, Artie?" She whispered in his ear, a slight squeeze accompanying her question.

He bobbed his head and stuck his thumb in his mouth. So much for conversation. Then again, there wasn't much to say.

When the men had first boarded, her fears and doubts had ratcheted to the point she thought she might faint. Their head-to-toe scans of her biker chick outfit left her feeling exposed and vulnerable. She'd fought the urge to cover herself and zip her leather jacket to the chin. But they'd tossed her jacket on the floor under the table, out of her reach. When she'd first spotted Artie climbing on his little chubby legs into the cabin, she finally understood with a sharp blast of clarity that left her gasping.

The pieces of the puzzle slipped neatly into place. Jo's soon-to-be ex-husband intended to abscond with the boy to prevent the U.S. courts from taking away his son. Which meant he intended to leave the country. The previous doubt vanished with the blink of her eyes at the tall man who held the boy's hand with a firm grip. Her visions began to make sense. The image of Jo consoling Artie gave her hope everything would work out for the best. She vowed to do everything in her power to reunite the boy and his mother. She resisted the urge to hold onto her purse, not wanting to draw attention to her ace in the hole. Hoping she'd have the courage to draw her gun if things went badly.

Todd Walsh glanced up at her, holding her gaze for several nerve-wracking moments. He looked down to her lacy halter top, blinked at the deep cleavage. She forced herself to not instinctively cover her breasts with her arms. Lifted her chin to keep her gaze firmly on the man undressing her with his eyes. A shiver wiggled down her back but other than that she held still. Daring him to make a wrong move.

A slow smile washed onto his face as he dropped his regard to rest on Artie. "Be strong, son. You're with me now."

Artie held onto Beth's wrist with his wet hand, the small fingers leaving white halos where he pressed his fingertips into her skin.

Glad the inspection had ended, Beth squeezed lightly with her arms around the boy, her eyes steady on his dad.

"Mr. Walsh, Artie is already strong after being with his mother." She watched the realization dawn that she knew his family. The slight widening of his eyes and the brief inclination of his head revealing his surprise.

"You know my wife." He shook his head slowly, calculatingly, his gaze taking in her leather and laced-up attire. "I suppose I shouldn't be surprised she'd take up with someone like you. She's probably told you how evil I am and a bunch of other lies."

"Something like that." What did he mean someone like her? *Jerk.* Judging her based on clothing alone. He had no idea who she was or what she was capable of. His bad. She suppressed a smile. She would use his error in under-estimating her capabilities against him. Artie squirmed in her arms and she relaxed her grip. "What are you doing? Why is Artie here?"

Todd closed the file of what looked like sales records and lists of some kind, and regarded her with twinkling eyes. "I'm taking him on a little trip with me. That's really all you need to know."

Practicalities pushed to the forefront of her concerns. The plan had been a quick hop to Colorado and then home again. "I was just exploring your nice little plane when these guys made me a prisoner. How long is this trip going to be?"

"I apologize for the inconvenience, sweetheart." He chuckled and shook a finger at her. "If you need anything, we'll see about providing it. But I wouldn't worry about it if I were you."

"Why not?" Beth blinked at him, trying to see his future but finding only a murky haze. Like turning a corner into a fog bank. Had he no real future ahead? A chill crept down her back. "What are you planning to do?"

The uncertainty lying in wait made her pulse beat a heavy tattoo. She'd wanted the excitement and surprise but not like this. Not without Mitch. Not when it endangered a small boy. What had she gotten them mixed up in?

Jo had taught her about situation awareness and mapping out exit strategies, or defense strategies if it came to that. Which it looked like it very well might. She didn't want to have to use her gun but she would. She'd gather her courage along with every protective instinct she possessed to do what must be done.

Two of the men had taken command of the cockpit, leaving the third to guard her and the boy. His huge frame squeezed into the seat on her left, his gun close at hand. Todd sat across the table from her and his son, reading through a thick file of papers and sipping scotch. Acting as though his actions were normal for any father and son.

"Miss…I'm sorry. What's your name?"

"My name is Beth Golden." She stared at him, searching his expression for hints of what might be in store for them.

"You're looking at me as if I were the devil himself." Todd sipped from his glass with his eyes focused on her. "Miss Golden, I won't do anything to harm my son. We're simply flying south to connect with another longer flight. At that point, I'll decide what to do with you."

"Assuming that's true, what purpose do I serve? You could have let me get off before you abducted me." The chill settled on her shoulders. A longer flight to where?

"I didn't abduct you, Miss Golden. You invited yourself aboard my plane." He sat back and shrugged. "A happy coincidence. You can look after him until you're no longer needed."

"Which would be when?" Did she want to know? Her fingers tightened on Artie's arm of their own volition. When he squirmed, she forced them to relax although every fiber of her being tensed.

"When we land, of course." He sipped his amber liquor and then set the glass on the small table between them. "You don't have the proper…credentials for the remainder of our trip."

"Then you'll let me go?" She'd be alone in an unknown location.

Dread crept through her. She'd wanted to travel but again not in this manner. Forced to fly somewhere not of her choosing, at night, with only herself to rely on. As long as she kept her purse, she had resources. Her muscles relaxed a tiny fraction at the thought.

"In a manner of speaking." The light in his eyes died as he studied her. "No more questions. Zeke here will keep an eye on you while I close my eyes. I need my rest before we land."

Zeke laid his pistol across his lap as he pivoted the leather chair to face her more directly. Obviously, he wasn't concerned about a stray shot. She blinked and glanced away from the severe expression. Todd smirked at her and then leaned his head back.

She rested a hand on the boy's shoulder, which prompted him to look up at her with trust shining in his eyes. How had he come to associate her with safety? Thinking back over the last weeks she pictured the many times he'd sat with his babysitter watching from the sidelines as she and Jo grappled. As she learned the ins and outs of sweeps and escapes, learned to shrimp and to block holds. Worked harder than ever before to become more flexible, better, stronger. Ready for anything.

After all the training she'd done, surely she could manage to keep the boy in her embrace safe until her visions became reality. If only she could see her own future, then she could choose a workable path forward. Without any foresight, she was left to figure it out on her own.

"I don't care about the damn money." Mitch growled at the bank rep on the other end of the phone line. "I need to find that plane and fast. Can you help from your end?"

He studied the anxious expression on Jo's face as he listened to the yammering of the man going on about finances and investments. Blah, blah, blah. Keith trotted across the expanse from the hangar office, his face grim.

Mitch harrumphed into the phone. "Look, man, I'll get your plane but it's going to take longer than I thought. They took off a little while ago, with my woman and a boy as hostages, and…"

Muttering and cursing blasted his ear and he held the phone away from his head. Punching the speaker button, he held the phone so all could hear as Keith halted beside him.

"You guaranteed you'd have that plane in Denver in two days and now you've lost it?" The nasal voice rang through the night air. "Get it back at whatever cost or you won't see a dime. Got it?"

"You're paying that cost, right?"

"Naturally." The tone indicated the man rolled his eyes. "Just get it back or it's my job."

"You'll get your plane right after I get those two hostages safely home." Mitch ended the call and shook his head, staring at the device in his hand. "If only there was some way to find her quickly, to know for certain which direction to start."

"I asked air traffic control and they confirmed it." Keith shook his head and then ran a hand through his short hair. "The flight plan they filed is for Brownsville, Texas."

Jo gasped. "He's really heading for Matamoros."

"A dangerous entry point into Mexico." Keith crossed his arms, glancing between Jo and Mitch. "Why there?"

"It's not the place to take a child." Horror filled Mitch at the thought of the toddler, let alone Beth, being subjected to the criminal elements both lurking in the shadows and boldly walking the streets of the border city.

News stories about the kidnappings and smuggling in the city echoed in Mitch's head. Crime proved so rampant the U.S. Embassy in Mexico City issued travel warnings.

Private citizens and organizations also issued tips on how to safely cross into and out of Matamoros to shop the local markets, visit the doctor, or to experience the amazing culture and foods of the country. The threat to Americans seemed highest in non-touristy areas so additional precautions were deemed necessary. If Walsh thought he'd be able to protect his young son in such an environment he was sadly mistaken. What proved even sadder was recalling how much Mitch had once enjoyed visiting Mexico and its wonderful people, food, art, and music.

"It's the perfect place when you don't want him to be found." Jo clutched her waist, staring at Mitch with terror in her eyes. "He hinted he'd take Artie and leave the country if I persisted with the divorce and sole custody. I never thought he'd actually endanger our boy."

"Even if they aren't simply mugged, they're likely to be subjected to car-jacking, extortion, abduction, and even homicide." Keith frowned and inclined his head at Mitch. "Remember that poor woman they found in the Rio Grande?"

Fear clawed into Mitch's chest at the reminder of the horrific incident. An elderly woman had been held up in a parking lot, choked to death with a belt by a gang of violent teens, and then discarded like a bag of trash in the river. He shook his head once at Keith. No need to share such a terrible death with Jo. The woman was scared enough already.

Mitch caught Keith's attention with a tilt of his head. "We need to go after them. Try and stop him from crossing that border."

"What do you need?"

"We need a plane that can catch that Lear. What's available?"

Keith pivoted to scan the hangars and planes parked along the taxiway, illuminated by a few tall lights scattered around. "With the show in town, there are quite a few possibilities. But only a few are going to be fast enough to catch that jet."

Mitch gazed out over the darkened airfield, searching for something suitable. He blinked at the row of fighter jets parked at one end of the runway. An idea formed. It just might work. He had to try and suffer the consequences. "Is one of the trainer jets here with the Blue Angels?"

Keith turned back to raise a brow at him. "They brought one FA-18 but it's not for rent, you know."

"Well, I was thinking…Say I reactivated my service…" Mitch's mind spun with possibilities, finally settling on the one that just might work. "I'm a bit rusty on my night flying. I need to put in some hours so…want to go?"

"You're a piece of work." Keith chortled and shook his head. He tapped Mitch on the shoulder with a fist. "We'll need orders to take it up."

"Let me work on that while you roust the flight mechanic to get it prepped. We'll aim to have wheels up in twenty."

"I'll be ready." Keith started to walk away, but Jo stopped him with one hand.

"I'm going." Jo kept her attention on Mitch as Keith turned back to address the newest wrinkle in their plans.

"No way. Keith will go. He's a trained pilot."

"No. It has to be me." Jo pleaded, her eyes bright and fierce.

"You can't fly in a fighter jet. You're not authorized." Mitch placed his fists on his hips, shaking his head at her steady regard. "I'm serious."

"So am I." She inched closer to poke him lightly in the chest to emphasize her words. "Artie's my son and I'm going after him."

"Not in that jet, you're not." Mitch looked at Keith, seeking his support.

"It's against regs for a civilian to be in that aircraft." Keith splayed his hands and shrugged. "Not our rules."

Jo lifted her chin and stared at Mitch. "You're bending the rules for your woman. Bend them for my son."

Mitch's jaw dropped open at the woman's sheer audacity. But she had a point. While he would much prefer to have his wingman with him, the boy was far more important to her. Perhaps she had a right to see his safe return. They both needed to rescue their people. He'd flown reporters for a demo ride in years past. With the right introduction, like he could provide, Jo would be alright. He'd see to it.

He snapped his mouth closed and nodded once. "Let's go."

Chapter Seventeen

$\mathcal{N}$ow Beth understood how the poor frog in her high school science class must have felt pinned down for dissection. At least the creature didn't live through the operation. Watched every second by Zeke the goon to her left, she felt like sticking her tongue out at him. Right before she knocked his legs out from under him and pinned *him* to the floor. She huffed at her own childish reaction, drawing a sharpened glance and quirked eyebrow. Artie squirmed in her arms.

"Down." He pushed on her forearms with his little hands, his legs inching sideways on her lap.

"Is it okay? He can't go anywhere." She directed her question to Zeke and he slowly nodded. She eased Artie off her lap and he toddled away to explore the cramped quarters.

She readjusted her position, sliding the bulk of the purse farther around her right side. If she'd been captured alone, her options would have been different. She wouldn't have worried as much about next steps with only herself to save. With the defenseless boy to consider she needed a much better idea than fighting her way to safety. An idea which chilled her to the core. She hadn't contemplated actually having to use her skills to save her own life let alone anyone else. More of a backup plan, one to keep on the back burner.

"Don't pull that." Zeke's gruff voice alerted her to trouble and stopped Artie's exploration cold.

The child's deep blue eyes glittered as he looked over his shoulder at the burly man. Without a word, he moved away from the red lever in question and headed toward the back of the cabin. Nothing back there for him to get into. Beth turned her attention to trying to figure a way out of the mess she'd found herself in.

How might she effect their escape? She looked slowly around the cabin, taking inventory and assessing her options. One door to the outside. A tiny bathroom at the back of the space with no possible escape hatch. Windows large enough to crawl through if they opened. Which they didn't. Four big men with guns between her and the lone door. Of course, her musings were moot. Escape wasn't possible as long as they remained in the air. Even if she managed to somehow take out the men holding her, where would she and Artie go? She'd have to fly the plane and then land it when she'd never done so before. Not a good option.

Artie babbled to himself as he peeked into the corners and crevices of the cabin. At least the tense situation didn't affect his good-natured roaming. Beth returned his happy grin as he toddled about, free to move around. All she could think about as she pivoted her chair to keep a watchful eye on the boy was searching for a solution to their predicament.

On the ground, her grappling skills would help her defend herself. At least from one of the brawny thugs at a time. But not all four. She sighed in frustration. Fighting her way out wouldn't work with the boy to consider. While she confronted one assailant another would grab the boy—or her—and it would all be for nothing.

If she pulled out her gun, she might—just maybe—be able to hold them at bay until she could whisk Artie to safety. How could she make such an escape possible let alone happen? She could aim and shoot, even hit the bull's eye most of the time. But shoot moving, living and breathing targets? All threatening herself and the child? Her breath hitched at the thought. Would she be able to pull the trigger on another human being? She couldn't even slap a person in the face. Hurt them intentionally? Take their life? Doubt seared her confidence. She'd have to wait for the right moment to attempt any form of escape. And pray for the will to follow through.

It proved very sobering to realize she might not be as badass as fictional heroines. She'd imagined so clearly being ready and capable of defending herself. She'd trained with that vision of herself in mind. Yet now that she faced the very threat she'd prepared for, she faltered. She hesitated to take the steps necessary out of a sense of inadequacy. But she would do whatever she could to protect Artie. Even from his own father.

She needed to be ready to run with Artie after they landed. Find a place to hide until she could devise another plan. A better way of keeping the boy safe until help arrived. Surely Mitch would come after them. Depending on where they found themselves. A frown settled on her brows, weighting her thoughts. Where were they heading? How on earth would anyone find her and the boy without any clue as to their destination?

Peering at the big man, she realized she had to use her brains instead of her strength or her weapon. "So, we might as well get to know each other since we're stuck on this plane for a while. Zeke, is it?"

"Yeah."

"Do you like your job?"

He blinked and shifted in the chair, the gun—a Ruger?—pointed at her where it lay beneath his hand on the table. "It has some great benefits, so yeah."

"Really? Like what?" Keep him talking and maybe she could find out where they were going and why. Then what? How would she use the intel once she had it? One step at a time…

"Travel to foreign countries, for one." His fingers caressed the metal barrel as he continued to study her. "Meeting beautiful women like you, for another."

Was he hitting on her? May as well play on that angle then. She smiled at him, batted her lashes a few times to gauge his reaction. He smiled back, his hand stilling on the gun.

"I bet you say that to all the girls, big guy." She mentally rolled her eyes at her own lame dialogue but it seemed to be working. Drawing the guard into conversation had his interest on her instead of the boy. "What countries have you been to for your job?"

"France, Canada, England, and now…" The man glanced sharply at the boy where he had flopped onto the carpeted floor in front of the storage cabinet, playing with something he'd found. Suddenly Zeke shot to his feet and strode to the boy. "Hey, kid, give me that."

Artie clutched the small gold object in both hands. "Mine."

"I don't think so." Zeke leaned down to snatch the thing but the boy pulled it aside, out of his reach.

"No!" Artie scooted backward, away from the increasingly irritated man toward the cabinet doors.

"Give it to me." The man scooped up the boy under one arm and pried the cylinder-shaped item from his grasping hands. "That's not yours."

Artie wailed when Zeke plunked him back on the floor, mouth wide open and tears streaming down his cheeks at the loss of his toy.

"What the hell is going on?" Todd bolted upright, a flush of angry surprise on his cheeks. "What did you do to my son?"

"N-nothing. He was playing with this." Zeke held up the bullet-shaped object between thumb and forefinger.

Todd shot a glance at Beth and then shook his head at Zeke. "Damn it. Put that away."

Zeke slipped the item into his pocket but not before Beth recognized it. When Mitch first started teaching her how to aim, he'd used one to help her sight properly. A chamber pistol boresighter. While the device was normally used to ensure the accuracy of a pistol, it also let her have a visual for aiming. What was it doing laying around on the plane? A chilling thought settled in her mind. What if the locked cabinet held a load of guns? Ones to be shipped south...to Mexico? All speculation, but it fit the bits and pieces of information she'd heard so far.

"How much longer?" Todd shifted in his seat to lift his glass and sip the watered down scotch. "We should be there soon, right?"

"Yes, sir. Another ten minutes and we'll land in Brownsville." Zeke resumed his seat and motioned at Artie. "I think it might be wise to secure the boy, sir."

Todd nodded and pointed at Beth. "Make yourself useful. Put him back on your lap and keep him quiet. I've got a headache."

"I don't work for you." Beth tensed but stood her ground. She might be his captive but she wasn't his slave. "I'll hold the boy because I like him and will protect him from brutes like you and your men. But you won't order me around."

"You think you're something, don't you? What, did Jocasta teach you how to wrestle and now you're our equal? Is that what she taught you? Well, you're not." He thumped the empty glass back on the table and glared at her. "You're nothing to me but a tool for my use as needed. Now, if you don't want to be useful, then I'll have to get another tool, won't I? I'll have to discard you. Is that what you want?"

She inhaled and held her breath before slowly releasing it. She had to keep calm or someone really would be injured. She glanced to the boy and smiled at him. "Artie, come here, sweetie." She held out her arms and the toddler walked to her. Lifting him onto her lap, she swiveled the chair to face the table and his father.

She regarded him in silence and then shook her head slowly. "I will do what I can for your son's benefit. If you'll leave him alone. The boy's scared enough without you threatening everyone around you."

"You're making deals with me?" He laughed out loud and leaned back in his chair. "That's rich. Just shut the hell up and stop asking questions. Got it?"

Hugging the warm body of the little boy, a flash of his future echoed in her mind. She could see him safely beside his mother, her arm around him consoling him. Confirming he'd survive the ordeal. But what might they have to endure before her vision became reality?

The jet engines roared to life as Mitch adjusted the throttles and taxied the FA-18 into position for takeoff. Nervous tension vibrated down his spine in accompaniment to the pulsing of the aircraft. While it had been several years since he last flew a fighter jet, he could fly the bird as easily as if it had been last week. Its presence at the air show had been a blessing since the aerobatic F-18s only had one seat. The FA-18 featured a second seat which normally was occupied by a trained pilot being shuttled to their own jet.

Jo's insistence in flying along instead of Keith worried him, truth be told. Her safety rested in his hands. He gripped the stick, alarm pulsing through him. He had to catch up to the Lear before Walsh made good on his threat to flee the country and take his son—and Beth—with him. All while keeping a civilian safe. No worries.

After reaching cruising altitude, Mitch spoke into his headset to Jo. "Are you okay back there?"

"Ye-e-s." Her strained voice reached out to him, seeking reassurance.

"The worst part is over, getting her up into the air. It's quite a rush, isn't it?" He wanted her to relax. Her white face when he'd settled the helmet on her head and adjusted her seat straps rose in his memory. "It's a short hop in this baby, too. We'll land in Brownsville in about 40 minutes."

"Good to know." Jo cleared her throat. "How far behind him are we?"

Mitch checked the dials and gauges before responding. "They had an hour's head start, but we'll catch up to them, don't worry."

Mentally he recalculated the distance and times. At top speed, the Lear would take a little more than an hour and a half to cover the distance from Roseville to Brownsville. The fighter jet, on the other hand, would make the same trip in a little more than half an hour. He should be on the ground in plenty of time to prevent Todd from crossing the border with his, Mitch's, precious cargo. Beth.

They'd finally grown close enough to give him real hope for a future with the beautiful blonde. Her gold and green eyes mesmerized him, drew him in like a fish on a well-baited hook. The firming and toning of her already tantalizingly shapely body had increased his desire for her. She'd worked hard to improve herself in her own eyes. From his view she needed no improvement. Still, she'd done it all because she wanted to work with him. He should be flattered, and in some ways he was, but at the moment he was terrified. He couldn't lose her.

"Do you know what happens in Matamoros?" Jo's panic echoed in her voice over the intercom. "Mexico has the highest rate of kidnappings in the world. Did you know that? Todd's crazy. I can't believe he'd be fool enough to endanger our son."

"If he keeps his bodyguards close he can probably survive, but it's still no place for a kid."

Jo's voice held steel drenched with tears. "There's no rhyme or reason to the violence in Matamoros, which means everyone is exposed to dangerous situations. Whether they're aware of them or not."

Mitch stayed quiet, not wanting to add to her worries by sharing everything he'd heard about the city. Gunfights, grenade attacks, and the threat of abduction anywhere and anytime. Even armed robbery, sexual assault, car theft, and murder. Then there were the nonlethal crimes of financial scams, petty drug crimes, as well as drugs and gun smuggling. Definitely not a place to raise a child.

The fear crawling down his throat focused on what Walsh might have planned for Beth. She'd be in his way, perhaps know too much of his doings for him to let her go. If he took her across the border it wasn't beyond the realm of possibilities that he'd sell her to a sex trafficking ring. A beautiful and feisty blonde would fetch a high price. The thought coupled with images of what she'd endure made him queasy. He opened the throttle and sped through the night sky, toward Texas and his woman.

"Keith called the FBI and local authorities and they'll meet us at the airport. We'll get them back." He would or die in the attempt.

"Did you wonder why he snuck Artie away while I was not around?" Jo chuckled with a most definitely unfeminine bite to the sound. "I'll tell you. He's deathly afraid of me."

"Why?" Mitch kept a steady hand on the stick, clearing his mind of the awful images of rape and torture of his woman.

"Because he knows I can kill him if he gets close enough." Jo snorted a laugh. "What he doesn't know may get him just as dead."

"What doesn't he know?" He remembered the types of lessons Jo would likely have taught Beth, the skills she might have imparted.

"Beth is just as lethal as I am." A soft chuckle carried through the headset.

He let out his breath, a rush of relief settling his upset stomach. His sweet and endearing Beth could literally kill someone with her bare hands? That may prove useful. He hadn't realized her training had taken her to such a level. Using those newly acquired moves would change her. Perhaps in unexpected ways.

He swallowed the hint of unease clogging his throat. "Let's hope we get there before she needs to test those skills."

Chapter Eighteen

The roar in her head came both from the Lear's engines and her racing pulse. Beth kept her eyes on the boy, holding him on her lap while the guards made ready to land. Zeke regarded her steadily before glancing to the other men in the cockpit. Todd reclined in his chair, hands folded on his chest, legs stretched out under the table.

Outside the window, the lights of a city stretched over a wide area. A necklace of lights marked where a large body of water met what she presumed to be the shore to the east. The plane angled, turning to approach the airport with its flashing white and red runway lights guiding the pilot in to land.

Soon she'd have to act. Depending on what the men did, she had a couple of ideas as to how to escape. Beth hugged Artie, a quick squeeze to reassure him. He looked up at her, trust reflecting in his beautiful eyes. How had such a lovely little boy come from such a mean father? Although, Todd wasn't a bad-*looking* man, just a bad-*acting* one. Jo suspected he was up to some shady dealings. What if he was transporting guns with the intent to sell them, probably to the highest bidder? The little she knew about gun running and the people who did it didn't make her want to be involved for one second. What the weapons might be used for didn't apparently bother Todd. But it bothered Beth.

If she could prevent the guns from trading hands she would, but her priority remained Artie's safe return to his mother. And herself safely home.

Todd sighed and opened his eyes, staring at Artie as a slow smile inched onto his thin lips. He pushed up straight and stood. "Zeke, anything from Jorge?"

"He's waiting with the truck and the papers to cross at Matamoros. Everything's on schedule." Zeke hefted his pistol, glancing at Beth and then back to Todd. "What do you want me to do with her?"

Beth held her breath even as her thoughts raced over the small bit of information. Mexico. Damn. Where exactly were they? A large body of water stretched darkly away from the city. Suggesting the Gulf of Mexico but was Brownsville on the Gulf? She didn't know the geography well enough to know. She'd prepared physically but had overlooked the necessary education to be effective. Another lesson learned about her inadequacy.

She shook off the pathetic pity party and concentrated on the situation at hand. The guns must be going on a truck to avoid the customs inspection at the airport. By off-loading the contraband in the States they weren't subjected to a customs inspection. And the truck provided transportation for Todd and his son over the border. She had to keep the boy out of the truck at all costs. She gathered herself to do what she must.

"Up to you what becomes of her. The less I know the better off I am on that score." Todd lifted his suit coat off the back of his chair and slipped it on. "As long as she can't tell anyone what she knows." He chuckled as he studied her with hard eyes. "She's heard far too much to let her simply walk away."

She straightened in her seat, Artie wiggling his seat bones into her thighs. Grimacing, she shifted the boy to a more comfortable position. "You said you'd let me go. Not that I guess I should expect you to keep your word."

"You're no princess. You snuck onto my plane and pretended to be a tourist, when we both know that's not the truth." He rested his palms on his hips, pushing his coat tails backward. "Did you really think I didn't know that Mitch Sawyer was trying to get my plane?"

"Mitch who?" How much did he really know? Was he fishing for information?

"I'm no fool. I know he works as a repo agent and a damn good one. I wasn't aware that he's friends with Keith Merryman, my former pilot. An oversight on my part." Todd crossed his arms over his chest and shook his head. "I've seen you with him, Miss Golden. Why on earth did he drag you into this dangerous business?"

Beth lifted her chin to lock gazes with him. "I volunteered to help him."

"Your funeral." He shrugged, dismissing her as easily as shooing a fly away. "After Arthur and I cross the border, you won't be my problem any longer. My conniving wife won't be able to influence the boy away from respecting his father. He'll be my responsibility and I'll teach him the way of the world."

"To be a criminal? Is that the kind of life you want for your son?" Beth held onto the boy who listened without understanding the tension sizzling in the air. "Running guns to Mexican criminals?"

"I'll teach him to be a profitable businessman. He's my son and he'll do as I say." Todd winked at the boy. "Right, Arthur? You love your father."

Artie obediently bobbed his head and reached out his hands toward his father.

Beth tightened her embrace. "He may love you but he doesn't understand how you intend to harm him like I do. I won't let you take him to Mexico."

Todd guffawed, a bark of sound that made the boy startle on her lap. "He needs to be raised to be strong and smart, not a namby-pamby looking to placate others." Todd dropped his arms to his sides and smirked at her. "He'll learn to be tough and able to defend himself anyway he needs to."

"Seems to me that's what Jo was teaching him how to do."

"I seriously doubt that, but if you're so deluded by Jocasta's chatter then it's best if you don't have anything more to do with my son."

Instinctively she grasped Artie closer as Zeke motioned for Todd to resume his seat.

"Time to land, sir." Zeke glanced between Todd and Beth, his gaze lingering on her and then the boy before he dragged it back to his boss. "The seatbelt sign is on."

Beth glanced at the window, rain splashes streaking across the glass. The plane bumped through the clouds, jostling her where she sat, glad she had her own seatbelt fastened.

"Fine, but after we land, the boy is with me." Todd sat and snapped the belt home, his eyes steady on Beth. "You take the woman, Zeke, and dispose of her however you see fit."

Beth swallowed the fear burning in her throat. No way would she let Todd drag the boy across the border or allow Zeke to dispose of her like unwanted scrap. She'd trained for this type of situation. Well, maybe not exactly, but she had her own skills and resources. Somehow, someway she would protect Artie and herself. She only needed two things: an opening and confidence.

Despite the rain beating against the plane, the landing proved fairly smooth. Beth tensed, unsure what would happen next but prepared to seek any opportunity for escape. They taxied for a long while. Beth stared out the large windows at the cluster of buildings at the far side of the airport. The passenger terminal brightly lit and busy. On either side, a series of other buildings housed a variety of aviation businesses. Unfortunately at such a late hour, most stood dark and closed. The plane bumped and rolled past the slim hope each building represented to Beth. If she could somehow reach one, perhaps she could find help.

Before the door slowly opened, Zeke had her up and out of her seat. She grabbed her jacket and slipped it on before picking up Artie. Holding him close against her with strong arms. Todd rose with a quick sideways glance at her claim on the boy, and then strode to the opening.

A man with grey eyes and slicked black hair, a bright yellow raincoat shiny with rain, appeared at the top of the steps. "Mr. Walsh, you're needed immediately inside."

"What's wrong?" Todd frowned at the man dripping on the carpet.

"There's some problem with the inventory..." He trailed off, spotting Beth and Artie. His frown deepened as he stared at them. "We weren't expecting more passengers either."

"Only the boy will go with me."

The gray-eyed man shook his head. "There's no room with the extra cargo."

"We'll see about that." Todd shot a frown at the man and then motioned to Zeke. "Take them inside the hangar office and wait while I straighten out this mess. I don't want the boy to catch a cold or something."

Zeke nodded once and Todd disappeared into the stormy night.

Zeke peered at her, his gun aimed at her while he motioned with his head toward the door. "Get moving, lady."

"Careful with that gun, it might go off."

"Keep that in mind." He pointed to the door. "Go."

She hugged the boy close and ducked out of the cabin, carefully making her way down the wet metal steps. She darted her gaze around the Learjet to determine her choices for escape. Rain coursed down the back of her neck, making her shiver despite the leather jacket. The jet stood near an L-shaped hangar at the end of the taxiway, the plane positioned at the inner joint of the building alongside a big panel truck. Two men scurried back and forth in the rain, lugging boxes from the plane to the truck. Beyond the hangar the airport taxiways and runways stretched into the night, defined only by landing lights intermittently spaced along the length of pavement. Behind the hangar the rest of the businesses remained out of sight but at least a hundred yards away. A long way for a woman with a boy to run. In the rain. At night. She drew in a deep breath, calculating her odds.

Zeke grabbed her arm and forced her into a jog toward the foot of the L to the part of the building that served as an office. The stuffy room provided welcome shelter from the drenching rain. She halted by the doorway and put Artie down while Zeke flipped a light switch. The overhead lights revealed a typical office, several desks and matching chairs with file cabinets lined against one wall. She held onto one of Artie's hands while she wiped the rain off his face with her fingers. Zeke took a position on the low porch outside, standing so he could keep his gun trained on her and watch for anyone approaching.

Shivering, Beth scanned the interior for some means of exiting without Zeke being able to stop her. One window faced the side of the building, large enough for her to squeeze through but high off the floor for the boy. No back door. No other way out. The only other way was through the front door. She moved to check the window but Zeke stepped inside.

"Stay by the door." He pointed to a spot two feet inside the open door. "No messing around in here."

"Where would I go?"

"You're not going anywhere." Zeke turned sideways to scan the surrounding area.

If she had any chance, it would have to be through Zeke. She swallowed the concern threatening her composure. She must think of an escape route. But how? And to where?

"Artie, sweetie, how fast can you run?" Beth squeezed his little hand in hers.

He blinked up at her, clearly confused by her question. "Why?"

"Never mind. When I say run, go as fast as you can. I'll be holding your hand to help, okay?"

"Why?" His perplexed frown made his lips purse.

"Because you want to see your mom again, right?" She tugged his hand until he nodded. "So we need to get away from these bad men."

He gazed at her with his deep blue eyes and cocked his head to one side. "Why?"

She sighed at his questions, realizing the never-ending nature of them. "I'll explain later. Just be ready."

"Okay." He popped his free thumb into his mouth and stared out the door.

Rain fell in sheets outside, drumming on the metal roof and making it difficult to hear the activity going on beyond the walls. The door stood wide open, but still she could only see a small part of what the men worked on. The longer they worked, the sooner Todd would come for the boy. She shivered again, rubbing the boy's shoulders with both hands to warm him and keep touch with the never-still body. Waited for a chance to slip past Zeke. Somehow.

Heavy footsteps approached the building. The man in the yellow raincoat stomped into view and stopped to talk to Zeke, drawing his attention away from his captives. Zeke frowned at the man and then they got into a heated discussion that quickly became an argument. She eased closer to the doorway and peeked around the corner. In the distance, perhaps one hundred feet away, Todd stood by the truck, talking to the driver with wild gestures of his hands. With the men's attention focused elsewhere, she steeled her nerve and then gripped Artie's hand.

"Shh. Let's go." She sidled out the door and half dragged the boy around the front corner and down the side of the building. Grateful she'd worn her low boots with her biker outfit. Trotting on the balls of her feet, she moved as stealthily as possible in the shadow of the building, Artie struggling to keep up. She paused only long enough to check a door now and again to see if it was unlocked before hurrying on.

If only she could reach someplace where she could hide, then she'd have time to plot an actual escape to safeguard the toddler beside her. Without a gun aimed at her and the boy. Without the threat of her own demise or whatever her guard had in mind. She could return Artie to Jo, where he belonged. If only… The roar of another jet approaching the airfield made her gasp. She didn't need the men spotting her when they looked to see what plane might be landing.

Panting, she paused to check a side door on the third office building she came to. She pushed on the heavy door and, much to her surprise and relief, she shoved open the door and pulled Artie inside. They were in a stairwell, lit by only one bulb high on the wall. She let the door swing shut behind them. Dropping onto a step, she strove to catch her breath and formulate her next move. Artie rubbed his wrist where she'd held on for dear life as they ran. At least he was safe and unharmed.

She needed a moment to think, to plan, to recover from the fear of her own failure. She'd found an opportunity and took it. A wave of pride flooded her chest at her ability to act in spite of her doubts. Faced the peril and took strides toward making things right. Leaving just one question. Now what?

Chapter Nineteen

Thankfully, the downpour he'd flown through on approach to the airfield had been brief. As soon as the FA-18 hit the wet tarmac, activity exploded near the air cargo hangars. Not only the men hurriedly closing the Lear's door but the flashing red and blue lights in the near distance leading a line of black sedans straight toward them. Mitch taxied the jet to the taxiway near the terminal and then helped Jo to the ground. He secured the jet before they dashed to join the police and FBI officers already halting in front of the farthest hangar. In time to block the path of the truck and prevent it leaving, the driver none-too-gently hauled out of the vehicle while agents inspected the cargo. All based on the tip Keith had phoned in before Mitch took off in the fighter jet with the intent to overtake the Lear.

He glanced at Jo, practically trotting beside his longer strides, as they hurried to search for Beth and Artie. He started to brush past the pair of officers standing with legs braced and one hand on their guns to reach the Lear.

"Hold up, you can't go in there." The blue uniformed officer blocked their approach to the hangar where the executive jet stood.

"I need that plane." Mitch pulled a crumpled folded paper out of his pocket and showed it to the officer. Hoped the contract would gain him access to the plane but also closer to finding his woman. "It's my job to confiscate that plane for the bank."

"Your claim will have to wait. That plane is evidence and will be impounded." The officer hiked a thumb toward a tall FBI agent giving directions to several other agents, one of them heading to the back of the truck. "Talk to him."

"Man, I'm never going to get paid for this gig." Mitch raked a hand through his hair as he peered at the officer, putting on his best hang-dog look. "Give me a break, will ya?"

"Talk to the FBI. They've claimed jurisdiction."

"I'm screwed." Mitch didn't really care about the money so much as Beth and the boy. "Were there civilians involved?"

He slid his gaze over the buildings glistening with rain. Thankful yet again that the downpour had stopped. Where could they be? What was happening to them?

"Not that I've seen, but I just got here." The officer glanced at his partner and, after seeing the quick shake of his head, shrugged at Mitch. "Why?"

"Where's my son? He was on that plane." Jo took a step closer to the first officer. "I don't see him or my husband."

"Like I said, miss, talk to the FBI. We're just guarding the perimeter for them."

"He's here, he has to be." Jo's white face and wild eyes warned of her verging on a maternal meltdown despite the rigid grip she had on her arms.

"I don't see Beth either." Mitch's frantic perusal of the area left him frustrated and worried. He could only imagine how terrified the woman beside him must feel. "How did we miss them? We were only a few minutes behind them."

The agent emerged from behind the truck with a box in both hands. He indicated the driver of the truck with a tilt of his head. "Arrest that man for smuggling."

"Not me! You want the owner of that Lear. Todd Walsh. He's the one in charge of this operation."

"Where is he?""

"He ran off when you guys showed up. Hey!"

The driver's cry of alarm when an agent cuffed him preceded a flurry of activity as the agents fanned out to search for the other men involved. Mitch pivoted away from the hangar, knowing the smugglers wouldn't have hidden inside where the evidence of their crime remained. He scanned the lighted area, listening and searching for any clues as to their whereabouts.

"I'm going to see if I can find anybody." He clasped Jo's hand for a moment, catching her wild eyes with his own forced calm gaze. "Stay here in case they come back."

She stared at him, eyes brimming with unshed tears. "No. I'm going with you. He's my boy."

"He's probably with Beth, safe from harm." He flashed a faint smile and nodded. "You taught her how to defend herself, so I imagine that's what she's doing for your son, too."

"I can protect myself, so don't worry about me." Jo motioned toward the agents searching between the buildings and testing the doors as they moved down the taxiway. "Let's go."

He started walking toward the silent and dark buildings along the right side of the taxiway, Jo pacing beside him, silent as death. His heart was in his throat as he neared the first hulking building. He inhaled, testing the air as he tried to open the door without any luck. No special scent reached his nose.

He hurried to the next building, peering into the dark shadows between the hangars as he strode past. Inhaling and exhaling, hoping with each breath. He could hear the agents' footsteps as they searched without any success. She had to be somewhere. But where? Then the wind shifted and brought the scent of spiced vanilla along with a cry that stopped him dead in his tracks.

Beth pulled her phone out of her purse, ready to call for help. Frowned at the blank screen. Dead. Damn. She'd forgotten to charge it overnight and now she had no way to reach out to the police. To Mitch.

They couldn't stay in a stairwell forever either. The door leading into the office spaces needed an electronic key, a badge of some kind, to enter. She'd trudged up the steps to the second floor only to find the same result. Locked out of the heart of the building. Where phones and people may be able to assist them. They'd have to venture outside or nobody would find them.

"Okay, Artie, we're going to go try to get to the terminal. We'll be safe there."

The boy pouted at her, unhappy with the climbing of the stairs and the echoing concrete room. "K."

"Buck up, dear. We're almost there. Come on." She kept Artie behind the door as she slowly pulled it open. Peered out into the dimly lit area and then pulled the boy from the safety of the stairwell.

She kept a firm hold on the little boy's hand as she hurried down the sidewalk toward the bustling terminal, brightly lit and inviting but far away.

"Arthur! There you are."

Beth spun around in horror, the dangerous man mere yards behind her.

Todd strolled closer, staring at her. She held onto Artie's hand as the boy squirmed at her side.

"Hush, now, Artie." Her whisper had little effect on the boy. She held his hand tighter, but he pushed against her grasp.

The weight of Todd's angry gaze pierced her, making her step back.

"Arthur?" Todd hesitated, arms crossed. "Come on, son. I don't have time to play games. Come here."

At the commanding tone, Artie yanked his hand free and ran to his father. "Daddy!"

Beth lunged only to grab empty air. "Artie! No!"

Todd clutched the boy to him while he recovered from the impact of the compact body hitting his legs. He blinked at her once and then smirked. "Well, well, Miss Golden. I thought Zeke was going to take care of you."

"He was busy." She racked her brain for some way to get Artie away from the man. "Not the sharpest crayon in the box, if you know what I mean."

"I'd trust him with my life, and do."

If she could move close enough, perhaps an opportunity to extricate the boy would present itself. Not that she wanted to be closer, but if she must, then she would. She flexed her hands, preparing for the fight. She inched closer, moving slowly so as to not raise an alarm in Todd's little brain.

"Artie, sweetie, come here." Beth reached toward the boy who shook his head and hugged his father harder.

"He's safe with me." Todd chuckled and peeled Artie's arms from around his leg, taking one hand instead. "More than I can say for you."

Beth stood as calmly as she could while facing the threatening man. "You don't scare me."

"I'm going to have fun making you pay for kidnapping my son and hiding him from me." He gripped the boy's hand until the child frowned.

"You're hurting him." Another foot closer, slowly and steadily shrinking the distance. She shifted her purse to the front of her, the concealed Glock near to hand. She unzipped the secret compartment. She'd rather not use the pistol if she could avoid it. But she would if forced. She swallowed the knot of fear pressing against her larynx. "It's me you want to hurt, not your son."

"True, but I need him with me." Todd smiled down at his son as he let go of his hand. "Stay close, Arthur."

Artie leaned against his father's leg, one thumb finding its way into his little mouth.

"What do you intend to do with him in Mexico?" A little bit closer and the man, who didn't see her as a threat of any kind, would be in range to take him down with a sweep. "He's so young. Who will take care of him while you're working?"

"Ever hear of nannies?" He chuckled and shifted his weight to one side, away from the boy.

Artie pulled his thumb out of his mouth and spotted something on the ground. Squatting suddenly to examine it more closely, Beth saw her chance.

She lured Todd away from the child with a sudden sideways leap and then swept the big man's feet out from under him. He fell with a thud and a grunt and she launched into a Jiu-Jitsu position. Muscle memory kicked in and she soon had him in a side control so she could put a choke on him until he passed out, falling limp with his head lolling and mouth open. After she was absolutely certain he remained unconscious, she turned to gather Artie, crying, into her arms.

"I promised to keep you safe and that's exactly what I'm doing." She hugged him close, relief flooding through her entire core when she spotted Jo in a formal gown and heels and Mitch running toward her with several men in FBI vests close behind. "Look who's here."

Artie looked up to see his mother racing closer. He smiled through his tears at Beth and then ran to his mother's embrace.

Beth rose slowly to her feet, tears smarting her eyes as her vision played out in real life. Jo comforted her crying son, bowed over him to wrap an arm around his shoulders and hold him close. When Mitch aimed a worried look her way, she smiled with relief and an intense joy at seeing him safe and sound. Her man had come after her just as she'd known he would. She loved Mitch more in that moment than she ever thought possible. Still, tears spilled over and trailed unheeded down her cheeks as she trembled and waited for him to reach her side.

Chapter Twenty

She entranced him with her teary smile, drawing him toward her with an increasing urgency. His powerful strides carried him to her, proud of her courage in the face of personal harm in order to protect the innocent child. Jo, the sparkling evening gown reflecting the lights, stood off to one side, her arm around her son's shoulders as she leaned over him and wiped away his tears. Such a good outcome from a very bad state of affairs. So why was his girl crying while watching them? His sweet kitten had turned into a ferocious tiger capable of taking down a much bigger adversary. Something he best remember after they married.

Married? He stumbled over nothing, casting a glance over his shoulder at the sidewalk as if it had tripped him on purpose. Yes, indeed. He pictured their life together, filled with love and respect for each other, but also laughter and fun. A passel of kids to adore and raise as upstanding members of the town. Would she have him even though he didn't know what kind of job he could find in the Roseville vicinity? He'd find a way to persuade her. After they were safely back home.

"Sweetheart, you're amazing." He clasped her hands to his chest as he drew her special scent into his lungs. Grateful to have her in reach again. "How did you do that?"

"I'm not sure. I just did." Beth sniffled as she contemplated the mother and son. "Reflexes?"

"Whatever, I'm glad you're safe." He peered closer at her, searching for any hint of injury. The cause of her tears. "You're not hurt?"

She shook her head and squeezed his fingers. "I'm fine. We both are. What about him?"

Mitch glanced at the prostrate man, sprawled on the pavement. "The FBI will take care of him. Thanks to you."

She shuddered as she stared at the man she'd defeated. "He was going to have me killed." She swallowed as she turned to peer up at Mitch's face. "What did I ever do to make him want to dispose of me? His words…"

A protective rage swept through him at the disbelief and pain in her eyes. The man had no scruples or sense of decency. The very fact he'd threatened to harm the woman standing before him made Mitch want to do the man some bodily injury of his own. The rage was soon replaced by a swell of love for her, uplifting and sustaining.

"Those were the words of a twisted individual, honey." Mitch released one hand to wipe the trail of her sorrow away with his thumb. "Don't shed tears on his behalf."

"I'm not, trust me." She blinked and pressed her cheek closer to his hand for a moment. Then regarded the man on the ground.

Todd rolled his head to one side, slowly blinking awake. Two agents speaking to the lead agent noticed, rousted him to his feet, and snapped handcuffs on him.

"You'll pay for this, bitch." Todd spat on the ground and the agent yanked him around to march toward his black sedan. He glared at Beth and then Jo as they led him away.

"Don't believe him, sweetheart." Mitch drew her attention with a finger to her chin. "They'll make sure he never has the chance to hurt you again."

"I'm glad he's gone." Beth shuddered and pivoted to put her back to the retreating angry man and the agents. "Now things can get back to normal."

Jo and Artie strode closer to where Mitch and Beth stood. He would swear he could feel the woman's relief radiating from her with each breath she took. Artie looked happy to be back with his mother as well. How confusing for the kid to be caught between his parents. With Todd's arrest and the ton of evidence in the crates of pistols once destined for criminals south of the border, Jo shouldn't have any trouble receiving full custody when her divorce was final.

"Hey, Beth, I hate to interrupt but I have to say thank you." Jo crossed to bear hug Beth for several moments before releasing her and taking her son's hand. "You saved Artie, and I can never thank you enough for that."

"I'd do it again in a heartbeat." Beth laid a hand on Jo's shoulder. "Thank you for teaching me so well how to defend myself so I could protect your son, too."

"Artie, what do you have to say to Miss Golden?" Jo tugged on his hand and he ran to Beth.

"Tanks." He wrapped his arms around her legs.

"Oh, you're so precious." Beth's voice choked into silence.

She dropped to his height and hugged the boy. Mitch's eyes misted at the sweet sight. She touched him in so many unexpected and wonderful ways. He'd fought his reactions to her when they'd first met but only because he'd been selfish and stupid. Living a quiet existence alone was no way to spend the rest of his life. Not that he wanted to be chasing Beth across the country, but he would without a second thought if that's what it took to make her happy.

Reluctantly, Beth released the boy and rose to her full height as he went back to Jo. She glanced between Mitch and Jo. "I suppose we should figure out how to get home."

"Before we worry about that, I need to ask you a question." Mitch inclined his head toward the small group of agents still working nearby to process the crime scene. Then he peered at Jo, the hint of a smile on his lips. "Can you give us a minute?"

"Sure. We'll wait over there." Jo took hold of Artie's hand and led him away to stand in the pool of light from the nearby office building.

Mitch regarded Beth, wondering how best to phrase his question. "Tell me one thing. Why were you crying?" Mitch searched her now dry eyes. "You smiled at me through your tears."

"Oh, that." She flapped a hand in the air as if brushing away a pest. "Because my vision finally came true and I was happy to see everyone safe."

"Your vision? What do you mean?" He stilled, sudden doubt and wariness mixing in his chest.

"Yes, my visions." She studied him as a light frown dipped her brows. "I'm a psychic. I can see events in people's futures."

"Seriously?" Mitch had never known a real psychic, but his sister had and that whole affair had not ended well. "You're kidding, I hope."

Her frown deepened as she stared at him. "No, I'm not."

Dismay tinged with anger seeped through him, leaving a cold trail inside. "I had no idea."

"What's the matter?" She peered at him, puzzled and leery.

He stepped back and ran a hand over his hair before shaking his head. "You're not the woman I thought you were if you think you can tell somebody's future and all that crap."

Beth crossed her arms, a defensive barrier. "It's not crap."

Mitch gazed out across the expanse of runways, their lights blinking a welcome. He looked back at Beth and shook his head. "I thought you were special but not a deceiver."

She gasped and reared back her head as if he'd slapped her. "How dare you…"

"Tell the truth? My sister fell for a woman's claims of being able to predict her future, could see her doing this and that." Mitch swallowed the knot in his throat. "All Wendy had to do was pay her four thousand dollars and she'd guide her through a very difficult time."

"Oh, no." Beth's eyes widened and her brows lifted to her hairline. "Tell me she didn't…"

He nodded once, quelling the churning in his gut. "All the money she had saved, her nest egg for when she started college. Gone." He snapped his fingers and shoved his hands into his jeans pockets.

"I don't tell anybody that I have these visions, Mitch. And I certainly don't charge anybody for anything."

"Look, I'm sure you think you have visions and such, but we both know it's not possible. Doesn't much matter whether you cash in on your playacting, it's still a matter of honesty. With yourself and others.

"Mitch, you don't understand." She peered at him, the hope shining in her eyes slowly dimming.

He heaved a sigh, releasing all his dreams and hopes of a future with her into the night sky. "It's late and we need to get you home. Your sisters will be frantic."

Several hours slid past in a blur of dejected agony. Emotionally bruised and beaten, Beth moved where directed and waited for the pain to subside enough for her to make sense of Mitch's rejection. He'd shut her out as effectively as a locked door without even a window to peek through. No hint of what he felt.

"You'll fly with me." Mitch caught her attention with a motion of one hand. His frosty tone sent ice shards into her heart. "I promised Roxie I'd make sure you got home safely and I'll do that much."

She nodded, not trusting her voice to not give away the turmoil roiling her stomach. He stood gazing down at her, shutters over his emotions. Even reaching out to him mentally gained her no insights as to how to convince him that she was not a charlatan, not lying or deceiving anyone about her abilities. An FBI agent appeared on his other side and Mitch turned away to speak to him.

Jo walked up, a frown on her face as she and Artie halted beside Beth. "What's wrong?"

Tears pressed the corners of Beth's eyes as she stared at her friend. "I don't know what to do."

"About?" Jo laid a hand on Beth's shoulder. "Talk to me."

"I love him but he's broken any chance for us." She sniffed and swiped away a stray tear. "He's blocked me out."

Jo firmed her lips and glanced at Mitch's back. "Did he say why?"

Beth drew in a long breath and let it out slowly, mulling whether to reveal her secret to her friend. She searched Jo's sincere expression and made her decision. "I told him that I'm a psychic, that I can see the future. He…told me his sister had been taken in by a lady claiming to be able to counsel her as to her future for a sum of money."

Jo rolled her eyes and shook her head. "And he equates you to this other schemer? How uncharitable of him."

"What do I do?" The hint of a wail laced her voice and she swallowed. She must stay strong. "I've worked hard to be with him and now he's shut me out."

Jo glanced down at Artie leaning against her leg, tired from all the night's drama. Then aimed her piercing gaze at Beth. "You either need to convince him you're telling the truth, or…let him go."

Beth's heart tumbled, bumping and banging all the way to her knees. She snuck a peek at Mitch's broad back tapering to his jean-clad hips, his tousled dark blond hair nearly within reach. Yet so far away. She tried on the idea of never seeing him again. Going through days without the anticipation of his ready smile, his teasing banter. His protective nature reminding her of how much he cared about and for her as a person and a woman. Until now.

"Jo, I need to find a way to make him believe me." She squared her shoulders and bit her lip. "I have never backed down from a challenge, and now is not the time to start."

"Good choice." Jo patted Beth's shoulder.

The contact flashed a new vision past Beth's inner eye. Jo and Keith walking hand in hand through a garden. They were laughing at some private joke. Then the vision dissipated. Beth blinked at Jo but remained silent. After all, she didn't know when or how the vision would actually come about. Best to keep it to herself.

Mitch finished his conversation with the agent and pivoted to stride over to the ladies. "Jo, you and your son will be taken home by the FBI. So if you'll go with that agent, you'll be on your way before too much longer."

"Thanks for arranging the transportation, Mitch." Jo regarded him for a moment and then shifted to face Beth more directly. "I'll see you later. Remember what I said."

"Right, I will." Perhaps the way to convince Mitch rested in the new vision. Then again, she had no way of knowing how long before the events of the peek at Jo's future would occur or even if they would. "Safe travels."

Jo hugged Beth farewell before Artie also gave her a little boy hug goodbye. Jo led her son away to meet up with the waiting agent.

"Shall we go?" Mitch peered at her, his eyes and mood unreadable.

"One thing before we do." Beth forced the doubt down her throat. She'd rather take the risk than not and regret missing her opportunity to prove her integrity. "A moment ago, when Jo touched me, I had a vision of Jo and Keith together as a couple."

Mitch lifted one sardonic brow as a smirk appeared on his lips. "Keith with Jo? That would be something to see."

"I don't know when they'll get together, but when it happens, then you'll know I'm telling you the truth about my ability."

"What about my future? How come you've never told me about mine? You've touched me plenty of times."

"That's a mystery to me." She slowly shook her head as she fell in step beside Mitch, walking back to the fighter jet. "I can't explain it."

"Should I be worried?" Mitch stared straight ahead as they closed the distance to the jet.

"I hope not." Beth chuckled at the sudden sharp glance he tossed her way. "I guess we'll just have to wait and see."

Chapter Twenty-One

The last whine of the jet engines faded as dawn arrived at the Roseville airfield. He parked the jet back in place with the other F-18s the Blue Angels used for their aerobatic air show and shut down. Glad to be home. Yes, Roseville welcomed him. The sun peeked over the horizon, slanting rays across the grass and runways. Mitch yawned as he unfastened his helmet. Quite a night they'd had.

"Beth, are you awake?" He opened the canopy while he waited for her reply, the refreshing morning air flooding inside.

"How do I get out of this thing?"

"Hold on." Suppressing a chuckle at the morning grumpiness in her voice, Mitch pushed out of his seat and went to help her with extricating herself from the harness straps and helmet. Despite the long night, she still looked beautiful even with her hair mussed and her sleepy eyes blinking at him. "Follow me."

Muttering to herself, she wiggled out of the seat and, placing her hands and feet in the same places he did, climbed down. Once they safely reached the ground, she stood peering up at him for a moment, dragging one hand through her long hair, before she propped her fists on her

217

hips. Still wearing her sexy biker chick outfit, the stance emphasized her womanly curves in all the right places. Curves he'd like to explore like a scenic country road. Slowly and with purpose. Feeling his way. Finding hidden delights around every bend. If only he could see a future with her after her revelation of the previous night.

He'd sort out what he'd do with his time and talents before officially settling down. Not that he had a date set for such a momentous occasion. Soon though he'd make a decision. Before he did, he should evaluate his options, but which direction to turn proved a more tangled question than he'd expected. Reserve duty, maybe. What else? Find a full-time gig somewhere? If so, doing what exactly? Keep doing repo work? No, not that.

She snapped her fingers before his nose. "Focus. Did you even hear me?"

He blinked in surprise and then looked at her, forcing all his wayward thoughts aside. "Sorry. I got distracted…"

"Men." She sighed melodramatically but couldn't hide the smirk. "I'm starving and you're ogling me like I'm the meal. I need food."

His laugh burst unbidden into the air. "First things first. Keith is going to need to check in the plane before anyone from the Blue Angels notice it was gone."

She frowned at him, a crinkling of her brow for an instant. "Will you be in trouble?"

"Possibly, but I think since I'm still a fighter pilot it won't be as bad as it might have been." He couldn't help himself. Her luscious lips beckoned, compelling him to plant a kiss on her upturned mouth. "I'd do it all again no matter the punishment in order to have you safely back with m…your sisters."

"I wouldn't want you to get in any trouble, but I sure am glad you came after us." She pressed a kiss to his mouth and then took a small step back to peer at him, a glimmer of hope lurking in the depths of her green eyes. "Thank you."

"I didn't do much. You handled the situation. Just don't make a habit of it, okay?" He smiled to soften the request to a mild joke and she quirked a brow in response. His heart squeezed at the mere idea of her putting herself in danger. But there was no doubt in his mind. He'd go after her no matter what kind of trouble she encountered. Surprise coursed through him at the thought. Apparently, the urge to protect her no matter what hadn't died despite her claims. "I don't think I could live with myself if anything happened to you on my watch."

"No worries on that score. I've learned my lesson." She studied him as he started walking toward the airfield office. "Be careful what you wish for because you may not like the reality."

"All things in moderation, huh?" He shot her a glance and then noticed Keith marching toward them. "Here comes trouble of a different sort."

The man in question halted in front of them, stopping their progress. A half smile hitched his mouth and his eyes twinkled with mirth. "What do you have to say for yourself, young man? Didn't I tell you to have her home by eleven? What's this landing at dawn business?"

"Very funny, *sir*. Did anyone miss her?" Mitch glanced back to the jet, then to his friend. "How much trouble am I in?"

"You should be glad I know the right people." Keith pulled a folded paper out of his breast pocket. "You flew that bird under orders to catch a known gun smuggler and free his kidnap victims."

"Mission accomplished." Mitch let out a long breath, letting relief drop his shoulders back into their normal position. He took the page and held it firmly in his hand, grateful to his quick-thinking and well-connected friend. "Should I ask how you wrangled orders?"

Keith grinned at him, shoving his hands into his front jeans pockets. "Probably not. But there's something else you should know."

Mitch tensed at the gleam in his buddy's eyes. "Good news?"

"You asked me to tell you if I came across the perfect job for you." Keith shrugged and turned to start walking back toward his office. "In exchange for the official paperwork, I've promised the colonel you'll do a little consulting for him."

"Consulting on what?" The sun climbed higher in the sky, warming his shoulders as they continued the short walk back to the airfield manager's office. Another nice day ahead for the air show's finale and the fireworks to celebrate Independence Day in style. "What could I possibly know that they'd want me to consult on?"

"Don't be so modest, Mitch." Keith chucked him on the shoulder, knocking him a little sideways. "You know plenty about jets and strategy. They want you to train new recruits."

If he became a consultant he could change course whenever he wanted to try something new, different, more interesting. Jump from one option to another, as long as it paid the bills. Not that he was hurting for money. Far from it. As a freelancer, he could set his own rates and choose which jobs to accept. He'd have freedom to come and go as he wanted. The more he considered the idea, the more he liked it.

Mitch shot a look at Keith and caught his eye. "Where would all this happen?"

"The airbase in Tullahoma, not too far from here." Keith glanced at Mitch and then Beth. "You'd be able to commute without any problem. Nice back country roads between the two places."

"I'll talk to the colonel about making that work." Mitch smiled at Keith, lifting a brow in question. "Why didn't they ask you?"

"Who said they didn't?" Keith laughed and shook his head. "I've got my work here to keep me fully employed. I will admit to selfish reasons for suggesting you."

"What's that?"

"It's been good to reconnect with you after so many years." Keith stopped in front of the door to his office. "I wanted you to stick around."

Mitch held out his right hand to clasp with Keith's in a confirmation of their friendship. "I'm glad I stumbled into Roseville."

"Me, too." Beth smiled at the two men.

Keith nodded as he prepared to go inside the small building. "Be sure you come back out tonight for the fireworks display. The organizers promise it will be spectacular. Tell all your family and friends, I need the money…"

"I'm sure my sisters would enjoy the show." Beth looked at Keith with a wide grin. "Probably a burger and grilled corn on the cob as well."

Keith chortled at her expression. "What else on the Fourth?"

"We'll spread the word." Mitch slapped his buddy on the back before the man hurried into the office. "Where do you want me to take you, Beth? Home or the store?"

The bookstore buzzed with activity. The air show drew people from all around but Beth hadn't expected they'd be in town shopping at the Golden Owl. Humming to herself, she straightened up the several stacks of flyers near the register. She'd already worked through the travel section with nary a twinge of desire to go anywhere. Not after her last unexpected trip.

Roxie repeatedly glanced at Beth, curiosity evident on her face. Beth ignored her and kept busy with straightening and arranging the handmaid jewelry hanging on a rounder.

"What's got you so subdued this afternoon?" Roxie finished ringing up another sale.

Tara glanced at her from the coffee bar as she made iced beverages—sweet tea and coffee—for the cluster of women at the counter. Beth acknowledged the group of ladies, a trio of friends who frequently popped in, their somber long skirts and plain blouses in sharp contrast to the shorts, colorful tops, and sandals of the other female patrons. Beth delighted in their friendly conversation and acceptance of each other. Their relationship was more like Beth and her sisters than of friends. Close and supportive and above all honest with each other.

"I've been curious ever since you walked through the door a little while ago." Tara handed the last of the cups to the ladies and then wiped her hands on her apron. "Far too calm for you. What have you been doing?"

Beth waved to the ladies as they chatted past and out the door, the little bell cheering them on their way. "You won't believe where I went last night."

Tara frowned at her, curiosity mixed with concern in her eyes. "You left? Why didn't you tell us?"

"I didn't have a chance to. It all happened so fast." Beth braced her hands on the glass countertop.

"I wondered where you were. Did you go somewhere with Mitch?" Roxie shook her head at her. "You need to be careful. You don't know him all that well."

"Well, he didn't go with me, but he did come after me. In a fighter jet, no less." Beth gnawed on her lower lip, reliving the events of the last twenty-four hours in her mind. "Wait until I tell you."

Beth recounted the kidnapping and the flight as well as everything that occurred in Brownsville. She left out no detail, no matter how small, experiencing the excitement and the fear all over again. Dawning horror reflected from her sisters' expressions as they gripped their hands together in silent agony on her behalf. When she got to the part where Mitch arrived in the jet to rescue her and the boy, their eyes widened at the same time in surprise and awe.

"You can't keep doing this airplane repo thing." Roxie frowned at her. "It's too dangerous. I won't permit it."

"You're right. I wished for excitement not threats on my life." Beth crossed her arms and gazed at her sisters. Love for them swelled in her chest. "I took on more than I could comfortably handle."

"But you did handle it. So that's vindication for your efforts. Right?" Tara smoothed her apron down with a slight tremor in her hands. "I'm proud of you for that."

"Thanks, but I don't think I want to continue with such a risky business." She sighed and then smiled. "I have enough surprises coming my way right here in Roseville after all."

"I know I'm surprised. I didn't know he could fly jets." Roxie dropped her hands to rest on the glass counter near Beth's. "He possesses some hidden talents. Like us."

"Does he know about your hidden talent?" Tara leaned against the counter, peering at Beth with a worried expression.

"He's not happy about my psychic abilities. He got pretty upset when I told him." Beth huffed a frustrated sigh and shook her head. "I've got to find some way of convincing him I'm not deceiving anyone with my visions."

"How?" Roxie grabbed a towel and wiped down the counter, more for something to do with her hands than necessity.

"I told him of a vision." She gulped and grasped her hands together on the counter. "When it comes true, then he'll have to believe me."

"What do you hope to gain?" Tara asked.

"His trust." Beth peered at her sisters in turn. "More importantly, his love."

The little bell above the door announced new customers entering. Beth glanced up and spotted Mitch striding through the door.

"Speak of the devil." She turned away from the checkout counter to saunter toward Mitch. "Hello."

"I won't keep you, Beth. Keith asked me to make sure you've asked everyone you can think of to be at the airshow for the fireworks tonight." Mitch nodded to Roxie and Tara before focusing on Beth again. "Mission accomplished."

"I told these two and texted everybody else I could think of." Beth aimed her most sincere smile at him, hoping he'd see her for the woman he knew. Not the one he thought she'd become. Only he remained unreadable in every way to her.

"Good, I'll let him know." He nodded once to himself as if confirming an already held opinion. "See ya."

"Wait." Beth laid a detaining hand on his forearm, stopping him from turning to walk away. "What happened with the Learjet? Did you get it back?"

He shook his head and rolled his eyes, then smiled at her. "The FBI is in touch with the bank rep to work out a deal. I may never see the payment, but at least everyone is home safe."

"One more thing before you go." Beth drew in a breath, hoping to draw in courage to ask what she most wanted to know. "Will you be at the fireworks as well?"

"I owe Keith that much for housing me." He gazed at her, inscrutable. "See you around."

She removed her hand from his arm as he strode out of the store. Tears formed in her eyes but she brushed them away. She'd not cry but stay the course. Prove to him she wasn't a bad person. She simply needed patience to wait it out. He said he'd talk to the colonel so an itty-bitty hope lit in her soul. Pivoting on one foot, she shot a happy grin at her sisters.

"Let's close early and go have some fun. What do you say?"

Chapter Twenty-Two

$\mathcal{F}$olding chairs and blankets crammed together across the field. Families and couples milled along the edges and in the food court. Children skipped and darted among the adults juggling paper trays of food and drink cups. Mitch found a place to stand out of the mix, the sight making him nervous. Too many people in too small a space for his liking. Scanning the people passing back and forth, he searched for Keith.

"Hey, Mitch, we found you." Beth marched up to him, dressed in red shorts and a blue shirt with white stars, her sisters flanking her like guard dogs.

So she'd told them about their argument. Roxie's expression warned him to proceed with caution. Didn't want her sister to have a broken heart like he did. Not that he blamed the sister from looking after Beth's interests. The close-knit nature of their relationship made it a tad easier for him to walk away from the hope he'd cherished.

"Hey, ladies." He nodded to all three of them, not wanting to single out Beth. It made his heart hurt to distance himself from her, but he also had to protect himself. "Have you seen Keith?"

"I think I saw him heading over to the fried chicken booth." With a toss of her head, Beth indicated the direction. "I wouldn't mind following him. I'm starving."

"Again?" Mitch shook his head at his blurted out response. "Sorry."

Beth shrugged away his apology. "Food?"

"This way, then." Mitch joined the trio, creating a path through the crowds heading toward their seats. "Won't be long until the show, so we should hurry."

"I'm hungry for a burger, so I'm going to that vendor." Tara pointed to a short line with only a handful of people waiting.

"Sounds good." Roxie glanced at Beth. "You?"

"I'm thinking chicken. I'll meet you back by the entrance to the court when I get mine and then we can find a place to watch the show."

"Works for me." Roxie spun around to catch up to Tara who had started for the burgers.

Beth turned a questioning gaze up at him. "Chicken?"

"Why not." Might as well be with her in a friendly sort of way if he planned to move to town. He'd see her from time to time without a doubt. He took her arm to ensure they stayed together in the crowded space. "Did you bring chairs or a blanket?"

"Chairs. We left them at Keith's office but he wasn't there." Her voice sounded faint against the noisy background. Suddenly, she dragged him to a stop.

"What?" He looked down to find her jaw dropped open with a huge smile on her face. He followed her gaze and then froze, blinking. "Oh my god."

Coming toward them through the parting crowd, Keith and Jo were laughing and holding hands, little Artic holding her other hand. They passed in front of a vendor's tent decorated with artificial flowers in red, white, and blue.

"Do you see that?" Beth smiled at the oblivious couple.

"Keith and Jo together, just as you predicted." Stunned barely described how he felt at the sight.

"And the other part?" Beth glanced at him and then waved to Jo.

He studied the surprising scene more carefully and then shook his head in amazed disbelief.

"The garden." Mitch stared and then smiled. Relief flooded him as he turned to pin his adoring gaze on Beth. "You didn't lie. Damn. I should have trusted you, honey."

She gripped his hand and lifted a brow at him. "Yes, you should have."

The threesome halted in front of Mitch. He lifted both brows at Keith and shook his head. "I never would have thought the two of you would get together."

"I didn't either. Not at first." Keith smiled tenderly at Jo. "She bumped into me earlier, wanting to thank me for my help in her and Artie's safe return."

Jo let go of Keith's hand to snatch Artie back to her side. "Stay close, son. I don't want you getting lost."

Artie glanced at her and then let his attention wander away again, but stayed pressed against Jo's legs.

"We were about to grab some dinner. Will you join us?" Mitch motioned toward the fried chicken booth.

Before very long they had trays of chicken, fries, and sodas to juggle on their way back to Keith's office. They gathered Roxie and Tara on the way, all talking and laughing over the patriotic outfits and face paintings on the people they passed.

Mitch helped Beth settle into a canvas chair, the several containers of their meal crammed onto a small folding table provided by Keith in front of them. "The show should begin in just a few minutes."

"Yum." Beth wiped her mouth with a paper napkin. "Don't mind me if I don't say much."

Mitch took a bite of his hot chicken, savoring the seasonings as he chewed. "Better than my mama could make."

"I wouldn't let her hear you say that." Keith leaned closer from the other side of Beth. "She takes her cooking very seriously."

"Good point." A test shot flared into the sky, streaking and squealing its way high above. "They're starting."

"Finish up eating, everybody. You won't want to miss a moment." Keith cleaned his hands on a napkin and then helped Artie gather the trash.

In short order everyone was ready and the show began. People oohed and aahed at the bursts and patterns set to patriotic music. Mitch found himself leaning toward Beth, aware of a sense of peace and calm inside. He'd never doubt her again. She shouldn't have had to prove her ability to him, not if he wanted her to trust him. She'd never done anything but strive to better herself and her life.

If she'd be his woman, his wife, they could find a home close to Roseville so Beth would be near to her family and work and he could make the commute to his new position as consultant. He could almost picture the cheerful cottage surrounded by lavish flowering gardens under immense shade trees. He'd get a dog of his own, too. Maybe an Airedale. Call it Earhart or Lindbergh. But he was getting ahead of himself.

He stared at the fireworks lighting up the heavens and knew with a deep certainty his next move. He cleared his throat, drawing Keith's attention and then the rest of the gang watching the show together. Beth watched him with a bemused, curious expression as everyone gathered to see what Mitch would do next.

Turning toward her, he took her hands in both of his.

She aimed her happy green eyes at him with a lifted brow. "Did you want something?"

"Very much." He smiled into her captivating eyes.

"What?" She licked her lips, a quick dart of the tip of her tongue.

"You. All of you, forever. I love you, Elizabeth Golden." He lightly squeezed her hands and steeled himself for her answer. "Will you marry me and spend the rest of our lives finding out what our futures hold?"

She blinked slowly, pushing tears out of the corners of her eyes as she smiled. "Yes."

She tensed and then laughed at him. Glanced around the group as they cheered and clapped. Roxie had tears standing in her eyes and Tara bobbed her head happily. Jo clasped her hands together, a smile trembling on her lips.

"Is something funny?" A white flash followed by a loud bang echoed into the night, making Mitch flinch. The fireworks, not her laughter. "You did say yes, right?"

"Of course I did, I love you more than I can put into words. But I've solved the mystery." She blinked at him several times as the smile grew. "Now I understand why I couldn't see your future."

Mitch regarded her with a slight frown as the light breeze lifted his shoulder-length blond hair to shift and fall back around him. "Why you couldn't see mine?"

"I was confused about my lack of sight where you're concerned. Thinking you had the ability to block my visions. If so, then you are the only person who had ever managed such a feat. All my musings on the matter didn't reveal the truth to me. Until tonight when you said you love me."

"I do, with all my heart. Why?" He gripped her hands, clamoring to know.

"I love you, too." She smirked up at him. "Which explains everything."

"What?" He slowly shook his head. "I don't follow."

"You're so full of surprises. All the more reason I love you." She kissed him, a long exploration of his mouth.

Ending the kiss with a light chuckle, she gazed at him. "I can't see my own future."

"So you've said. What about it?"

She shrugged lightly, the smile never leaving her face. "Think about it for a minute." She crossed her arms and grinned wider. "You're a smart guy."

Mitch rubbed his stubbly jaw, musing over her words, trying to understand the implications. Then his eyes widened and he snapped his fingers.

"You figured it out?" She lifted one brow.

He winked as a matching grin flashed onto his lips. "I do believe so."

"Tell me, hot shot."

"I'm your future?"

She kissed him, a light peck on the lips. "And since I can't see my own future, I can't see ours joined together. It's like a veil draped over my visions where our love is concerned."

He drew her into his embrace and kissed her, his tongue exploring the deepest parts of her mouth while their love wound itself around them and the fireworks finale began above. He'd never be without this woman and she would never need to crave excitement again. He'd be all she needed to satisfy her cravings.

The End

Thanks so much for reading *Veiled Visions of Love*! I hope you enjoyed Beth and Mitch's story. In the fifth and final book in the series, Roxie is confronted with the return of her childhood sweetheart, Leo King, who has come home against his wishes to bring her a mysterious gift.

To find out about new releases and upcoming appearances, please sign up for my newsletter via my website at www.bettybolte.com. I send out a monthly newsletter with book news to share with my readers, upcoming events and signings, and even a few favorite recipes, puzzles, and other doings!

I'd love to hear from you! Feel free to send me an email at betty@bettybolte.com, find me on Facebook at AuthorBettyBolte, follow me on BookBub, or connect with me on Twitter @BettyBolte.

You can always find an updated list of the titles in this series, as well as all of my other books on my website, at www.bettybolte.com/books/.

Thanks again for reading!